D1057931

SLEEP WHILE I SING

Also by L. R. Wright

NEIGHBORS
THE FAVORITE
AMONG FRIENDS
THE SUSPECT

SLEEP WHILE I *Sing*

L. R. WRIGHT

VIKING

VIKING
Viking Penguin Inc., 40 West 23rd Street,
New York, New York 10010, U.S.A.
Penguin Books Ltd, Harmondsworth,
Middlesex, England
Penguin Books Australia Ltd, Ringwood,
Victoria, Australia
Penguin Books Canada Limited, 2801 John Street,
Markham, Ontario, Canada L3R 1B4
Penguin Books (N.Z.) Ltd, 182–190 Wairau Road,
Auckland 10, New Zealand

First published in 1986 by Viking Penguin Inc.
Published simultaneously in Canada

LIBRARY OF CONGRESS CATALOGING IN PUBLICATION DATA
Wright, Laurali, 1939–
Sleep while I sing.
I. Title.
PR9199.3.W68S56 1986 813′.54 86-4034
ISBN 0-670-81089-4

Printed in the United States of America
by Fairfield Graphics, Fairfield, Pennsylvania
Design by Liz Fox
Set in Times Roman

Second printing November 1986

This book
is for my daughter,
Katey

AUTHOR'S NOTE

The author wishes to acknowledge the advice, suggestions and information provided by Brian Appleby, Elaine Ferbey, Aristides Gazetas, Brian Martin, Marti Wright, and John Wright; any inaccuracies are her own.

There is a Sunshine Coast, and its towns and villages are called by the names used in this book. But all the rest is fiction. The events and the characters are products of the author's imagination, and geographical and other liberties have been taken in the depiction of the town of Sechelt.

SLEEP
WHILE
I SING

PROLOGUE

The clearing lay fifty feet from the two-lane Sunshine Coast highway. It was roughly circular, surrounded by thick-trunked cedar trees. In the summer it was a cool and fragrant place.

But despite its proximity to the road it was infrequently visited, except by raccoons and squirrels and garter snakes and rabbits and many varieties of birds; no well-trodden paths led toward it through the woods and brush that pushed against it on all sides.

Few drivers pulled off the highway here, although there was a grassy area which made this possible. The clearing, which was on the west side of the highway, was only two miles north of the town of Sechelt; anybody heading down the road was usually intent on getting to Sechelt, or to Gibsons, twenty miles farther south, or to Langdale, the terminal for the ferries that ply their way across Howe Sound between the Sunshine Coast and Horseshoe Bay, just north of Vancouver.

And even if someone had pulled off the road and gotten out to stretch his legs and look around him, he would not have known that the clearing existed. Not without pushing through six-foot stands of blackberry bushes so dense that the thorns would have raked blood from his face and arms.

It wasn't a secret place. Some people knew about it. They had come upon it by accident, from the side opposite the highway, where the brush was mostly salal, as tall and thick as the blackberries but much less wounding.

There wasn't anything special about it. It was too close to the road to be a satisfactory hiding place for children. And nothing particularly interesting grew there—except mushrooms, and the blackberries; and blackberries grew in ferocious profusion everywhere on the Sunshine Coast.

So the clearing managed to keep itself to itself, most of

the time. Particularly in winter, when the rains came and nobody in his right mind went stumbling aimlessly through the coastal forests, pushing blindly through the whip-cracking brush.

Only in hot sunlight did the place provoke thoughtfulness, and perhaps a mild elation, in those who happened upon it. Then, summer sun-spears flung themselves like challenges through the cedar boughs, but only succeeded in intensifying the coolness and the seclusion of the clearing.

Late one November evening, rain was falling upon the Sunshine Coast. It bounced and pattered upon the sea, painted the highway a glistening black, made soggy the lawns around houses in the several towns and villages that stretch along the coastline between Langdale and Earls Cove. It murmured in the tops of the tall evergreens and rustled in the undergrowth, and it fell with an adamance that suggested it was never going to stop. There wasn't a square inch of the clearing that wasn't at least damp, despite the fanlike branches of the cedars, layer upon layer of them, which sheltered the ground beneath the trees.

Through the rain a car could be heard, approaching from the north. This was not unusual. Traffic wasn't heavy on the coast highway during the winter, especially at night, but cars and trucks and an occasional bus did trundle past now and then.

The car slowed as it approached the clearing, inching along until the grassy area off the road was visible in the peripheral spill of the headlights. It pulled cautiously onto the grass and for a few moments it just sat there, inexplicably, with its engine running and its lights on.

A pair of raccoons curled up in a hollow log on the floor of the clearing awoke and listened warily, and watched the unwelcome light that filtered through the screen of blackberry bushes.

A gust of wind cut through the underbrush from the west, causing the salal bushes to shudder.

Then the car's passenger door was flung open and a figure

leapt out and ran away from the highway toward the prickly wall which hid the clearing.

The raccoons raced pell-mell out of their den and through the salal and disappeared into the woods that led eventually to the sea.

"Help!" cried the woman who had jumped from the car. Her voice sounded weak and disbelieving, alarm threaded with uncertainty. She was stumbling forward with outstretched hands when she ran into the blackberries. Her almost timorous cries became involuntary shrieks; she clawed at the bushes to disentangle herself and whirled around, facing the car. Its lights were still on; its engine continued to purr. "Oh God," she said, wiping at her face, using the rain to soothe the scratches on her skin.

Suddenly the headlights were extinguished, and the motor was silenced. The rain sounded louder now. The woman waited, half crouched, by the wall of blackberry bushes. The driver's door opened and for a moment the inside light went on, and then the driver was outside, in the rain, and he closed the door and the car was dark again.

"Oh God," whispered the woman. There were light posts along the highway, but the nearest one was some distance away. All that could be seen was the man's shape as he made his way around the back of the car. And then he turned on a flashlight.

Within the clearing the sound of the rain was somewhat muffled. It fell fitfully through the many-layered canopy of cedar boughs and made almost no noise at all when it struck the ground, which was thickly carpeted with the sheddings of the trees. But the salal clattered at the western fringe of the clearing and the blackberries rustled at the other side and high up in the treetops birds made themselves small and still, rocked in the cradles of cedar branches, remote from whatever was to happen below.

The woman shouldered her way into the barrier formed by the blackberry bushes, her head averted, hands up to protect her face, and in the clearing her muffled gasps were heard;

from the clearing the bushes could be seen to shake and brandish themselves in an effort to stand firm. But she catapulted through them, a woman wearing a red plastic raincoat, her blonde hair torn and tangled, her wrists and hands and one side of her face scraped and scratched. She stood still for a moment, blinking and panting, then stumbled quickly across the clearing. In the rain and the darkness she collided with the salal and recoiled with a cry; then she cursed it and pushed blindly through into the woods.

The flashlight beam poked cautiously through the blackberries, through the gap in the thorny barrier which had been carved by the flailing woman. Soon the man stepped carefully through, sideways, head down, brushing against broken vines. Once in the clearing he turned off the flashlight and stood erect and still. The rain whispered in the trees and rattled the bushes, and in the invisible distance the woman could be heard blundering through crackling brush, tripping over things. And then she called out, loudly, "Help! Help!"

The man flicked the switch on the flashlight. He held it in his right hand, down by his side, pointing upward, so that he looked like a streak of light himself, hard-edged and glittering; as though he had created the surrounding darkness in his own negative image.

He swung the flashlight up and out and moved quickly across the clearing, as if going to the woman's rescue.

From beyond the salal came sounds of struggling, and frantic swearing. The man pushed roughly through the bushes, and the clearing was once more empty.

In the darkness beyond, the flashlight beam swept back and forth until it found her, a hunched, twitching shape upon the ground. She began to sob. She was caught, ambushed by a tangle of moss-covered branches pitched to the ground in a long-ago storm.

"What is it with you?" she said frantically. "Have you gone crazy all of a sudden?" Her voice tried to pierce the night but rain and darkness like a shield deflected it, hurled it back at her. She kept on struggling to loose herself, groping ineffectually at the deadfall that had entrapped her.

The man walked slowly toward her, shining the flashlight, which he held now in his left hand, into her face. In his other hand there was a knife.

The woman saw the knife and raised one hand against it, fumbling behind her with the other, clawing frantically for a weapon, trying to wrench free some part of the intricate confusion of branches in which she was snared.

"Oh God," she said, "don't," and she tried to push herself farther in, to cage herself around with tree limbs.

He slashed at her, aiming carefully. She flung up both hands. He stepped back and she looked at her palms.

"Oh Jesus. Oh God." She was panting and sobbing. Her eyes were dark, enormous. The flashlight carved black chalk shadows under her eyes, beneath her chin.

He slashed again and again, moving quickly away each time, beyond the reach of her bloody hands.

The sounds from the woods entered the clearing on the rain and the wind but there was nothing there to hear them; even the birds had fled.

There was nothing, no one, there to watch the man as he stumbled backwards through the salal, dragging the woman by her feet. Nobody saw him prop her against a thick-trunked cedar. Nobody watched as he crossed the clearing, thrust himself through the blackberry bushes, and returned a few moments later carrying things he had brought from the car, which waited silently on the grass by the side of the highway.

The rain continued to fall.

Within the clearing the man was humming a tune old and nostalgic.

It was a sweet, distracted sound.

CHAPTER I

"What the hell are you doing here, anyway?" said Corporal Sanducci to the waitress, wishing he had time for another cup of coffee. He was twenty-eight, tall and dark-haired, and his R.C.M.P. uniform fitted him extremely well.

"Well, what do you mean? Why shouldn't I be here?" She reached for a cloth and began scouring the countertop. Sanducci was the only customer in the place.

"I mean, you ought to be in school somewhere," he said.

"I was in school. I graduated." She looked up at him quickly. "In June," she said, lifting the sugar bowl to wipe beneath it.

"And is this what you want to do with the rest of your life?" said Sanducci, but softly, so the cook wouldn't hear. The cook, who was also the girl's father, had been peering at them through the serving hatch ever since he'd arrived to help out his daughter, fifteen minutes earlier. Sanducci hadn't approved of a young woman looking after a roadside cafe on a dark, rainy night all by herself. Yet he had observed her father's entrance with sorrow.

The girl laughed and moved, still wiping, down the counter, away from him. Sanducci could see that she was flustered but he didn't care. She had a lot of things going for her, he was sure of that, even though he'd only talked to her maybe half a dozen times. And waitressing was a dead-end job. Not good enough, he thought, for a girl called Sunny, plump and yellow-haired and freckled, with eyes the color of a summer sea and breasts as soft and warm—he was certain—as down-filled pillows.

He shook his head and sighed. She ought to be going to a college or a technical school, he thought. She ought to be learning how to be a secretary or a dental hygienist or something. Something that had a future.

He dug into his pocket for some change. She came back to take his money, which he held in his outstretched hand so that she had to pick it up coin by coin. He felt her fingers on the skin of his palm and watched her face flush.

He could easily imagine her on her own in a little apartment in Vancouver, humming to herself in front of a mirror as she took out the elastic band which held back her hair and then shaking her head, letting her hair fly free. That's where she ought to be, all right, he thought. Not mired here in the small-town life of the Sunshine Coast, isolated from the excitement of cities by the waters of Howe Sound.

"I'm going on a holiday," she said, closing her hand around the coins he had given her. She looked up at the clock on the wall above the counter, which read 10:05. "Only two more hours. Less than two hours." The cafe closed at midnight. She beamed at him. "I've been telling everybody. It's my first real holiday. Without my dad. We're leaving tomorrow morning, on the seven-thirty ferry. Me and a girlfriend." She laughed out loud. "Hawaii!" she said. "We're going to Hawaii!"

"For how long?" said Sanducci, dismayed.

"Almost three whole weeks. We don't get back until the twenty-first. Three weeks in the sun. The sun!" She laughed again.

The corporal heard an enormous truck pull up, straining and coughing, into the parking lot outside the coffee shop.

Sunny deposited his change in the till, closed the drawer, and, still smiling, absently brushed some hair away from her forehead. Sanducci felt an ache in the center of him and stared hungrily at what he could see of her body; he hardly ever got to see her below the waist, because she was almost always standing behind the counter when he came in. There were four tables in the coffee shop, each with four chairs, but most people preferred to sit at the counter. Sanducci tried to think of some way to get her out from behind there, but he couldn't.

Seventeen days until he'd see her again. Maybe eighteen. She probably wouldn't go to work the day she got back.

What the hell, he thought, picking up his peaked service cap from the counter. There are other girls. Lots of other girls.

The bell above the door rang out excitedly as the truck driver came in, calling a greeting to Sunny and the cook.

It was a logging truck. Sanducci passed it as he hurried through the night, through the rain, to the patrol car. He thought briefly about accidents, as he unlocked the door and got in behind the wheel. He thought about a logging truck that had lost control one July evening. The skies had cleared after a day of rain and the driver was blinded, coming around a corner, by glittering sunshine slanting onto wet pavement; the truck had gone off the road and toppled over, dumping a denuded forest upon the highway and demolishing a bright red Toyota. Sanducci remembered blood glistening, and he remembered that there was a wind, and that the wind had picked up the sound of screaming and tossed it around so that for a few seconds after he'd arrived on the scene, he couldn't tell where the screaming was coming from.

He started the motor, turned on the lights and the windshield wipers, and pulled out from the cafe at Halfmoon Bay onto the road heading south to Sechelt. There wasn't another vehicle in sight.

Not many logging truck accidents, though. Mostly it was drunken high school kids, or tourists unused to the twists and turns of the two-lane highway; they crashed regularly off the road and into trees or houses or one another.

But late on this rainy November Sunday there weren't any tourists around, and so far he hadn't encountered any drunken high school kids, either.

The rain was neither storm nor drizzle but something in between. It fell heavily but meant no harm. It was an unpremeditated rain, an aimless patter on the roof of the patrol car; the wipers swished contentedly back and forth, the tires sprayed rainwater, the highway rippled black and shiny, divided by a solid yellow lane marker like the wide yellow stripe down the legs of Sanducci's uniform.

Occasionally the radio squawked at him, and he exchanged a few words with the dispatcher, grateful for these interruptions, for they helped him stay awake.

The inky pavement snaked ahead, eluding the grasp of his headlights, and it seemed to be moving, unrolling, undulating in a manner which Sanducci suddenly found extraordinarily sensual. He tumbled into gloom. It sometimes seemed that he found everything on God's earth sensual. In this matter adolescence clung to him—though not, he told himself, in any other.

He shifted position behind the wheel and realized that he was tired. All this driving, a voyage into colossal boredom; it wasn't surprising that the highway had begun to move. It wasn't surprising that his mind was all at once splintered by glimpses of women: a bare thigh, a profile, a black-hosed calf, breasts hidden behind the pink-and-white checkered uniform of a waitress.

Sanducci groaned and clutched at the steering wheel.

He was strongly tempted to floor it, see what this buggy could really do; he was flooded by a wave of machismo that embarrassed and excited him. The road twisted before him like a lithe and living female.

Reluctantly, he lifted his foot slightly from the accelerator. He began to sing out loud. It was a Newfoundland fishermen's song taught to him by his father, an Italian immigrant whose major disappointment with his adopted country was the paucity of indigenous folk music he'd found there.

But Sanducci remained mesmerized by the yellow-striped curves of the highway, lulled by the metronome that was the windshield wipers, the pattering of the rain, the husky splashing of the tires. He began to feel drowsy.

When the figure materialized on the road in front of him, Sanducci for a moment thought it was a dream or an hallucination. He peered incredulously through the windshield and didn't at first think to slow down; when his brain finally flipped into gear it was too late to slow down, so he hurled the car off the road before slamming on the brakes. The car came to a stop between two large trees, its hood smothered in broken greenery. Sanducci sat there holding onto the steering wheel, his heart pounding, and the wipers continued their losing battle with the rain.

Then he got out and looked down the highway. The man was visible in the rain-smudged glow from a light post. He was moving away quickly, either oblivious of Sanducci or ignoring him.

"Hey!" shouted the corporal. "Hey! You!" But the man kept on going, getting steadily smaller, and now Sanducci noticed that he was weaving as he walked.

"Drunken son-of-a-bitch," muttered Sanducci, furious. He got back into the car, backed it onto the highway, turned on the siren and the rooftop beacons and roared down the road.

It took him only seconds to catch up with the imprudent pedestrian, who continued his dogged but erratic trek as though blind to the patrol car straddling the center line beside him, deaf to the wailing of the siren in his ear.

When Sanducci, hollering fruitlessly, recognized the man, he accelerated and pulled off the road. The corporal turned off the siren and got out of the car. He walked swiftly up to the man and took him by the arm. "What the hell are you up to, Alfred? You nearly got killed back there. Are you soused or what?" But he knew when he looked at him closely that Alfred Hingle wasn't drunk.

"I'm not saying a damn word," said Alfred. Rain dripped from the brim of his baseball cap and glistened in his black beard. He attempted to move on, but Sanducci tightened his grip.

"What are you doing out here on the highway in the rain, for Christ's sake?" said Sanducci.

"I'm going home," said Alfred. He seemed twitchy, which put Sanducci on automatic alert.

"From where?"

"That's none of your goddamn business." Hingle shivered, despite the heavy Cowichan sweater he was wearing over his work shirt.

On the wind there drifted toward them a long, terrifying howl.

"What the hell is that?" said Sanducci. He let go of Hingle

and advanced toward the trees at the side of the road. He took his flashlight from his belt and aimed it at the impenetrable forest. "Alfred? Did you hear it?"

But Hingle had resumed his march down the highway.

"Alfred! Goddamn it, come back here!"

Hingle had reached the patrol car when Sanducci caught up with him. The rooftop lights flashed silently, red and blue; another howl cut through the sound of the rain.

And coldness clutched inexplicably at Sanducci's spine.

He grabbed Hingle by the shoulder and spun him around. "What the fuck's going on, Alfred?"

"Nothing's going on," said Hingle angrily, shrugging off Sanducci's hand. "I don't know anything."

Hingle wasn't a tall man, but he was big. His face was streaked rhythmically with red, then blue. Sanducci couldn't see his eyes; they were shadowed by his visored cap.

"If I was anybody else," said Alfred, "you wouldn't be bugging me like this."

"I'm not bugging you," said Sanducci. "You tell me you're going home but I know damn well your house is *that* way," he said, indicating the woods to the west of the highway. "You're so out of it, walking down the middle of the road, I nearly ran you down, for Christ's sake. What's the problem, Alfred? That's all I want to know." He'd left his hat in the patrol car. The rain slid down his face. It poked cold inquisitive fingers under his collar.

"For twenty-five years you guys've been bugging me," said Hingle, his voice rising. "If I was anybody else out here, you'd just leave me be."

"I didn't even recognize you," Sanducci protested, exasperated but defensive, "until I drove up next to you with the siren blaring."

Again, a howl—desperate: laden with fear, or menace, or grief.

"That's my dog," said Hingle, watching Sanducci. "That's Clyde you're hearing." He let Sanducci see him smile, teeth glistening between mustache and beard. "Did you think it was a wolf, maybe?"

Sanducci realized that not a single vehicle had passed. He did not like standing in a dark, wet world with only Alfred Hingle for company. The rain struck his skin like stings, cold splinters of a shattered black night. The dog howled. And it felt to Sanducci more like Hallowe'en than Hallowe'en.

"What's the matter with him?" he said. He thought he sounded calm, authoritative even.

Alfred hesitated. "I'm not talking to a corporal," he said.

"You're not talking to a corporal about what?"

"About what my dog found in those woods."

Sanducci became aware that the night was filled with sounds, wind and rain conducting the forest in a mournful, thick-tongued chorus. He wished that Hingle would move away from the car, out of range of the lights that washed his face with blue and red.

"Get Alberg," said Hingle. He leaned against the front fender of the patrol car, pulled his cap farther down on his forehead, and folded his arms. "I'm not talking to any goddamn corporal."

Sanducci opened the door and fumbled for the radio, while from somewhere in the blackness of the coastal forest Alfred Hingle's dog howled yet again.

CHAPTER 2

Alberg hunkered down in front of the body and trained his flashlight beam directly upon the face. The victim's expression seemed inappropriate, to say the least. She looked attentive, politely questioning—as if she'd fallen asleep while being spoken to, but, in obedience to the powerful demands of an innate courtesy, had left her eyes open.

Her hair was combed, her face was clean and unmarked—except for some shallow scratches on the right cheek, and because of the way her head had slumped these were practically unnoticeable.

Below the chin, though, it was a different story.

"Jesus Christ," sighed Alberg. He stood up, flicked off the flashlight and thrust it into the pocket of his poplin jacket. "Anybody know her?"

"Nope," said the sergeant heavily. "Not so far."

"Any sign of a purse? Handbag?"

"Nope." Sokolowski glanced around the floodlit clearing, where several uniformed officers were searching the area. "If it's here, we'll find it."

"Where's Hingle?"

"Over there by those goddamn blackberries. Sanducci's with him. You want to talk to him?"

"In a minute." Alberg looked down at the body. "Christ. Somebody really carved her up. But not the face."

"The face is too clean," said Sokolowski. He squatted down and shone his flashlight on the ground around the body. "No blood." He glanced at the bushes bordering the eastern side of the clearing. "She must have been killed somewhere else. That's how she lost one of her boots. Maybe got dragged in here from the road, through the damn blackberries."

The rain fell erratically upon the clearing, the body, the crime-scene officers meticulously at work. The undergrowth encroaching upon them from all sides gleamed coldly in the light from the high-intensity flood lamps. Alberg ran his hands through his blond hair, which was dripping wet.

"It's weird," said Sokolowski, "the way he propped her up against the tree like that."

"Yeah," said Alberg. "Weird. I don't like 'weird.'"

"Hey, Staff. Can you come over here for a minute?"

Alberg and the sergeant made their way across the clearing. "What've you got?"

The constable pointed to a break in the underbrush. "It looks like somebody plowed through here. What do you think?"

Sokolowski fingered the rain-heavy leaves. "It's salal," he said. The other two looked at him blankly. "That's what it's called, this stuff. Sort of like laurel. The Indians used to sell it to florists. So much a fistful. They call it wood spurge. The Indians do."

Alberg looked gravely at the sergeant, who was a huge, muscular man. "That's extremely interesting, Sid," he said.

They aimed their flashlights at the bank of salal. "Maybe this is where Hingle and his dog came through," said Sokolowski.

"Sanducci!" Alberg called across the clearing. "Bring Alfred over here."

The rain fell and the woods made sounds. At least these no longer included the wailing of the dog, whom Hingle, under police escort, had taken home.

"Is this where you came into the clearing, Alfred?" said Alberg, pointing his flashlight at the gap in the salal bushes.

"No," said Hingle. "We came in over there a ways. There's a kind of a pathway. Not much of a one, but you can find it if you know it's there."

"Okay. Just stay here with Corporal Sanducci a few more minutes, will you? I won't be long."

Cautiously, he shouldered through the broken bushes, which shuddered and crackled and sprayed upon him rain which felt several degrees colder than that which was falling from the night sky. Sokolowski and the constable were close behind.

Beyond the salal bushes Alberg saw, surrounded by forest, a barren landscape of logs, and huge moss-covered rocks, and spiky, shivering undergrowth. The rain fell more freely here, outside the domain of the cedar umbrellas.

The three men fanned out and picked their way cautiously, flashlights moving slowly across the ground.

Rain caught in Alberg's eyelashes and made his flashlight slippery in his hand. He stepped between two slim logs and, when he tried to step out, found that his foot was caught. "Shit," he muttered, and wrenched himself free, only to feel his other foot slip out from under him. He grabbed frantically at another log, this one at least four feet around, and the beam from his wildly swinging flashlight caught for a second on a red rain boot.

When he'd regained his balance he hoisted himself up

cautiously until he was straddling the big log, which proved to be the wet and slippery trunk of a fallen tree. He shone his light slowly back and forth over a disordered heap of mossy branches. He couldn't tell how many trees had toppled, their limbs helplessly entangled. The flashlight beam made silver shards of the rain and glinted green when it struck moss; it showed him broken ferns and, finally, the boot.

"Sid," he called out softly. "Better get some lamps in here." He climbed awkwardly down from the log and wiped his hands on his jean-clad thighs. "Right here, on the other side of this tree," he said, as the other two approached. "I want this area searched as thoroughly as the clearing. Blood, the weapon, a purse—maybe we'll get lucky. I'm going back to talk to Hingle."

He found Alfred standing where he'd left him, beside a weary and impatient Sanducci.

"The doc's here," said Sanducci. "He wants to move the body. Okay?"

"Has the photographer finished up?"

"With the body, yeah."

"Then sure. Take her away."

Sanducci left, and Alberg turned to Hingle. "Sorry to keep you waiting, Alfred."

"It's my wife I'm worried about. He said he'd call her. She gets off work at eleven, and I was supposed to pick her up."

"Who was supposed to call her; Sanducci?"

"The corporal. Yeah."

"If he said he'd call her, I'm sure he did. Do you want me to check?"

Hingle hesitated, then shook his head. "Let's just get it over with."

Alberg led him across the clearing, through the blackberry bushes, and down the highway past several patrol cars until they got to Alberg's Oldsmobile. Inside, he turned on the motor and the heater and the dome light and took a notebook and a pen from the inside pocket of his jacket. "Okay," he said, turning to Hingle. "Let's hear it. From the beginning."

Alfred took off his baseball cap. His hair, a silvery shock after the blackness of his beard, was flattened to the top of his head and stuck out around the sides. The cap had also left a crease across his forehead. He stroked rain from his mustache.

"I took the dog for a walk," he said. "I don't know what time it was. Couldn't have been much later than ten or so, because I knew I had to pick up Norma at the hospital at eleven." He watched the rain streaming down the windshield.

"And?" said Alberg.

Hingle was slowly shaking his head. "I didn't want to do this. I just wanted to go home. Leave her laying where we found her. I don't need this kind of trouble."

"Yeah. And maybe some kid would have found it, on her way to school."

Hingle sighed. "We came out of the house, Clyde and me, and it was raining. So instead of going down to the beach I decided we'd go into the woods, where there's more shelter. Clyde was running on ahead of me like he does. And all of a sudden he starts this howling." He shuddered. "Never heard him make a sound like that before. So I called him. He usually comes when I call him but this time he just ignores me, keeps on howling and howling. And so I followed the sound of it, and got onto the path leading to the clearing, and in the clearing there he was, standing halfway between that tree and the woods, just a-howling away. I went up to him and put my hand on his collar and that's when I saw her."

"And what did you do then?" said Alberg.

"I got out of there," said Hingle. "What the hell do you think? Through those blackberries"—he stretched out his hands, which were covered with scratches—"out to the highway. Clyde was still howling. He took off when I did, but he ran into the woods. I started down the road. Just went down the road. Going home the long way. Then the corporal showed up."

"Why didn't you tell him about the body right away?"

Hingle's eyes were such a dark brown they looked black. "Why the hell do you think?" he said.

"Had you ever seen the woman before?" said Alberg.

Hingle shook his head vigorously. "Never. Never laid eyes on her before in my whole damn life."

"In the woods," said Alberg, "did you see anybody? Hear anything? Besides the dog, I mean."

"I—maybe I heard a car," said Hingle carefully. "I'm not sure. Maybe it was just the rain. But maybe it was a car."

"When?"

"Before Clyde started howling. Sometime before that."

"But you're not sure."

"No," said Hingle. "But maybe."

Alberg closed his notebook and put it away. "Okay, Alfred. I'll run you home now." He turned off the dome light and switched on the headlights. "I'll want to talk to you again," he said, pulling out onto the highway, "once we've got the time of death. See if we can't narrow things down a bit more."

"I know what it looks like," said Hingle. "But I didn't do it. I don't want cops breathing down my neck again just because my dog found a goddamn body."

"Now, Alfred," said Alberg. "We suspect everybody, at first. You know how it is."

"Not everybody," said Hingle grimly.

They drove in silence for a few minutes.

"Not everybody," he said again.

"Come on, Alfred," Alberg said with a grin. "Don't get all self-pitying on me." He glanced at Hingle. "After all," he said softly, "you only live—what is it—a mile, a mile and a half from the clearing? Even if you hadn't found the body, you'd have been a suspect anyway, wouldn't you."

CHAPTER 3

Several hours later the sky had begun to lighten to a flat, dull gray; a listless segue from night to day. Why bother with day at all, thought Alberg, staring bleakly from his office window. The clouds lay low and heavy and leaked persistent rain. It was days like this that caused him to long for real winters. Snow-choked streets, black ice on the highways, cold that numbed the bones and paralyzed the muscles—but also blue skies and sun; Jesus, what he wouldn't do for some sun.

This part of British Columbia was famous for sun, and for a balmy climate in which roses and eucalyptus trees thrived alongside giant Douglas firs and wild rhododendron. The richness of the land was equaled only by the richness of the coastal waters, which contained an abundance of fish—especially salmon—and a variety of shellfish.

But in winter the sun often disappeared for days or weeks at a time. And then Alberg couldn't easily recall how brilliantly blue the sea could be, how bright and hot were the days of spring and summer and fall.

He rubbed wearily at his eyes and turned from the window to sit behind his desk. He couldn't even see the tops of the mountains, the clouds were so low.

There was a knock on his door and Isabella Harbud, the detachment's secretary-receptionist, came in. She was carrying a tray with a mug of coffee, a paper napkin, and a plate of glazed doughnuts. Alberg's mouth began to water.

"I figured," said Isabella, putting the tray on his desk, "that you'd be needing some quick energy."

He saw that she'd put cream in the coffee. He took a sip: sugar, too. "Thank you, Isabella," he said. He picked up a doughnut and studied it lovingly. "I am beholden to you, Isabella. I think my spirits are beginning to rise."

"By rights I should have brought you an apple and one of those little boxes of raisins," said Isabella. She had folded her arms in front of her and was watching him eat. "And a glass of milk."

The staff sergeant glanced up at her and nodded humbly. Isabella was wearing a bulky cardigan with horizontal orange and red stripes. He thought she must have knitted it herself; he couldn't imagine any store selling such a thing.

"But I knew you wouldn't eat an apple," she said. "Or raisins."

Alberg nodded again, his mouth stuffed with doughnut.

"I don't know what this town's coming to," said Isabella heavily. "That poor woman." She shook her head. "Let me know if you want some more coffee. I've got things to do. It's a madhouse out there." The Sechelt R.C.M.P. detachment didn't get a lot of homicides. It was an almost alarmingly peaceful posting, to those senior members who had served in more volatile communities.

Alberg told Isabella to wait five minutes and then send in Sokolowski and Sanducci.

He ate all three doughnuts. He didn't even have to feel guilty about it. Isabella had brought them to him herself. He munched contentedly.

To his enormous irritation, she had recently appointed herself watcher over his weight. She was even trying to make him drink his coffee black. She would hide the cream and sugar and then watch his face keenly as he ranted and raved at her; she could always figure out when he was posturing, his outrage enfeebled by guilt, and when he was so determined to have his way that his anger was real.

He pitied her chiropractor husband.

But he loved her golden tiger's eyes.

Alberg wasn't much overweight. Maybe ten pounds or so. And he could get away with it, he told himself, because he was tall and he carried himself well. For a man of forty-five, he was in pretty good shape.

He'd be in even better shape, he thought glumly, if he

had the self-discipline necessary to jog four or five times a week instead of the once or twice he usually managed.

He drank the pale coffee to the last, sweet drop.

"Come in!" he hollered, almost cheerfully, when there was a knock at his door. "Sit down," he said to Sanducci. "You look terrible. What's the problem? No stamina?"

Sanducci threw him a dour glance as he sat in the black leather chair opposite Alberg's desk. His uniform trousers were rumpled and smeared with dried mud. His hair was in disarray. His face was the color of the slaty sky, and the lines from nose to mouth had deepened. Alberg noticed these things with some satisfaction. He himself had gone home to change, and was now thoroughly revived by carbohydrates.

"When's the autopsy?" he said.

"Ten o'clock."

"Good. You'll have time to spruce yourself up a bit."

Sanducci opened his mouth to speak, then changed his mind.

"It won't be your first, will it?" said Alberg incredulously.

"No."

"That's good, then," said Alberg, grinning at him.

Sokolowski came in dragging a metal chair, which he set down between Sanducci and the door. He looked patiently at Sanducci until the corporal got up and sat on the metal chair, leaving the leather one for the considerably wider sergeant.

Alberg picked up the tray and stood to put it on top of the filing cabinet, shoving aside a pot of ivy. He sat down and picked up a file folder. "Okay. Let's go over it again. Sanducci, you start."

"Hingle was wandering down the highway like a drunk," said the corporal wearily. "I pulled over to talk to him. He farted around for a while, finally told me his dog had found something in the bush. Said he wouldn't talk to anybody but you. So I radioed in. That was at ten thirty-three."

"While you were waiting for us," said Alberg, "did he say anything?"

"No."

"Nothing about hearing a car?"

Sandueci looked at him blankly. "A car? When?"

"Before his dog sniffed out the corpse."

"He didn't tell me about the corpse, Staff, remember? He said he'd only talk to you. He didn't open his mouth again until you got there."

"Okay," said Alberg agreeably. "Sid? What've you got?"

"What we've got so far," said Sokolowski, flipping through his notebook, "is not much. Blood in the moss on those fallen trees, where we found the boot. That's where she bought it, all right. What the hell she was doing in there—who knows. No footprints. Too much crap from the trees. No tiremarks on the grass between the highway and the clearing. Except ours. No purse, no weapon. The guys are still at it, but it's pretty clear that the place where the boot and the blood were found is as far as she got into the woods."

Alberg opened the file and started reading. "A rusted tire iron; three cigarette packs, empty; a soggy box of crackers, empty; a tin of salmon, empty; some broken china; a yo-yo, for Christ's sake; even a couple of condoms." He tossed the folder back on the desk. "I didn't think anybody used those things anymore. I thought every female in Canada was on the pill." His daughters in Calgary crept into his mind and he pushed them away. "What about her clothes, Sanducci? Anything there?"

"The raincoat's plastic. The lab's going to check it for latents. Nothing in the pockets except a stone."

"A what?"

"A stone. A rock. Like you'd pick up on the beach."

"Anything else?"

Sanducci shrugged. "We got the brand names of the clothes. Only the raincoat and the boots look like they could be new, though. Doesn't look too hopeful."

"What about missing persons?" said Alberg to Sokolowski.

"Nothing," said the sergeant.

"Shit," said Alberg.

"There's only one house anywhere near that clearing," said Sokolowski.

"I know, I know," said Alberg irritably. "Hingle's."

"I think he did it, all right," said Sanducci decisively.

"Then why was he on the highway?" said Alberg. "Why didn't he go home the back way, through the woods, where nobody would have seen him?"

"Maybe he got spooked," said Sokolowski. "Didn't like the sight of her, after he'd done it. Got rattled by the dog. Something."

"For Christ's sake," said Alberg in disgust. "There was no blood on him, right? And who the hell would take a dog along on a homicide?"

"He'd already been home, maybe," said Sanducci. He leaned forward in his eagerness. "Probably he took her there in a car. Then after he killed her, he drove the car home. Showered, got rid of his clothes."

"And then wandered back to the crime scene, dog in tow? Jesus, Sanducci."

The corporal flushed. "He could have taken the dog for a walk afterwards," he said stubbornly. "The dog runs off, finds the body. Hingle panics. It could have happened."

"You checked his house, right, Staff?" said the sergeant. "When you drove him home."

"Yeah. Nothing."

"He would have gotten rid of everything by then," said Sanducci.

Alberg gave him a bleak stare.

"Was it sexual?" said Sokolowski.

"It doesn't look like it," said Sanducci reluctantly. "The doc won't know for sure until the autopsy." He glanced at his watch.

"The next closest place to the scene," said Sokolowski, "is that old folks' home. I just sent two guys out there to interview the old people."

"There's nothing but woods on the other side of the highway, right?" said Alberg.

"Right," said the sergeant.

Alberg leaned back in his squeaky chair and put his feet on the desk.

"She's got scratches on her face," said Sokolowski. "Could be she came through those damn blackberries, from the highway. Maybe she was a hitchhiker. Got picked up by a loony, jumps out of the car and tries to get away; he takes off after her."

"Jesus Christ, I hope not," said Alberg. "I don't want to be dealing with any goddamn loony, thanks."

The sergeant shrugged. "You don't want a loony. You don't want Hingle. You're hard to please."

Alberg grinned at him.

"Why the hell did he lean her up against a tree?" said Sanducci.

The other two looked at him with tolerance. "That's the big question, all right, Corporal," said Alberg. "That, and why the hell did he wash her face?"

"Maybe he did it with spit," said Sokolowski disapprovingly.

"More likely with rain," said Alberg, and the sergeant looked relieved. Alberg stood up and stretched. "Until we find out who she was, we are running on no gas." He went to the window and looked out upon the gray day. "We've got to get some kind of a picture out. Plaster it up and down the coast, get it to all the ferry terminals, and into the Vancouver papers, as well as the local rag."

"It's gonna have to be a sketch," said Sokolowski. "Can't do a photograph. Not with her neck all sliced up like that. Couldn't do one anyway, of course. No paper's gonna run a picture of a corpse."

"I don't like to use Vancouver except when I have to," said Alberg. "Besides, those guys make live people look dead, for Christ's sake. Who do you know around here who draws?"

Sokolowski shook his head emphatically. "Nobody. No. Body."

"Don't look at me," said Sanducci.

Alberg sat down at his desk. "Well, Jesus, somebody must know somebody."

"Staff?" said Sanducci.

Alberg looked at him warily. There was a sly note in the corporal's voice.

"I know somebody who'd know somebody."

They looked at him expectantly. Finally, "We are not playing 'Twenty Questions' here, Corporal," said Alberg coldly.

"The librarian," said Sanducci.

Alberg assumed his most enigmatic expression. He waited, staring at Sanducci, knowing that his face was perfectly smooth, that his blue eyes had become wintry. He said nothing. He heard Sokolowski clear his throat. He wondered remotely whether Sanducci would have the sense to now shut his mouth.

But the corporal couldn't resist. Exhaustion had made him rash. "She knows all the arty types on the peninsula," he said softly. "Or so I hear."

Alberg looked him steadily in the eyes, and after a while Sanducci began to shift uneasily, and eventually his gaze faltered and he looked away, out the window behind the staff sergeant's desk. Dimly, Alberg was aware of phones ringing in the main office.

Sokolowski stood up and poked Sanducci in the shoulder. The corporal, startled, stood up, too. Sokolowski gestured with a thumb toward the hall, and Sanducci left the office.

Alberg felt the sergeant eyeing him uncomfortably but sympathetically. He was mortified and furious.

"It's a good idea, though," said Sokolowski casually as he backed out into the hall, closing the door gently behind him.

"Shit," said Alberg. But he looked at his watch; she would still be home. He was dismayed by the ease with which he remembered her number, and the eagerness with which he picked up the phone.

CHAPTER 4

Cassandra Mitchell was sweating her way through the *Twenty-Minute Workout,* trying to reject a comparison which threatened to undermine her resolve: people who flailed themselves about in front of the television set like this were surely akin to those who, senseless with religious fervor, flailed themselves before altars.

But she had put on twelve pounds since the summer. It was the first time infatuation had caused her to gain weight instead of lose it. As the freakishly supple instructor gushed and simpered at her to bend farther, faster, Cassandra wondered if it was her age that was to blame. Maybe when you were past forty, lust suddenly became fattening, like everything else.

As she flung herself upright, a few drops of sweat flew from her forehead. She could feel her blood churning through her veins, wrenched from lethargic meanderings into a purposeful flood. This was satisfying—though she noticed that her knees had begun to quiver in protest against holding upright an overweight body in remorseless gyration.

When the phone rang she almost didn't answer it, so determined was she to get through the whole twenty minutes for once. But Cassandra had never been able to let a telephone go unanswered.

It wasn't Roger.

It was Karl Alberg.

"Can you spare me a few minutes?" he said. "I need some advice."

Distractedly, Cassandra grabbed a dish towel from a rack on the end of the kitchen counter and blotted her forehead with it. "I've been doing my exercises," she panted. "I'm out of breath."

"You're supposed to cool down afterwards," said Alberg. "Walk around. Stretch."

"I know that," said Cassandra irritably. "But it's hard, when you're on the phone. What kind of advice do you want?"

"Have breakfast at Earl's with me before you go to work." Earl's was a cafe down the street from the library.

"Not breakfast. I don't eat breakfast," said Cassandra. "I could have coffee, though."

She hadn't missed much of the workout, she thought, as she flicked off the television set. Just the last couple of exercises. She felt tingly and virtuous.

In the shower she thought about Alberg. He hadn't called in months. She'd seen him only when they happened to meet in the post office, or on the street, or somewhere.

Last summer they had begun weaving, cautiously, the tenuous threads of a friendship rich with sexual possibilities. And then in September Roger Galbraith entered her life, like a rocket. Alberg had immediately and frostily retreated. Cassandra regretted this but didn't know what to do about it. He was wary, unyielding, suspicious, and sober. Against Roger's sunny recklessness, he hadn't had a chance.

She had met Roger on a bright hot Sunday afternoon in September when she got out of her car outside Golden Arms, Sechelt's apartment complex for senior citizens. She was making her regular weekly visit to her mother, and it turned out that he was there to visit his mother, too: she had retired to Sechelt from Vancouver several years before.

Cassandra noticed him because he was good-looking, and close to her own age, and different. He wouldn't have been different in most places, but he certainly was in Sechelt.

He wore baggy cotton pants and a loose sleeveless top and his hair was black and curly and his skin was pale. He was slim, he walked with an easy, fluid grace, he wore a small gold ring in his ear, and when he smiled at her he revealed impossibly white, extraordinarily straight teeth. And when he spoke to her it was in a voice so rich and melodious that she felt it like summer sunlight on her skin.

He told her he was an actor, an expatriate Canadian who lived in Los Angeles. She remembered, then, why he had looked vaguely familiar to her. She had seen him on television.

He was taking a sabbatical, he said, laughing. Had to get out of the rat race for a while, take a look at the real world again. Cassandra remarked that Sechelt was a corner of the real world that often wearied her, but she admitted that it could be soothing in small doses.

He was staying, he said, with his sister and her husband. He didn't know how long he'd be there. Until they got tired of him, he told her, laughing again.

It was good to meet someone who laughed so freely and so often.

She had been seeing him regularly and exclusively since then. She hadn't intended it to be exclusive. She'd looked forward, guiltily, to seeing them both, Roger and Karl, the actor and the cop, but that hadn't worked out.

It was just as well, she thought, as she entered Earl's Cafe half an hour later and shook rain from her umbrella, looking around for Alberg. Roger Galbraith, she thought, was not a man with whom Alberg would ever feel comfortable. And Roger had certain tastes which, as a policeman, Alberg was better off not knowing about.

"You're looking good," said Alberg, who had been waiting for her at a corner table where two mugs of coffee steamed comfortingly.

"So are you," she said. She had a craving for cream and sugar but was trying to get used to drinking her coffee black. This was somewhat easier on mornings when she'd exercised. She looked at him more closely. "You've put on some weight, though, haven't you?"

"A bit, maybe," said Alberg distantly. "I've started to jog again, though."

Cassandra nodded approvingly. "Good."

"What I want from you," he said, "is the names of some people who can draw."

Cassandra was astonished. "What, you mean artists?"

"Yeah. Artists. I need somebody to do a sketch."

"You personally? Or the R.C.M.P.?"

"I need somebody to do a sketch of a woman's face. The problem is, she's dead."

"Good heavens. Dead how?"

"Dead murdered. Somebody cut her throat."

"My God," said Cassandra. She set her coffee mug down carefully.

"She was found last night. No identification on her. So we want to run a sketch in the papers."

Cassandra was nodding. "Is she, uh . . ." She cleared her throat.

"It's kind of messy, yeah. But we'll hide it as well as we can. It'll be all right."

Through the front window of the cafe she saw a pickup truck pulling in next to the curb. The sides were splashed with mud and in the back rode a large, short-haired, red-brown dog. A bearded man wearing hiking boots, a Cowichan sweater, jeans, and a baseball cap got out of the truck and slammed the door. He let down the tailgate so the dog could jump out, and the two of them made their way through the rain and into the cafe.

As soon as he got inside, the dog shook himself, jangling the license tag that hung from the thick leather collar around his neck. Rain from his fur splattered two men sitting on stools at the far end of the counter, and one of them yelped and complained. "Jesus, Earl," he said to the Chinese man behind the counter. "You shouldn't allow dogs in a public eating place." He glanced at Alberg. "It's not legal."

The man with the dog ignored him. He sat at a table by the window, and the dog lay under it.

The owner of the cafe took a menu to the man at the table, who waved it aside and ordered hotcakes and sausages.

"Jesus," grumbled the man at the counter to his companion. "It's fucking unsanitary, is what it is." He turned suddenly and yelled at Alberg. "Well why don't you throw him out, for Christ's sake? Throw the fucking dog out!"

Alberg turned and gave him a slow smile. Cassandra had never seen such an unfriendly smile. She felt a coldness on the back of her neck.

The man threw a dollar bill on the counter. "Fucking dogs," he muttered, pulling the door open. "Fucking Mounties," he shouted over his shoulder as he went out.

The Chinese man shrugged at Alberg. The man with the dog stared out at the rain and ignored them all.

"How's your cat?" said Cassandra suddenly.

Alberg smiled again. This time it was a resplendent thing, warm and joyous.

"She's good," he said. "Had five kittens. I think each of them had a different father."

"Did you keep them, or what?"

He looked horrified. "Christ, no. I gave four of them away." He gestured to Earl, who came over with the coffeepot and refilled their mugs.

"And the fifth?" said Cassandra.

"Well, I had to keep that one." Alberg frowned at her. "So what do you think? About the sketch."

Cassandra sighed. She dumped sugar and cream into her coffee and stirred, thinking. "You could try Marietta Paige in Gibsons," she said finally. "She does a lot of pen-and-ink stuff. We hung a bunch of it in the library for a couple of weeks last spring."

"How do you figure she'd react to a corpse?"

"Forget Marietta Paige," said Cassandra quickly. She shook her head. "How would anybody react to a corpse, for God's sake? Isn't there somebody in your detachment who can draw? What do they teach you in police school, anyway?" She drank some of her coffee. "Oh for God's sake. Look what you've made me do." She pushed the mug away from her. "I've put cream and sugar in it," she said with disgust.

"Might as well drink it, though," said Alberg, encouragingly.

"I can't think of a single soul," said Cassandra, "who could look calmly at a corpse and calmly draw its face."

"He doesn't have to be calm about it," said Alberg. "He just has to do it."

Cassandra looked moodily across the cafe and out through the window. Soon the bearded man pulled a wallet from his pants pocket, put money on the table and stood up. So did his dog. The man looked over at the staff sergeant.

"Take care, Alfred," said Alberg casually.

The man nodded, and he and his dog left the cafe. Cassandra watched as he let the tailgate of the pickup down so the dog could jump into the back. Then he got into the truck and drove away.

"Was that Alfred Hingle?" said Cassandra.

Alberg nodded. She couldn't read anything in his face. She wanted to ask him about Hingle—surely facts were always less harmful than gossip. But she hesitated. Were they still friends, she and Alberg? At the moment he was too much of a policeman for her to be sure.

"You could try Tommy Cummings," she said.

"Who's Tommy Cummings?"

"He teaches art at the high school. They've got a couple of his paintings hanging in the new Bank of Montreal, over near the shopping center."

"Is he any good?"

"I don't know. What do you care?" She put more sugar in her coffee. She saw Alberg open his mouth, as if to protest. But he thought better of it. "How am I supposed to know if he's any good? One of the paintings in the bank is of a deer. You can tell it's supposed to be a deer, all right. Isn't that all you need?"

Alberg sighed. "I don't know. I guess so."

"At least he probably won't pass out on you."

"I'll call him," said Alberg. "I'll let you know what happens."

"Yes," said Cassandra, offhandedly. "Please do." She reached for her umbrella, which lay on the floor next to her chair.

"How's your friend?" said Alberg when they had left the

cafe. She saw that his car was parked in front of the bookstore across the street. She'd left hers in the parking lot of the library, a block away.

"What friend?" said Cassandra. "I have several friends."

"That actor," said Alberg, shoving his hands in his pockets. "Is he still in town?"

He was, thought Cassandra, looking at him, a very substantial man. Big and broad and solid. Sexy, in his Nordic way.

"He's still in town." She thought she might be smiling, just a little. "He's staying with his sister and her husband," she added, just in case Alberg had the wrong idea.

He hunched his shoulders against the rain. "I'd better get going."

"My God, Karl," said Cassandra angrily.

"What?"

"Nothing. Go on. You're getting soaked." She began marching up the street toward the library. Before she got there, he drove past her and didn't even wave. Furious, she told herself she was lucky not to have gotten any more involved with him than she had, before Roger showed up.

CHAPTER 5

At lunchtime Alberg drove up the hill north of Sechelt to the high school.

It was a nondescript single-story building surrounded by forest and reached by a rutted loop of a road carved into the bush like an afterthought, as though the real purpose of locating the school up here might have been to enable the villagers to forget that it and its inmates existed.

He stood in the drizzle in the parking lot and looked around. The woods had been pushed back behind the building to accommodate a playing field. There was no sign of life outside; either the last morning class hadn't yet been dismissed, or the school's inhabitants were already huddled in a lunchroom devouring their sandwiches.

Alberg wandered away from the building and along the unpaved road leading downhill, where it joined the residential street that linked houses flung at random upon the hillside. He stepped off the road into a small, muddy clearing and found that behind the trees was somebody's back yard. He saw a plastic tractor lying on its side. It was just about the right size, he thought, for a four-year-old boy. Or girl, he quickly had himself add.

From the school came a rude, flat blast which Alberg figured must be the dismissal signal.

He walked back up to the parking lot and across to the front of the building.

The doors were flung open and a bunch of students rushed out. He stood to one side as they careened past him.

Inside, groups of kids clustered in the lobby, talking loudly and excitedly about nothing in particular. Others sat huddled together on the kind of armless couch usually seen in medical waiting rooms. There were a few plants, tall and spindly. The leaves of some of them had turned brown.

Alberg went into the office.

It was quieter in there. A teenage boy sat sullenly on a bench against the wall, staring at his large, dirty sneakers. A woman wearing eyeglasses typed industriously away at a desk in the corner. Alberg saw that the door to the principal's office was open, and that there was nobody inside.

He waited patiently, but nothing happened. Finally he knocked on the counter. The woman at the typewriter looked up. "Yes?" she said.

"I wonder if you could help me," said Alberg, his tone gentle, his smile, he hoped, winning.

"Yes?"

"I'm looking for one of your teachers," Alberg began.

"They're in there," said the woman, gesturing behind her. She resumed typing. Alberg, trying to remain patient, noted admiringly that she typed even faster than Isabella did.

"In where?"

"In the staff room," said the woman, without looking up.

Alberg turned to the kid on the bench. "Is that it, then?"

The kid lifted his head. "Huh?"

"Am I supposed to march right in there, or what?"

The boy shrugged. "I don't know, man."

Alberg found the gate in the counter and went through. He threaded his way among the desks that cluttered the office area. When he reached the woman at the typewriter, he stopped. "Down there?" he said, pointing to a short hallway that ended at a door marked STAFF ROOM.

"Yes, that's right," she said, and flashed him a look of contempt which, brief as it was, froze Alberg in his tracks.

Who did she think he was? A parent? A visiting teacher?

"What's your job here?" he said curiously.

"I'm a secretary," she said, attacking her machine.

He looked over her shoulder. "Not a very good one," he said regretfully. "That page is filled with typos."

As he went down the hall he heard the page being ripped from the typewriter.

He knocked at the staff room door.

"Come!"

He went in. Twelve pairs of eyes stared at him, four female, eight male. The teachers were seated at a long wooden table in the middle of the room. It would have accommodated several more people. The empty chairs on both sides of the middle of the table created a barrier between the teachers who smoked and those who didn't. There was a large, orange, exceedingly ugly ashtray at one end. The scents of coffee and tuna effectively obliterated whatever smell of tobacco might have lingered in the room.

Alberg, surveying the place, was astonished. The table was littered with crumpled brown bags, sandwiches wrapped in wax paper, little plastic bags with cookies or pieces of cake or pie inside them, oranges and apples and bananas, thermoses, coffee mugs. He regarded the scene humbly; teachers, it seemed, didn't fare a hell of a lot better than cops.

"Can I help you?" It was the same voice that had invited him in. It belonged to a man of about thirty, short-haired, clean-shaven, who sat at the head of the nonsmokers' end of the table. He wore a sweat suit and sneakers and was eating a large sandwich that contained slices of tomato, among other things.

"I'm looking for a teacher."

They laughed.

"You've come to the right place," said the sweat-suited man. "Any particular teacher, or will any of us do?" He grinned at Alberg in a friendly fashion.

"Tommy Cummings," said Alberg. He looked at the eight men seated around the table. There was one suited gentleman with dandruff on his shoulders. A man in his twenties, good-looking, was deep in conversation with the young woman who sat next to him. An elderly man wearing a bright woolen vest over a bright yellow shirt slurped at his coffee with a loudness that Alberg found disconcerting. He saw a weary, middle-aged man push his lunch aside as if the sight of it nauseated him. Another was absorbed in a book, turning the pages with one hand and feeding himself carrot sticks with the other; perhaps, thought Alberg, he had only recently joined the nonsmoking section. And there were two men at the smokers' end of the table sharing the morning newspaper: one, in his fifties, with a lot of gray hair, wore suspenders and a white shirt and a dark blue tie; the other, bald, kept running his hand over his head as if this apocalyptic event had occurred mere seconds ago.

"Tommy Cummings," said the jock in the sweat suit, staring thoughtfully at the staff sergeant.

"The granola head," said the man in his twenties, lifting his head for a moment from the young blonde who sat beside him. She giggled, and he whispered in her ear, and she giggled again, looking at Alberg.

"He's not one of you, then," said Alberg, after a minute in which he had rearranged his thinking.

The sweat-suited man grinned. "You could say that," he said, and a murmur went around the table.

"Perhaps you'd be kind enough to tell me where I can find him," said Alberg softly.

"Why do you want him?" said the bald man, stroking his head.

Alberg smiled at him. "That's none of your business, fella."

All of the teachers looked at him then, even those who had to turn around to do so.

"Hey, hey," said the jock, uneasily.

"I'll get him for you," said a woman about fifty, dressed in yellow. She started to push herself away from the table.

"No," said Alberg. He smiled again. "Just tell me where I can find him."

"In the art room," she said.

"And where's that?" said Alberg, patiently.

"Go out of the office, across the lobby, turn right down the hall. It's Room 204."

"Thank you, madam," said Alberg.

As he left he heard the murmuring start again, subdued but excited.

The door to Room 204 was ajar. Alberg knocked and stuck his head in. "Hi," he said to the man seated at a desk by the window.

"Hi. What can I do for you?"

"Are you Tommy Cummings?"

"Yes."

Alberg went into the room and closed the door.

Cummings looked at him inquiringly. He held a small knife laden with cheese in one hand, and a cracker in the other.

"I'm sorry to butt into your lunch hour," said Alberg. He pulled his identification from his jacket pocket. Cummings' eyes widened, and he looked quickly up at the staff sergeant. "I'm here to ask you a favor," said Alberg.

"Good heavens," said Cummings. He put the knife and the cracker down on a paper towel. There was a container of soft Philadelphia cream cheese, and a plastic bag with crackers in it, and several small slices of meat.

"How come you aren't in the lunchroom with the rest of them?" said Alberg.

Cummings gestured to the window. "I like to look outside. The windows in the staff room are small, and high up in the walls." He wiped his fingers on a corner of the paper towel and stood up. "What favor is it that you want from me?"

He was a good-looking man in his late thirties, maybe early forties, wearing a tweed sports jacket over an open-necked shirt. Brown hair, brown eyes, about five feet nine, 175 pounds, Alberg figured.

"Sit down, for God's sake," said Alberg. "Eat your lunch." He looked around at the desks with drawing boards attached and opted to half sit and half lean against the window ledge. "We need somebody to draw something for us."

"Really?" said Cummings. He slathered the cheese on the cracker. "What do you need drawn?"

"Actually, it's a body."

Cummings' hand froze in midair. Carefully he put the cracker down. "A body." There was no expression in his voice.

"A homicide victim."

The teacher's face paled. He looked fixedly at the cracker as if wondering why it wasn't in his mouth.

"Now it won't be too bad," said Alberg, uncomfortably. "But if you don't want to do it, hell, you just say no, that's all."

"Why can't you just take a photograph?"

"Photographs of dead people look like photographs of dead people. We need something the papers will print. Something that will make her look like she's alive."

Cummings nodded. "I see."

"I misled you, actually, when I said 'body.' We don't need you to do her whole body. Just her face."

"A portrait," said Cummings.

"Yeah. A portrait," said Alberg, brightening. "That's exactly what we want."

The teacher sighed and sat back in his chair. "Oh boy," he said.

"Yeah, I know. But look. I'll have her put in a hospital bed. It'll be okay," he said with a confidence he didn't entirely feel. "What do you say?"

Cummings looked up at him and smiled. "What if I pass out?"

"I'll give you some smelling salts," said Alberg with a grin. "Then I'll take you home."

Cummings nodded, still smiling. "Okay. I'll give it a shot."

Alberg got off the windowsill to shake his hand. "Thanks. I really appreciate this. Come to the hospital after school tomorrow. Ask for me. Karl Alberg."

"Karl Alberg," said Cummings. "Okay."

CHAPTER 6

The following afternoon a nurse and an intern pushed a gurney through the hospital, from the morgue in the basement to a private room on the second floor. Alberg followed. His heels clicked on the shiny tiled floors, and the white shoes worn by the other two made muffled squeaking sounds, and the wheels of the gurney squealed whenever it had to negotiate a corner.

They encountered nobody at all as they passed in silence along the hall in the basement, and nobody in the elevator either, and on the second floor the nurses had made sure that all the patients were in their rooms; a couple of nurses glanced curiously at the shrouded cargo on the gurney as it wheeled along the corridor but most of them pretended that the gurney, the corpse, and its three attendants simply were not there. Alberg was slightly unnerved, as though he had been cast as a character in something by Edgar Allan Poe.

In the room the nurse and the intern pulled back the sheet covering the corpse. They lifted the body and placed it on the bed. The intern pushed the gurney out into the hall, and Alberg heard him roll it away.

The nurse covered the dead woman with the bedclothes, which had been folded back to the end of the bed. She tucked the covers around the corpse's chin. Then she straightened and looked at the staff sergeant.

"It's a sad business, Mr. Alberg," said Norma Hingle steadily. She was in her fifties, small and trim. She wore her graying hair in a braid coiled and pinned beneath her white nurse's cap. Alberg had been dismayed when he saw that it was she who would help take the body upstairs.

"Uh, yes. It is. Very sad," he said inadequately.

As the door closed silently behind her he swore under his breath.

He wandered over to the window and looked down at the parking lot. But he didn't know what kind of car the art teacher drove. It was early, anyway, he thought, and he sat down in a chair that had aluminum arms; its red padded seat exhaled a long breath as it accepted his weight.

The bed was directly in front of him. The corpse was almost at eye level. He knew that if he stared at it long enough he would see its chest begin to rise and fall. He blamed this on his Irish heritage. There was no way the Scandinavians on the other side of his family could have anything to do with the bouts of black imaginings which occasionally plagued and disconcerted him.

He stood up, wishing he could have a cigarette while he waited, and went again to the window. The rain was still falling, but less heavily than yesterday, and he thought the clouds had lifted somewhat, too. He scanned the sky for signs of further improvement but saw none.

At least the window admitted lots of natural light, which he thought might be necessary. That was just one of the reasons he'd had the body moved up here. The other was that a morgue was no place for an amateur.

His stomach growled, and he realized that he'd had no lunch.

He could hear himself breathing, and the beating of his heart.

He turned from the window, linked his hands behind him, and walked over to the bed to look down at the corpse.

Her hair was parted in the center. She wasn't a natural

blonde, but the color had suited her. He could see faint lines in her face—from the sides of her nose to the edges of her mouth, and along her forehead. Alfred Hingle's wife had inadvertently bunched the covers a bit, right under the dead woman's chin, in her attempt to conceal the wrappings around the throat. To Alberg it now looked as though the corpse had done it herself, as though under the sheet she had gripped the covers in her fists and pulled them up before finally settling into her death. But he knew that her arms lay at her sides.

It bothered him greatly that her face had been cleaned, that the blood that must have been spattered there had been wiped away.

And why had she been moved from the place where she'd been killed?

If Hingle had done it, surely he wouldn't have been found meandering dazedly along the highway while his dog howled at him from the concealment of the woods. That just didn't make sense. It *did* make sense that, having found the body, he would hightail it away from the scene as fast as his legs would carry him—and not through the sighing, rustling forest, either.

The perpetrator could have been dragging the body to a car when he heard something—Alfred's dog, or traffic on the highway—and panicked.

Except that she had been found propped tidily against a tree, rather than unceremoniously dropped upon the ground.

If he'd been interrupted in something other than an attempt to cart her away, what could it have been? What else had he intended to do? Strip off her clothing? Wash off the rest of her? What?

There was a tap on the door, and a very young nurse came in. "Mr. Cummings is here," she said, holding the door open. She looked back over her shoulder and smiled. "Come on in," she said cheerily, and opened the door wider.

Tommy Cummings came reluctantly into the room. The nurse patted him encouragingly on the shoulder and left.

"She was in one of my classes," said Cummings, his

brown eyes riveted on Alberg's face. "That nurse. Ginny, her name is. Several years ago, now. Apparently I taught her biology. I seem to remember teaching biology. It was only for one year, thank God." He laughed, a high-pitched sound that apparently startled him, for he cut it off as abruptly as he'd turned it on.

The staff sergeant stretched out his hand. "Thanks for coming."

Cummings hesitated, then shook hands. "What is it exactly that you want me to do?"

Alberg gestured to the hospital bed. "Like I told you, I need a sketch of this woman, here. So we can broadcast it around and find out who she is."

Cummings continued to look concentratedly into Alberg's face. He obviously wasn't ready to confront the corpse. So Alberg went on.

"She had no I.D. on her," he said, relaxed, taking his time. He shoved his hands into the pockets of his corduroy pants. "So far, nobody who's seen her can identify her." He gave the teacher an encouraging smile. "So we need a picture, a sketch, that we can spread around the peninsula, get to the ferry crews and the mainland police and the newspapers."

"Somebody murdered her, you said."

Alberg nodded.

Cummings looked beyond Alberg, out the window. "Usually I do better with inanimate things," he said.

"She's pretty inanimate," said Alberg.

Cummings glanced at him sharply.

"Sorry," said Alberg, gently.

The art teacher went over to the chair and set down his battered leather briefcase. He opened it and took out a large sketch pad and a thick pencil. "I don't know," he said. "I'll try."

He stood there for a moment, his back to the bed, and then turned decisively around. As he focused for the first time on the body, his hands began shaking and what little color there was in his face vanished. Oh shit, thought Alberg, and took a few swift steps toward him, but Cummings shook his head, without taking his gaze from the dead woman's face. Alberg stopped, but continued to watch him carefully.

Cummings went on shaking and his pallor gleamed, and Alberg, watching his profile, saw a sparkling in the man's left eye. He waited.

Eventually Cummings cleared his throat and said, "She was a very beautiful woman." He turned to Alberg. "Don't you think so?"

"Yes, I do," said the staff sergeant politely. He didn't, actually. She was so thoroughly dead that the matter of how attractive she might once have been was irrelevant to him.

Cummings walked slowly around to the other side of the bed. "How did she die?"

Alberg didn't answer.

"Maybe you don't want to tell me," said Cummings, looking down at the body. He studied the dead face in silence for a while. Then he turned away, looked around, and put his sketch pad and pencil on the floor. He pulled a package of pocket Kleenex from his pants pocket and blew his nose. He dried his eyes, put the tissues in his pocket, picked up the pad and pencil, and said to Alberg, "All right. I think I can do this." His voice was tight and there was strain in his face, but he was obviously in control of himself.

"Good," said Alberg, relieved.

"I suppose you couldn't step out into the hall . . . ?"

"I'm afraid not," said Alberg. "I'll try to be as inconspicuous as possible."

Cummings turned back to the body. "I'll do some preliminary sketches here," he said. "Then I'll finish it at home."

"Why don't you want to take photographs?" said Alberg curiously. He had called the teacher that morning and offered the use of a Polaroid camera.

"They don't work for me," said Cummings, glancing at the window, then back at the body. "I seem to end up copying the light and shade I see in the photo. And then I get flat surfaces."

"Ah."

"I'm afraid I'll have to ask you to crank up the bed." He turned and looked apologetically at Alberg.

"Oh. Sure." Alberg turned the handle slowly, watching to see whether the head was going to loll to one side, fervently hoping that the doctor had wrapped the slashed neck firmly. "Is that enough?"

Suddenly the covers slipped a little, revealing the bandaged throat. Alberg heard Tommy Cummings gasp. But when he spoke, his voice was steady.

"That's fine. Thank you."

"What are you using there? Is that just an ordinary pencil?"

"Just an ordinary pencil," said Cummings. He was sketching rapidly, concentrated on the pale still face that was almost the same color as the pillowcase. He hardly looked at the paper at all, Alberg noticed admiringly.

"What color are her eyes?" said the teacher hesitantly. "Do you know?"

"Blue. Kind of a dark blue. I can get the eyelids propped open for you, if you like."

Cummings looked at him in horror. "No no no. No. That won't be necessary. Blue. That's all I need to know." He made some notes on the edge of the paper and resumed sketching.

"How long will it take?" said Alberg, craning his head in an effort to see what was taking shape on the sketch pad.

Cummings stopped and looked at him. "Please, Mr. Alberg. Could you please wait over there by the door and not say anything?" He was still pale, but he spoke firmly.

Alberg retreated. "Sure," he said, and folded his arms and waited, comfortably, in silence.

CHAPTER 7

It was Wednesday morning, so when Norma Hingle heard the knock at her front door she knew who it was.

As she crossed the room to let him in, she ran her hands over her cheeks and patted the braided coil at the back of her head.

Roger was leaning against the doorjamb with his arms crossed. "A wee present," he said, "from one Scotsman to another," and produced from next to his body where he had hidden it under his jacket a jar of Robertson's marmalade.

She was flustered, but her face was mostly all smiles as she looked up at him. It was, she told herself, not his tinny television self she admired but the real one. She had never met a person so filled with exuberance.

"I do thank you for it," she said.

"It's a small thing, lassie," he said in his put-on burr, "for a' the cups of tea I've drunk in your kitchen."

"Well, come in out of the rain," said Norma, "and I'll give you another."

He filled up her kitchen with his body—which she privately admired. She saw him looking around with bright, curious eyes to see if anything had been added to the shelves. She had told him of Alfred's penchant for collecting things.

He scraped a chair across the floor and straddled it. "You're as beautiful as ever," he said. "It's a pleasure to look at you."

It didn't go to Norma's head when he talked this way. She knew that just about any female person was beautiful to Roger Galbraith. She enjoyed his company no less because of this.

She poured tea and put some cinnamon buns on a plate.

"My God, would you look at that," he said, reaching for a bun before she'd had a chance to set the plate down.

"A person would think you were starving," said Norma, "if she didn't know better. How many snacks do you get given to you, anyway, in the course of a single day?"

He just winked at her, with his mouth full.

His visitings had started at Golden Arms, he had told her. Where his mother lived. A lot of women on their own lived there. After he'd been to see his mother a few times and met her friends, he'd begun dropping in on some of them without her, just to say hello. He became much admired for this.

Then he went to the library and started dropping in on the librarian.

God knew how he'd first encountered the others.

Norma had met him when she and Alfred were out walking Clyde, and he'd stopped to talk to them—he was quite a talker, Roger was. "Full of baloney," Alfred had grumbled later when they were on their way home.

Soon afterwards, Roger came in to the emergency ward at the hospital. He'd had a fall and cut his head. It wasn't serious but it was bleeding a lot. The librarian brought him in to have it stitched up, and Norma was on duty. They'd had a chat, Norma and Roger, despite his paleness and the trembling of his hands. She'd kept him distracted, talking.

And a few days later he'd shown up at her door, still bandaged, which she thought made him look rakish, now that he had some color in his cheeks.

She was rattled, at first. She wasn't used to having virtual strangers pay her calls, especially people whose faces were familiar from her television screen. But she let him in and she offered him tea and he told her some jokes and a lot of funny things about being an actor and she told him that her maiden name was McKenzie and she was Scottish on both sides of her family and it turned out that he was, too. She was thawed and then she was charmed, she didn't mind admitting it.

Since then he'd come by regularly, every Wednesday, which was one of Norma's days off.

He also visited the bank manager's wife, and the wife of the elementary school principal, who had two toddlers whose diapers Roger occasionally changed—Norma didn't know the school principal's wife to talk to, but Roger had told her about the diapering and she had no reason to disbelieve him. Last month the principal's wife had persuaded him to go to the school and do a kind of a performance for some of the children. Norma had heard about this from one of the nurses whose small daughter had been in the audience. He'd read to them from *Alice in Wonderland* and acted out all the parts. Norma could just imagine it, too. He was always going on like that, quoting things.

Sometimes she wondered if there was some hanky-panky occurring between Roger and one or more of all these women he visited. There hadn't been a single thing improper in his visits to Norma, but she was too old for him; the principal's wife, and the bank manager's wife, and the librarian, though....

She wondered how on earth he ever got time to do any acting, down there in California.

"What's the week brought you, Norma McKenzie Hingle?" he said, wiping his fingers on the paper napkin she'd given him. He turned the chair around and sat down properly, stretching out his long legs. "What's happened in your life, since I saw you last?"

"One week's much the same as another, around here," she said, putting the Robertson's marmalade away in the cupboard with the honey and the peanut butter.

Then she turned. There was no point pretending it hadn't happened. "Did you hear about the poor woman who got murdered?" she said.

He cocked his head, as though he hadn't heard her properly. "Murdered?"

"I saw her in the hospital. Her body, that is." She bent slightly toward him. "Whoever did it cut her throat."

Roger looked at her with distaste. "You're kidding."

She was disgusted with herself for the excitement she couldn't help but feel—despite Alfred's situation and the worry it caused—passing along the news to one who hadn't yet heard it. She resolved not to say another word about the whole horrible business.

She sat down at the table and glanced at Roger, and was

surprised to notice how lined his face looked. She decided this was because he wasn't laughing or smiling, as he usually was; you hardly ever got a really good look at him, actually. He was an extremely good-looking man, she thought. Very trim in his body. She liked his dark eyes, and the narrowness of his face. She liked his astonishing mass of black curly hair, and his straight, white teeth. She'd even gotten used to the small gold earring he wore. As she watched him Norma felt a stirring in her; she wasn't all that much older than he, really, only twelve years or so. Firmly she damped the flickering before he could look at her and maybe see it.

He certainly did look older, though, than he appeared on television.

The highlight of Norma's day, when she wasn't working the three-to-eleven shift, was sitting down to watch reruns of *The Rockford Files*. She didn't know where she'd been when the series first came out but she'd missed it completely. Now it was on at six o'clock. She always set the table and started the dinner before it began, but Alfred still sometimes complained about having to wait until after seven for his meal.

It was on *The Rockford Files* last year that she'd first seen Roger.

She still remembered the episode in which he'd been introduced. He played Jim Rockford's cousin, whom Jim hadn't seen in years. He was a sunny young man named Brian, the son of Rocky's younger brother Matthew, and at first Jim was dismayed by him because Jim wasn't much interested in family, except for his dad, but then he became fond of him so it was upsetting when he found out that Brian was a kleptomaniac. He stole things all the time, and not things that he needed or wanted either, necessarily. He stole things like Band-Aids and photograph albums and stuffed animals and pruning shears. And bigger things, too, like footstools and ugly lamps and, once, a birdbath. He caused a lot of trouble for Jim, who finally sent his cousin off to a blind female psychologist from whom he stole a Braille alarm clock.

Brian came back several times during the season, and Norma had been delighted after she met Roger to be able to tell him that his character was appearing in an occasional program this year, too. Roger immediately looked gloomy; Norma couldn't figure out why. She had told him rather sharply that *The Rockford Files* was the main reason he found it easy to get into so many Sechelt kitchens.

He was looking now at the sampler which Norma had long ago hung on the wall between the refrigerator and the door to the mudroom. Suddenly he smiled at her, animated and cocksure, as though he had the power to change her life.

"I've got a song for you," he said, and then he was on his feet, standing straight and tall. He took her hand and sang:

Bonnie lassie, will ye go,
Will ye go, will ye go.

"Go on," said Norma, pulling her hand away. She was laughing and she knew that her face was red. He was unsettling. He seemed to have expanded. He and his voice had become far too big for the confines of her small kitchen.

He pulled her to her feet, still singing, and put his arm around her shoulder. He held her tight, close to him, and swayed gently from side to side, and she had to sway with him.

Bonnie lassie, will ye go
To the birks o' Aberfeldy?

"Roger, don't be foolish," she said, embarrassed, but she wished she'd put on a dress that morning instead of her plain brown washable slacks and a white sweater that had seen better days.

"Now simmer blinks on flow'ry braes," sang Roger, placing Norma gently in a kitchen chair,

And o'er the crystal streamlet plays;
Come, let us spend the light-some days
In the birks o' Aberfeldy.

He grinned at her, to let her know he was just playing, and then he was kneeling in front of her and had hold of both her hands.

Bonnie lassie, will ye go,
Will ye go;
Bonnie lassie, will ye go
To the birks o' Aberfeldy?

His voice was dark and Scottish, and he sang right to her, thinking only about the words, she could tell, and not at all about how he was looking or even how he was sounding. He sounded perishingly good, she thought. She'd had no idea that he could sing so well.

While o'er their head the hazels hing,
The little burdies blythely sing,
Or lightly flit on wanton wing
In the birks o' Aberfeldy.

Now he got up and stood behind her, with his hands on her shoulders, and sang almost in a whisper, bending close to her; she could feel his warm breath on the side of her face.

Bonnie lassie, will ye go,
Will ye go, will ye go;
Bonnie lassie, will ye go
To the birks o' Aberfeldy?

The song ended with some notes that went down and a final one that went up, like a question. Norma wished she had some words to sing as an answer.

He gave her a hug and sat down. "I've got a friend in L.A. who plays the bagpipes," he said. His forehead was glistening; his curly black hair looked soft enough to touch.

"Del McCrimmon down in Gibsons plays the bagpipes," said Norma, breathless. She noticed some bits of fluff on the sleeve of her sweater and began picking them off.

"Robert Burns wrote that," said Roger, and Norma nodded solemnly. "Did you know that Robert Burns died when he was only thirty-seven?" Norma nodded again. "I read a book about him," said Roger. "It said he died"—he straightened up in the chair and put a hand on his chest, quoting—"'of a rheumatic affliction of the heart caused or assisted, it would seem, both by work and by drink; so you could say that he was never anything but young, and that his youth was sustained by his art, his friends, and his lovers.'"

They laughed softly together.

"'. . . never anything but young,'" said Roger dreamily.

The outside door from the mudroom opened and Alfred and Clyde came in. Norma looked at them in astonishment. She hadn't heard the pickup. She'd completely forgotten that Alfred was coming home for lunch today. She'd forgotten all about it, even though it was to be the first time they'd really seen each other since Sunday night, when she'd been picked up at the hospital by a policeman and driven home to a distraught husband who had, incredibly, discovered a dead body in the woods.

Alfred looked straight at them, through the mudroom and the doorway into the kitchen, and for an awful moment Norma wanted to giggle, so surprised he looked. She had never before seen so much astonishment on one person's face.

Clyde, a reserved but amiable dog, went straight to Roger, his tail wagging, and began curiously sniffing at the slim-cut legs of Roger's dark blue pants. Roger had met him only once before, but he slapped him on the flank and said a friendly word or two.

"What's this, then?" said Alfred in a tone of massive disapproval.

"You remember Roger Galbraith, Alfred," said Norma. She was exceedingly discomfited, although she thought she had no reason.

"We met on the beach one day," she said. "Back in September it was. Roger's from Los Angeles, up here visiting his mother and his sister."

"The actor fella," said Alfred, scowling. He pulled off

his cap. "What's he doing in my wife's kitchen?" Talking like Roger wasn't even there.

"He's paying me a call," said Norma. She thought this sounded peculiar, although it was the absolute God's truth.

"I was just about to leave," said Roger, getting up. He grinned easily at Alfred.

That wasn't such a good idea, the grin. Norma looked quickly at her husband, and even in her inexplicable nervousness noted for the umpteenth time what a distinguished head he had. Lots of hair, pure silver at the front and the sides, darkening toward the back, and a beard and mustache that were almost completely black, except for some silver threads here and there. He had dark eyes, and heavy gray brows, and what Norma had always thought was a very pleasant smile.

But he wasn't smiling now. He pulled himself up straight, so that he was almost as tall as Roger and you didn't notice his large belly as much as you saw how huge his arms were, how thick his neck.

"You're not leaving fast enough," he said ponderously, glowering at Roger.

"Oh for heaven's sake," said Norma, suddenly impatient. "Sit down, Alfred. Sit down and let Roger finish his tea, and have a cup yourself, and one of my cinnamon buns, while I fix your lunch."

She went to the cupboard to fetch another cup. Roger sat down again. Clyde padded into the mudroom and with a long sigh lay down upon the mat. After a minute Alfred tossed his baseball cap onto a hook on the wall and reluctantly sat down. Norma put a cup of tea in front of him and began to get sandwich fixings out of the fridge. She thought about inviting Roger to stay for lunch but decided against it. He'd have the sense, she told herself, to leave before things got more awkward than it seemed they already were.

"So," said Roger. "Norma says you've had a murder around here."

Norma glanced over at Alfred, who turned to look at her, shock and betrayal all over her face. "I was telling him that I saw the poor woman in the hospital," she said quickly. "That's what I was telling him about." She gave Roger an uneasy smile. "Alfred doesn't know about that. I've been working three to eleven," she explained. "We don't see much of each other, Alfred and me, when I get that shift. He's off to work before I get up in the morning, and I'm off before he gets back at night, and by the time I get home he's fast asleep." She spread pieces of bread on the counter and began buttering them.

"Why was she in the hospital," said Roger politely, "if she's dead?"

"She was in the morgue," said Norma, arranging chunks of ham on the buttered bread.

"What the hell were you doing in the morgue?" said Alfred.

"We had to wheel her up from there into a private room," said Norma. She slathered mustard on the ham. "Cover her up, try to make the poor creature look half alive."

Alfred made a smothered sound of dismay.

"Now that's a very strange thing to do," said Roger, slowly, "it seems to me."

Norma wiped her hands nervously on a paper towel. She felt uncomfortable, with both of them staring at her. But now that she'd begun, she couldn't find a way out of it. Reluctantly, she sat down at the table. "Do you know Tommy Cummings?" she said to Roger. "The art teacher up at the high school?"

Roger shook his head.

"We know him a little bit, don't we, Alfred?" Alfred slowly nodded agreement. "We see him on the beach sometimes, drawing," said Norma, "when we take Clyde for walks there. Well, the police called him in to draw her picture."

Alfred stared at her. "Jesus," he whispered, even though he knew that blasphemy offended her. He looked shaken.

"So they couldn't very well have her lying on one of those slabs in the morgue," Norma went on. "The poor man, after all. So they moved her into a regular bed."

Alfred nodded soberly, studying his big hands, which were clasped together on the tabletop.

"Cops," said Roger contemptuously. "They've got no respect for the dead. Or the living." This earned him a glance from Alfred that was half suspicious and half approving.

"It's because they don't know who she is, you see," said Norma. "They need a picture to put in the paper and show around to people. She was a lovely woman, too, poor thing. Blonde."

"Pretty creepy stuff," said Roger. He moved restlessly and stood up. "I've got to get going." He put out his hand to Alfred. "Nice to see you again."

Alfred looked at the hand, then got up and shook it. Stiffly, he muttered something unintelligible.

"Thanks for the tea, Norma," said Roger, winking at her. "Don't see me out. I know the way." He turned toward the hall that led to the front door.

"That's the librarian's car out there," said Alfred suddenly.

Roger stopped in the kitchen doorway. "Right. That it is."

"She's given him the loan of it, Alfred," said Norma. She left the table to stand between the two men. "Now let him be. Let him get on his way." She put one hand on the small of Roger's back and pushed him gently. At the same time Alfred stepped grudgingly back.

When they had heard the front door open and close, Alfred said, "What the hell was that fella doing here anyway, in broad daylight, visiting my wife?"

"Would you sooner he came calling at night?" said Norma.

She went back to the counter and began tearing off lettuce leaves to go on top of the ham.

"I'd sooner he not come at all, that's what I'd sooner," said Alfred loudly. Clyde, worried, was watching him intently.

"I didn't tell him that you found her body, Alfred," said Norma quietly. "What do you take me for?" When he didn't say anything, she went on. "I've got no neighbors nearby. And I'm not excited about having to ride my bike into town in all this rain if I want a bit of a natter."

"You natter all day long at the hospital," said Alfred,

whose face, she noticed from the corner of her eye, had gotten red. He was also swinging his large hands around in the air. "You natter all the time at me."

Norma turned quickly from the sink. "Don't you go getting hot under the collar, Alfred Hingle. It's a harmless friendship. He likes my tea and my cinnamon buns. And he's a Scot." She went back to the sandwiches, slapping them closed with the top slices of bread. She was blinking her eyes rapidly, and realized this was because she didn't want to cry.

She felt again the emptiness of a life without sons and daughters. But of course it was better this way. How could they have borne it all, she and Alfred, if they had had children?

She heard Alfred breathing heavily behind her and knew he was in a little struggle. After a minute he put his hands on her shoulders and turned her around. In his embrace she felt his big belly pushing firmly against her. He patted her back and she knew that meant he was sorry for his rudeness, for having almost lost his temper.

CHAPTER 8

As Alfred Hingle began eating his ham sandwiches, and Roger Galbraith sped toward the bank manager's house, where he was expected for lunch, Karl Alberg was knocking on the door of Tommy Cummings' apartment above the Sechelt hardware store.

"Sorry to break up your lunch hour again," he said when Cummings opened the door.

"It's no trouble," said the art teacher. "Come in. I've made some coffee." Alberg went inside and Cummings closed the door. "Sit down," he said. He crossed to a drawing board on the other side of the large living room.

"We're very anxious to have it reproduced," said Alberg,

"and get it distributed. I didn't want to wait any longer than I had to."

"I should have dropped it off on my way to school this morning," said Cummings. "I'm sorry I didn't think of it." He turned and walked toward Alberg, holding a stiff piece of paper about eight inches by ten. He handed it to the staff sergeant face down.

Alberg took it and turned it over.

The shock was physical.

He felt the adrenaline rush through him, carrying with it a discomfiting admixture of pleasure and dismay.

"I didn't expect it to be in color," he said. He sat down, the picture in his hand. "I expected a black-and-white sketch."

"I thought it might be more useful," said Cummings. "For showing it to people. They might be more inclined to remember her." He went into his small kitchen, separated from the living room by a counter.

The portrait was head and shoulders, about eight inches by ten. Her shoulders were turned slightly away, but her eyes gazed straight at Alberg.

"Do you take cream and sugar?" said Cummings.

"What? Oh, yeah. Thanks."

There were almost imperceptible indentations at the corners of her mouth, as though she had often found it necessary to suppress a smile. But not now. Now there was no trace of smiling.

"Jesus," said Alberg.

He remembered Cummings asking the color of the woman's eyes. He'd gotten them right. They were a much darker blue than Alberg's.

When he looked closely they appeared to contain a reflection, perhaps of a nearby window; there had to be a window nearby, he reasoned, even if none appeared in the picture, because sunlight was coming in from somewhere.

"Is it all right?" said the art teacher, appearing before Alberg with a tray bearing two cups of coffee, cream and sugar, and an ashtray.

"Oh yeah. Yeah, it's fine. It's good. Very good."

Her hair, parted in the center, fell to her shoulders. She was not young, but she was beautiful. One side of her face was sunlit; she had high cheekbones and a strong jawline.

"Just fine," said Alberg.

Her throat was unmarked. Her blood remained captive behind her skin, where it belonged. He could see the flush of it. He could see the color she had been—a complicated combination of white and gold and rosiness—before she was slaughtered.

"Jesus," he said again. "How did you do it?"

"Pastels," said Tommy. He smiled and shrugged. "Color. Light. Shade."

Her lips were slightly parted. Behind them Alberg caught the gleam of straight white teeth.

He stared hard at the portrait, trying to see how pastel crayons had created compassion, invented melancholy.

He thought her voice would be slightly husky.

She was suddenly real to him, and her truncated life clamored at him, filling his mind with a bewildering tumble of shapes, sounds, and colors that lacked delineation of any kind. She was alive, but everlastingly inaccessible, and Alberg found this baffling and frustrating. She looked so tangible that he felt she ought to be able to speak, to solve her own murder.

It was a kind of apparition he was looking at, he thought uneasily. Perhaps it wasn't the live woman he was seeing at all, but the dead one; perhaps what was in her face was whatever she had observed, discovered, across the chasm of death.

Alberg shivered. He put the portrait carefully down on the coffee table and lit a cigarette.

"Drink your coffee," said Tommy. "I ground the beans fresh."

Alberg took a sip. "It's good coffee."

"I drink a lot of coffee."

"So do I. But it isn't really coffee. It gets brewed in a great jeezly pot. I don't know what the hell it is, but I'm damn sure it isn't coffee."

"Would you like some lunch? I'm a pretty good cook." He was smiling, tentatively.

"No thanks," said Alberg. "I've just got time for the coffee. But look, go on, get yourself something to eat. I know you have to get back to school."

"It's all right. I've got a spare period right after lunch." He picked up his coffee cup.

Alberg let his eyes wander around the room. It had windows in two walls and a large skylight in the pitched roof. On the other walls were paintings and pen-and-ink drawings. "Did you do all those?" he asked.

"Not all of them," said Tommy. "Most of them."

Alberg stubbed out his cigarette and went over to look at them more closely. There were several watercolors of places he recognized: the sea and Trail Islands from the beach at Davis Bay; the stone breakwater at Selma's Cove; the jungle of masts that was Gibsons harbor at the height of summer. There was a Douglas fir soaring in solitary splendor above a deciduous woodland; driftwood on the beach; a pink climbing rose in full bloom, smothering a trellis. Alberg was surprised to find that, without knowing why, he didn't much like any of them.

He stood back and scanned the walls again. "There aren't any people here," he said.

"I don't do many portraits," said Tommy. He stood and went into the kitchen for the coffeepot.

Alberg looked at the art teacher curiously as he refilled their cups. Today he wore a dark green turtleneck sweater beneath his sports jacket. His clothes were of good quality; his shoes were shined. His brown hair was cut short at the back and the sides, in a style that suited him. He was somewhat round-faced, with a full lower lip and a slight cleft in his chin. It was a pleasant face.

The teacher was in good shape, too—no flab around his waist—and although he moved awkwardly as he returned the coffeepot to the stove Alberg figured that was because he wasn't used to having police officers in his apartment. The observation caused him some dismay; he'd forgotten for a moment that that's what he was: a police officer.

He noticed a scar, almost hidden beneath the hair that fell over Tommy's forehead.

"What happened to your head?" he said.

Automatically Tommy's hand went to his forehead and he brushed the hair back. It was an ugly scar that extended into his hairline. "I was in a car accident," he said, "oh, a long time ago now, more than twenty years ago. It was before they put the four-lane highway in from Vancouver to Horseshoe Bay. I guess you weren't here then. It was a terrible road, treacherous, two lanes and always lots of traffic. Anyway, there was an accident. The boy who was driving—it was his car—he was killed. I got pretty badly banged up. I was in the hospital for ten months, in a coma for three. I guess they thought I was going to die, too." He shrugged.

"Was he a good friend of yours?" said Alberg.

Cummings looked at him serenely. "Yes. He was. A very good friend."

Alberg nodded, slowly. "I'm sorry," he said. "It must have been a bad time for you."

Cummings didn't reply.

Alberg picked up the portrait from the coffee table and started for the door.

"Aren't you going to drink your coffee?"

"Thanks, I've had enough." He stretched out his hand. "I appreciate this. I know it wasn't easy for you. Send us a bill, would you?"

Tommy shook Alberg's hand and quickly let it go. "I couldn't possibly send you a bill," he said. "I couldn't possibly. Just promise me you'll never ask me to do it again." He laughed. "That'll be payment enough."

Alberg slapped him lightly on the shoulder. "Okay. Whatever you say. Thanks. But we owe you one."

Tommy smiled at him. "I'll remember that," he said.

Alberg went down the steps to the sidewalk, the portrait tucked under his jacket to protect it from the rain.

CHAPTER 9

When Roger arrived at Cassandra's house for dinner that evening, he brought a bottle of wine and some flowers.

She had worked it out that he brought flowers every time he intended to sleep with her. She didn't think he realized it, but that's what he did. This time it was a potted chrysanthemum, the blossoms bronze-petaled. When she looked at them she saw their dark brown centers and thought of her nipples, and felt them rise beneath her blouse. She must have expected the flowers, for she hadn't worn a bra.

"Jesus, what a town," said Roger, going ahead of her into the living room. "I was coming out of the liquor store and Mrs. Hendricks was going in. She lives in Golden Arms, two doors down from my mother, and she does like her gin. She's English." He threw himself onto the white leather sofa, which was one of Cassandra's most prized possessions.

Cassandra put the pot of flowers on the glass coffee table.

"She stopped me, right there in the doorway to the liquor store," said Roger, "pulled next week's *TV Guide* out of her purse, and asked me to autograph it."

"You ought to be used to that by now."

He sat up. "Shit, Cassandra, I did that stuff ten years ago." He spread his arms wide and looked down at himself. "I ain't the same fella."

"They don't think about that. They think it's the makeup that made you look younger."

"It ought to be funny," said Roger, lying full length on the sofa again. "A riot."

She got them drinks from the kitchen and put them on the coffee table. Then she switched on a lamp and pulled the drapes against the black sky and the rain that shimmered silver in the light from the streetlamp outside her house.

"Come over here," said Roger. "Let's fool around." He swung himself upright with a smooth, almost menacing grace that was infused with sexuality. It was one of the first things she had noticed about him, one of the first things that had attracted her to him. Every movement he made was effortless and unstudied, yet suggested consciousness of power. Cassandra had come to believe that his body, perhaps through an actor's training, had become unquestioningly obedient to his mind, and that his muscular litheness aroused her because his mind wanted things that way.

"I don't want to," said Cassandra. Resisting him, even temporarily, gave her the illusion of maintaining some control over her life.

He picked up his drink and took a healthy swallow. "I've got to be back around nine," he said. "My sister needs her goddamn car." He stood up to remove his jacket, soft, supple suede the color of nutmeg. Beneath it he wore a white silk shirt, collarless, and jeans.

"I'd better get dinner on the table, then," said Cassandra, preparing to get up from her easy chair by the window.

"Dinner's not what I came for," said Roger. He knelt at her feet and took her hands. She could see a few glints of gray in his black curls. He began kissing the backs of her hands. "I'll do you some poetry," he said. "That'll get you in the mood."

"I don't want to be in the mood," said Cassandra, laughing. "Not yet." She wondered why she was doing this. "I want to talk."

"Talk!" said Roger, looking up at her. "You mean, love talk? Or—" he looked away, assuming an expression of enormous distaste—"conversation."

"Conversation," said Cassandra.

He sighed and got up—slowly, heavily, painfully, to make Cassandra laugh—and hobbled over to the coffee table. "For conversation, I need more to drink," he said, finishing off his scotch. He went to the kitchen for a refill and sprawled once more on the sofa. "Conversation about what?"

"Well I don't know," said Cassandra helplessly. "Tell me what you did today."

"Christ, Cassandra," he said to the ceiling. "What do I do every day? Come on. Life on the rain-drenched Sunshine Coast ain't exactly one thrill after another. You're the only thrilling thing I've found around here, and I've come to you in my best duds, smelling of Brut, booze in one hand and flowers in the other, and you won't even roll around on the floor with me." He reached for his drink. "Fucking's the only entertainment there is in this place. You oughta indulge in it every chance you get."

"Thank you," said Cassandra coldly, "for the advice. I'll certainly keep it in mind."

He got up. "Shit." He grabbed his hair with both hands. "Screwed up again." He hit himself softly on the jaw, first with one fist, then the other. "When will you learn? Shitface. Shitface."

She started to laugh. "Sit down, for God's sake. You're going to damage the goods."

"Don't you want my body, Cassandra?" He peered at her worriedly. "I thought you liked my body." He knelt at her feet again. "I've got good hands," he said, stroking her calves. "I've never known a woman to wear dresses so much." He ran his hands along the insides of her knees, her thighs. "You could take these pantyhose off, though. Bare skin is better."

"Cassandra," he said later, "I've gotta tell you something." They were in her bed. She hadn't closed the curtains, and dim, gray light filtered into the room through the rain spreading itself against the window.

"What?"

"You know I'm not up here for good."

"I know."

"I think it's time I started thinking about getting back." He paused. "I'm getting restless, you know? And besides, I'm running out of bucks."

Cassandra's throat felt raw; grief hovered around the edges of her heart. "When do you think you'll go?"

"A couple of weeks, maybe."

They were lying side by side on their backs, and his arm was around her.

"I talked to my agent a couple of days ago. The son-of-a-bitch finally thinks he might have some work for me."

"I'll miss you," said Cassandra.

"I know. I'll miss you, too. But I've got to get back. It's not much. A one-shot thing in another fucking series. I can't even remember which one." He drew her closer to him, so that her head rested on his shoulder. "But maybe then I'll try to get some theater work. I used to get offers from dinner theaters, regional theaters. Up here, too."

"Don't you get them anymore?"

"They stopped asking when I stopped saying yes."

"Why did you stop saying yes?"

He hesitated. "Oh, I got involved," he said vaguely, "with some things."

She'd never asked him about women. Not even Sechelt women. She wasn't going to start now.

"You're very good in *The Rockford Files*," she said. "Really. Do you ever watch it, at your sister's place?"

He laughed. "Are you kidding?" He sat bolt upright and stared into the darkness of the bedroom. "Who *is* that jerk?" he said incredulously, pointing at an imaginary television screen. "Do I know you from someplace?" He fell back down on the bed beside her. "I got three movies after that series, you know. My agent told me, 'This'll make your name a household word.' Three times he told me that."

"Have you ever thought of moving back up here?" said Cassandra, casually. "There are lots of movies made up here. The papers are always writing stories about them. And there are several theaters, too. In Vancouver. You know, doing plays."

He shivered. "Too cold. It's too damn cold up here. It's too cold and wet up here for me." He raised himself on one elbow and looked down at her. She couldn't see his face clearly; it seemed to be constructed of shadows. "You're the only thing here that keeps me warm," he said, and as he bent to her she wondered how many more times this would happen, and it was a thought which hurt dreadfully, even though she knew she didn't love him.

CHAPTER 10

"So what's the grand total?" said the woman, rolling her eyes at her friend. It was Thursday afternoon.

"Twenty-five dollars and forty cents," said Cassandra.

The woman whipped her head around to stare at her. "Say what?"

"This is a whole lot of books," said Cassandra, resting her hand on them. "All overdue since August. It kind of adds up, doesn't it?"

"It was the end of the holidays. School was starting. He forgot." The woman had begun to smolder, sullenly. "He's only thirteen."

"Come on, Noreen, pay the fine and let's get out of here," said her friend.

"I haven't got the damn fine. Twenty-five dollars and forty cents. Since when have I got that kind of money to spend on library fines?"

The other woman dug around in her handbag. "I've got it. Here."

"Shit," said Noreen. She handed thirty dollars to Cassandra, who opened the cashbox and gave her the change, which Noreen thrust into her friend's hand without looking at her. She pushed a pile of books and her library card toward Cassandra. "Wait till I get my hands on that kid. I'll kill him."

"I'm sorry, Mrs. Murphy," said Cassandra gently. "He's still got six books out. I can't let you have any more until you bring them back."

Noreen Murphy had been slouched against the counter. Now she jerked herself upright. "What are you talking about? Those're his books, not mine." She thrust her selections closer to Cassandra. "These books, these are for me."

"But you let him use your card," said Cassandra. "So I'm afraid they're your responsibility. I'm sorry."

"My responsibility shit!" roared Noreen Murphy.

"Come on, Noreen," said her friend, tugging at her sleeve.

"I don't know where the damn books are. Maybe he sold them, for all I know. So what do I do about that?"

Cassandra looked at her thoughtfully. "Let's see. You could search his room. Or you could report the books lost and pay for them. That would probably cost you—oh, about fifty bucks, plus another thirty or so for the fine, of course; there's kind of a stiff fine, now, when books are lost."

"Fifty bucks! Eighty bucks! You can't name me six books anywhere worth eighty bucks!"

"What I really think you should do, actually," said Cassandra, "is report the kid to the cops. He sounds like he's more trouble than he's worth."

Noreen Murphy looked at her, speechless. She swept both stacks of books, hers and her son's, onto the floor behind the counter and slammed out of the library, closely followed by her friend.

Cassandra dropped onto a stool, thrust her hands in her hair, and yanked.

"Things can get pretty exciting around here," said Alberg admiringly.

She looked quickly around and saw him standing next to one of the fig trees by the windows that made up the front wall of the library. "What are you doing here?"

"Getting some books," he said, and she saw that he had an armful of them. In his other hand was a manila envelope.

Cassandra tried to smooth her hair. "I don't know what's the matter with me. I was so rude to that woman."

Alberg put his books down. "She was a lot ruder to you. You should have decked her." He took something from the envelope and laid it on the counter in front of her. "Ever seen her before?"

Cassandra picked up the copy of the portrait. "She's beautiful," she said.

There was a tag attached to it which read, HAVE YOU SEEN THIS WOMAN? Telephone numbers were provided for R.C.M.P. detachments on the Sunshine Coast.

"Is this the woman who was killed?" She glanced at Alberg and saw him nod. She studied the portrait in silence for almost a minute; she felt her chest tighten, and tears gather, ready to shed themselves for a stranger. Hopelessness overwhelmed her. "No. No, I've never seen her before." She handed the picture back to Alberg. "Tommy did that?"

"It's pretty good, isn't it?"

"She looks like she's breathing."

"Yeah," said Alberg.

"What are you going to do with it?"

"We've had a lot of copies made. We'll put some up at the ferry terminals, the post office, the marinas—anyplace we can. Send some to the papers. And we've got men going door-to-door."

He moved out of the way as an elderly man came up to the counter carrying several large-print novels. Cassandra checked them out and handed them back with a smile.

"You can put one up here, if you like," she said. "On the bulletin board."

"That's why I brought it," said Alberg.

"Here," said Cassandra, reaching for it. "Let me." She went through the hinged section of the counter and over to the large free-standing bulletin board that stood next to a rack of books marked NEW ARRIVALS. The board was covered with notices: storytelling classes for preschoolers, poetry readings at the creative writers' club, a show by a Vancouver painter at the arts center, the current ferry schedule, several plaintive queries about lost pets. Cassandra moved things around and carefully tacked the drawing in a prominent place in the middle of the board.

"Remember last summer," said Alberg as she went back

behind the counter, "when you took me along the beach to George Wilcox's house? And he looked at you and said, 'You've brought the Mountie.'"

"I remember." She began blindly checking out his books. She suddenly wished desperately for June; her longing for summer was so great as to make her dizzy.

"He didn't like that," said Alberg thoughtfully. "He didn't want to think that you might be getting involved with me."

Cassandra sat heavily on the stool and rubbed her temples. She blinked rapidly and put her hands flat on the counter. "I hate this weather. The clouds are so low they might as well be fog."

Alberg covered her hands with his. She hadn't realized until she felt his warmth how cold she was.

"When it's summer again," he said, "I'll teach you how to sail."

"I already know how to sail."

She liked his face. It was smooth, enigmatic; intriguing.

"Good," said Alberg, grinning at her. "That's even better."

And there was no point in denying it, she was also attracted to him. It was too bad, she thought, that they'd never gotten beyond one session of adolescent groping in her kitchen. She remembered that he had turned out the light, so they could see the moon shining over the water, beyond the Indian cemetery across the highway. And he had pressed her so close to him that she felt the beating of his heart against her cheek. She thought she might not have gotten involved with Roger at all, if things had progressed further between her and this cop. This police officer.

"What are you thinking about?" said Alberg.

"Nothing," she said. "I was thinking that I've never seen you wearing a uniform." She pushed the pile of books toward him. They were an odd choice, she thought absently, for a policeman.

"Cassandra."

"Yes?" she said.

"Let's have dinner or something."

She knew immediately that she was going to say yes. Relief and anticipation had just made themselves known to her when the library door opened and her mind started to stutter, because it was Roger who was coming in.

She couldn't believe she deserved this. The sight of him made her weak and she felt her face start to burn. Would she have grown weak at the sight of Karl Alberg if she'd ever gone to bed with him? She was sex-drugged, hypnotized, and when she glanced quickly back at Alberg she knew that he saw it.

She wanted to grab his sleeve and whisper quickly, conspiratorially in his ear: "Just hang in there, Karl, he'll be leaving town soon, he's practically gone already, and then I'll be normal again, whatever that is."

But she said nothing.

He nodded to her as he stepped away from the counter, a gesture of recognition and acceptance.

Roger gave Alberg a smile as they passed each other, but Cassandra was sure that Alberg hadn't even looked at him. She watched Karl leave the library, carrying the books about painting and portraiture.

Roger vaulted over the counter and put his arms around her. "You got any tea? Coffee? Cookies? Is there a couch in your back room? Wanna fool around?" His color was high, his eyes were bright. His lips looked swollen; she wanted to touch them with her tongue. But she lifted the hinged section in the counter and pushed him firmly through it.

"Okay. Okay, we'll wait. When do you get off work?" he said. "I'll wait. I'll find myself something to read." He looked around the empty library. "Doesn't anybody ever come into this place? Who was that big dude, some kind of library inspector?" He wandered to the nearest stack, pulled out a book, looked at it, put it back.

Cassandra ran cool hands over her face and fixed a shirt button that had come undone. "Not exactly. He's a policeman."

Roger looked at her in astonishment. "A cop? A Mountie? What the hell does a Mountie want in a library?" He went back to the counter and leaned over it. "I bet he wants the librarian. Right?" He watched her reaction and roared with laughter.

"He wanted to put a picture on the bulletin board," said Cassandra. "That's all."

"What kind of a picture?" He glanced at the bulletin board. She saw him become still. Then he laughed. "What the hell is that?" He sounded exasperated. He moved closer, closer still, his eyes on the picture. "What the hell is that doing here?"

With his back to Cassandra, Roger stared at it. He read slowly aloud: "HAVE YOU SEEN THIS WOMAN?"

"She's dead," said Cassandra. "Somebody killed her. And nobody knows who she is."

He was still staring at the portrait. "Shit. Fuck." His voice had lost its resonance; it was tense and strained.

My God, thought Cassandra, looking at his shoulders, hunched and tense. She stepped away from him. "Roger," she said. "You recognize her. You *know* her."

CHAPTER 11

"Of course I don't know her," Roger snapped, still with his back to her.

"What's the matter with you, then? Why are you so upset?"

Finally he moved away from the bulletin board. "Norma Hingle told me about it. Somebody cut her throat, right? They got some guy to draw a picture of her after she was dead, for Christ's sake." He was white-faced, and his hands were trembling.

"Oh Roger. Look at you. You're shaking." With an effort, she went to him. He put an arm around her.

"She looks like somebody I know," he said. Cassandra glanced involuntarily beyond him at the portrait. "That's all." She felt him shudder. "Jesus. I thought I was going to have a fucking heart attack."

"Maybe she *is* the person you know," she said.

He shook his head. "No way. It just looks like her, that's all. Jesus."

"Roger," said Cassandra. "Maybe you should go to the police. Just in case."

He pulled away from her. "Forget it. It's not her, I told you." He slumped into a chair next to the Sociology section.

She hesitated. Then, "Who is it that she reminds you of?" she said.

"A friend, that's all," said Roger impatiently. "A friend. Her name's Sally. She lives in L.A." He looked over at the bulletin board. "But that's not her," he said, more confidently. "It's just—it's a spooky resemblance. Christ." He looked up at Cassandra and tried to laugh. "Shook me up some."

"Why don't you call her? Have you got her number?"

"Yeah."

"Why don't you phone her, then? Just to be absolutely sure. I mean, it's possible, isn't it? Anything's possible."

"Yeah, yeah. I will. I'll call her." His eyes kept wandering to the picture.

"Here," said Cassandra, going behind the counter. "There's a phone right here."

"I'm not going to do it now," said Roger irritably. He stood up and ran his hands through his hair. "Shit. I wish I had a toke on me."

"Roger, for God's sake, I don't understand you. You said she was your friend."

"That's not her, I told you!" he shouted, pointing at the drawing. "No way. No bloody way."

Cassandra studied him. "Why are you carrying on like this," she said quietly, "if you're so sure?"

"Because of the goddamn picture. Because it looks like her. Because it gives me the fucking creeps, that's why." He looked out the window. "Jesus Christ, it's still raining. That's all it does around this godforsaken place is rain. I came to ask if I can borrow your car again."

"Why don't you borrow your sister's car?" said Cassandra stiffly.

"Her old man's got it. It's his day off or some fucking thing. How about it? I can get the four-thirty ferry, be back tomorrow."

"What? You want it overnight? How am I supposed to get to work?"

"I don't know. I thought maybe you could get a ride with somebody. Forget it." Restlessness radiated from him; she saw it as heat waves. "I just wanted to get out of here for a while. Into a city. Forget it."

Cassandra was still behind the counter. She picked up the books flung to the floor by Noreen Murphy and began furiously thumping them onto a cart.

"I could have it back by noon," he said. "Pick you up after work. Take you out to dinner somewhere."

"Great," said Cassandra. "Terrific."

"I'm not dealing with that guy anymore. He makes me nervous. I want to see if I can score in town. Somebody gave me a name."

"Oh wonderful," said Cassandra bitterly, slamming down the last book.

"I thought you'd be relieved," he protested. "Your car stands out like a neon sign around here. What would your cop friend think if he saw it where it's got no business being?"

Cassandra sat down on the stool. She wished somebody would come into the library. "Take the damn car," she said.

"How will you get here in the morning?" said Roger. Cassandra was fumbling in her purse. His hand was already out to accept her keys.

"I'll get the volunteer to pick me up." She raised her head to look at him. The car keys were in her hand. "I still think you should tell the police. If you don't want to call your friend, they'll do it for you."

"Tell them what, for Christ's sake? 'Oh, excuse me, sir,

but that picture in the library? It looks an awful lot like somebody I know.' 'Oh, really, Mr. Galbraith? And where does this person live?' 'She lives in Los Angeles, sir.' 'Ah. Los Angeles. Well, thank you very much, Mr. Galbraith, don't call us, we'll call you.'"

"Right," said Cassandra, nodding. "I'm sure that's exactly what would happen."

"Well, shit on it."

"I saw your face when you looked at that drawing."

For a minute he just stared at her, tense and cold. "I don't like cops," he said finally. "L.A. cops, Vancouver cops, Mounties—means fuck-all to me where they come from. I don't like any of them."

Cassandra waited.

"Are you going to give me those keys or not?"

Cassandra gave him the keys.

CHAPTER 12

That evening Alberg took himself off to talk again to Alfred Hingle.

Alfred's house didn't have anything like an actual driveway leading up to it. There was an access road about five hundred feet away, wandering toward the beach, and from the road to Alfred's house a rutted trail had been blazed by his pickup truck. This trail branched into a circle in front of the porch.

Hingle's place was a never-ending source of fascination for Alberg. His visits, though infrequent, were usually pleasurable.

Not this time, though.

Alberg parked on the soggy grass off the access road and plodded through the rain toward the lights from Alfred's house. He tried like a turtle to huddle into the shelter of his upturned collar, he thrust his hands into the pockets of his zippered jacket, and he kept a careful eye on the trail ahead of him, but the rain got into his ears and wet the thighs of his pants and sloshed in muddy puddles around his ankles. He heard it rustling in the woods behind the house, chattering on the roof, thudding on the pickup parked at the top of the circle, pinging from the tarpaulin that was stretched over a pile of boards beside Alfred's shed.

The dog began to bark as he neared the porch. He knocked at the door and heard Alfred give a command. The dog quieted and Alberg waited, looking down morosely at his sodden shoes.

He saw fear in Norma's face when she opened the door. He felt like a storm trooper.

"My goodness, Mr. Alberg," she said, "you're soaked through; where's your car?"

"I left it on the road. Wasn't sure I could get it turned around in here." He shook raindrops from his smooth blond hair and stomped his feet on the sisal mat.

"Take your jacket off," she said when he was inside. She closed the door behind him. "Here, give it to me, I'll hang it up in the kitchen." She went down the hall, calling loudly, "Alfred, Mr. Alberg's here. Come along, Mr. Alberg," she said over her shoulder. "Come in where it's warm."

"I've interrupted your dinner," said Alberg from the kitchen doorway. It was past seven; he'd been sure they would have eaten. "I'm sorry." He stood there dismayed as Alfred rose from his chair, crumpling a paper napkin in his hand.

"It's all right," said Alfred. The big dog thumped his tail on the floor under the table where he had been told to lie down. "I'll finish, though, if you don't mind, before we talk. Sit down. Norma will get you some coffee."

Norma had hung his jacket from a hook on the wall above a heat register. Now she got a cup and saucer from the cupboard and poured coffee from a pot on the stove.

"It's miserable weather, just miserable," she said, setting the cup in front of him. She sat down and picked up her napkin, smoothed it over her lap. Her face was flushed and Alberg thought he could see the pulse beating in her throat. "Every morning I wake up and before I even open my eyes please God I say don't let it be raining, and I haven't even got it said before my ears hear it, pittering away out there." She loaded her fork with mashed potatoes. "I'm riding my bike to work these days, you see, Mr. Alberg, and home again too, because my Mini's in the shop." She put down the fork, still laden, and energetically sprinkled salt over the potatoes, the Brussels sprouts, and the half-eaten slice of meat loaf on her plate.

"Norma," said Alfred.

"Well, I wear something on my head," she said, apparently addressing the meat loaf, "one of those plastic things, you can buy them in the drugstore, they have them right next to the checkouts these days, along with the pocket Kleenex, because good lord it just goes on raining and raining, but they break, you know, the seams are not well sewn, I have it in mind to make one for myself, just about anything you make yourself, the quality's bound to be better."

"Norma, eat," said Alfred.

Alberg shuffled his feet uncomfortably. He bowed his head and tried to think of Norma's torrent of words as rain, or a rushing stream, or the wind in treetops, but there was too much tension in her voice.

"It's a terrible thing, what happened," said Norma, emptying the potatoes from her fork and spearing a Brussels sprout. "That poor girl. And such a shock, now, to see those pictures up everywhere you turn, looking alive and fit to speak, while really she couldn't be deader, could she?" She looked suddenly at Alberg, and he had to turn away.

"Norma," said Alfred again, sounding tired.

Beneath the table the dog sighed, heavily. The rain gossiped at the window. A wind-up clock ticked busily from the kitchen counter. Alberg wondered if Alfred had rescued it, and the small desk and chair which sat in a corner of the kitchen, too. His eyes wandered to the sampler hanging on the wall and Norma must have seen a look of incredulity on his face as he read the words inscribed there in needlepoint, for she laughed and said in her speeded-up voice, "Oh my, what must he think, Alfred, reading that thing?"

"Oh, no," said Alberg weakly. But he did find it abrupt and astonishing. *Heigh o! Heigh o!* it read. *What'll I do wi' ye? Black's the life that I lead wi' ye.*

"It's part of a lullaby, you see, Mr. Alberg," said Norma, leaning earnestly toward him. "A Scottish lullaby. I did it when I was a young girl—you see how big and awkward the lettering is?"

"Norma, stop your goddamn nattering," said Alfred.

"I was supposed to get the next four lines in there, too," she said to Alberg. "But I'd used up all the space. The next four lines explain it, you see. They say, 'Mony o' ye, little to gie ye. Heigh o! Heigh o! What'll I do wi' ye?'" She was looking at him expectantly.

"I see," said Alberg. He looked at the sampler and nodded, feeling clumsy. "A lullaby. That's very nice."

Alfred threw down his fork and pushed himself out of his chair. "We'll go to the shed now," he said. He put on his Cowichan sweater and handed Alberg his still-wet jacket. The dog, who had raised his head to watch, got up when Alfred opened the door and followed him out into the rainy night.

Alberg hesitated. "Thanks for the coffee," he said.

Norma looked up at him. "You're his friend, aren't you, Mr. Alberg?"

He thought friendship was too big a word to describe the relationship that existed between them. But he did like Alfred Hingle. So he said, "I am, yes."

Norma nodded. "I'll just do up the dishes," she said, picking up her dinner plate, "while you're talking."

Alberg went outside and closed the door softly.

He made his way along a well-trodden path toward the shed; a light shone from inside, and he could see that the door had been left partly open for him.

Alfred's home had been imposed upon the woods. About a mile due west lay the ocean. Alfred could walk through the forest and down a small sandy cliff straight onto the beach. He often went there, with his dog, at low tide, and collected things left on the shore by the sea.

Alberg had heard about Alfred Hingle soon after he arrived to take over the Sechelt detachment, two years ago. First from Isabella. And then from the R.C.M.P. files.

Alberg's house in Gibsons had contained, when he moved in, an old wringer washing machine. He was pleased to see it there; it reminded him of his childhood. But he couldn't get it to work properly, and when he mentioned this to Isabella she'd told him there wasn't a hardware store on the Sunshine Coast likely to have wringer washing machine parts in stock. But she said that Alfred Hingle might. So Alberg had sought him out.

Alfred was a collector of all sorts of things. The clearing in which his small house stood was surrounded by objects. A pile of boards of varying lengths and thicknesses. A doghouse, in which Clyde had no interest. Several oak barrels which filled with rain and then let it pour or dribble out the top so that shallow troughs had been carved in the earth around them.

Alfred had also at one time had a wringer washer and, fortunately for Alberg, had frugally saved various bits and pieces of it in carefully marked boxes which he kept on a shelf in his shed.

Hingle had also acquired a double-size bedspring and that, too, was in the yard, along with half a dozen plaster flamingos whose pink paint had by now almost completely flaked off. And there were three large rolls of chicken wire, and several sections of drainage pipe. The house stood on a slight rise. Alfred had so far had no problem with accumulations of rain-water seeping into the crawl space and causing mold to grow on the inside walls of the house; this was a situation encountered by some people he knew, and he'd told Alberg that he had a horror of its happening to him. He said he felt reassured every time he looked outside and saw the row of pipe sections sitting there next to the shed.

There had been a lawn, once, around the small house. But Alfred and Norma had let it revert to nature. Dandelions and buttercups and wild roses and giant lupins rioted around the house in the summer; dead weeds and muck surrounded the place in winter.

The house itself, however, was kept in excellent repair.

Alberg reached the shed and went inside, closing the door against the rain.

"Come on over here and get warm," said Alfred.

Alberg went to the Franklin stove and held his hands out toward the fire.

Hingle pulled up two folding chairs, one metal and the other made of canvas, which he placed at either side of the large mat directly in front of the fire. Then he whistled, and the dog, who had been standing by the door wagging his tail expectantly, padded across the shed and arranged himself upon the mat.

Alfred Hingle was what in more sophisticated communities had come to be known as a sanitary engineer; in Sechelt, he was a garbageman. He drove his pickup to the town offices five mornings a week, got into a garbage truck, and set off on his rounds. He liked working alone and would never have considered moving to a big city, where sanitary engineers were assigned in teams. He also liked taking Clyde along with him, which wouldn't have been possible in most places. He was content in Sechelt, where he drove at the end of the day out to the dump, unloaded his truck, and had plenty of opportunity to poke through his collections when he felt like it.

"Sit down, Mr. Alberg," said Alfred, pointing to the canvas chair.

Alberg sat, and got out his notebook and pen.

Alfred had pulled a pipe from his pocket. He reached for a tin of tobacco on the shelf behind him. He seemed remarkably calm.

"She was killed between seven-thirty and ten-thirty P.M.," said Alberg.

Alfred took a tamper from his pocket and tamped down the tobacco. Alberg held out his lighter, but Alfred shook his head and used a wooden match from a box on the shelf. He lit the pipe, puffing, and smoke billowed toward the ceiling.

"Norma was at work," Hingle said. "You already know that. From three o'clock on. I drove her to the hospital because I wanted to check out the Mini. So I did that. Turned out that it's leaking brake fluid. She took it in to the shop before she went to work the next day."

The shed wasn't a shed at all, but a long, narrow garage. Hingle had installed two rectangular windows, side by side, in the wall behind Alberg, which faced the house. The garage doors at one end were still operable. The remaining wall space was covered with shelving.

"You took Norma to work at three," said Alberg. "And then you checked out the Mini. Then what?"

"Then I fixed one of the lamps in the living room. It needed a new plug."

On the shelves were items requiring repair—a wooden tobacco stand that was missing a leg, electrical appliances including a toaster, a heater, a mixer, and several lamps, and a small wooden box. Alberg also saw a large number of cans of indoor and outdoor paint, paraphernalia for applying wallpaper, and sandpaper, scrapers, tins of paint remover, and a selection of stains and brushes.

"I just sort of puttered around in here," said Alfred, "until I got hungry." He was frowning at the wood fire in the Franklin stove; his forehead was creased. "Was this woman sexually molested?" He sounded like he was quoting from a textbook.

"No," said Alberg.

"Oh well," said Alfred dryly. "I mightn't have gotten around to it. Maybe somebody was coming. Maybe I got scared. Could be lots of reasons for that."

"Sure," said Alberg agreeably. "What time was it when you got hungry?"

Alfred shot him a sideways glance. The reflection from the fire flashed briefly in his eyeglasses. "You figure I went out and found this woman somewhere, and killed her in those woods, and sat her up against that tree, and then went home and got my dog so he could find her body? Is that the kind of damnfool thing you're figuring?"

"I don't figure anything, Alfred. Not yet. I'm just going around getting information, right now."

Alberg's right side was warm and dry. The fire crackled

behind its screen, and there was a pungent scent like licorice in the air, from Alfred's pipe tobacco. He had a sudden craving for a glass of brandy.

A kid, he thought, looking around the shed, a small boy, would love this place. On the floor under the shelves were cartons of various sizes labeled SMALL APPLIANCES, HARDWARE, SMALL FURNISHINGS, and TOYS, among other things. These contained objects restored to their former usefulness. When he figured that the shed wouldn't comfortably hold anything more, Alfred would reluctantly take these cartons to the Salvation Army.

"So?" he said. "What time did you eat?"

Alfred shrugged. "I don't remember looking at the time. It was dark. But it gets dark about five, now. And I like my supper early."

"You didn't have an early supper today," said Alberg.

Hingle snorted. "That's because of the goddamn *Rockford Files*. She always has to watch the goddamn *Rockford Files*."

"When do you figure you finished eating?"

"If I can't remember when I started," said Alfred irritably, "how the hell can I remember when I finished?"

"Make a guess," said Alberg.

Hingle sighed. "Say about six-thirty. That's probably about right."

"And then what did you do?"

The other man shrugged, defeated. "I cleaned up my dishes, fed the dog, watched TV, and about ten I took Clyde for a walk and you know the rest." Clyde raised his head and studied Alfred's face attentively. Alfred reached down and rubbed behind the dog's ears.

On the wall to Alberg's left were more shelves, and from a nail hung a scarred, chewed Frisbee which he knew was the dog's.

"How did you come to call him Clyde?" he said.

"It seemed to fit him," said Alfred. His pipe had gone out. He got up to knock it gently against the fireplace hearth.

"Did anybody phone?" said Alberg. "Or drop in?"

"Nope. I don't get many people phoning me, or stopping in. Norma does. She's more of a social animal than me. But that night—no." He looked at Alberg and again the fire burned in his glasses. "We'll change places, now. Get the other side of you dried off." He stood and picked up his chair, and Alberg did the same. The dog waited until this had been accomplished, then got up, stretched, turned around and laid himself down so that he was facing Alfred.

Alberg's eye was caught by a piece of paper that had been tacked to the wall he was now facing, between the windows. He couldn't quite make out what it was.

"It was a long time ago," Alfred was saying. "Do you know how long?"

Alberg couldn't remember, so he shook his head.

He thought it looked like a piece of drawing paper. He squinted, trying to see it more clearly.

"It was twenty-five years ago," said Alfred. "Twenty-five years." He shook his head. "I guess I'll never get to the finish of it. Not unless I change my name and move away. And I'm not that type of person." He looked over at Alberg. "I still think I should have just left her there. Even though you would have come after me for it anyway."

"Can you remember anything more about that car you might have heard? Before Clyde found the body?"

Alfred stared into the fire. "I think I did hear it," he said slowly. "I think I did. But I can't be sure."

Alberg put away his notebook. "I'd better be going."

"Thanks for coming yourself, anyway," said Alfred. "I appreciate it. Some of those snot-nosed constables you've got—I don't take kindly to them."

Alberg stood up and went over to look at what was pinned to Alfred's wall. When he was close enough to see what it was, he felt an unpleasant prickling at the back of his neck. "Where did you get this?" he said.

Alfred shrugged. "Where do I get anything?"

A pencil sketch hung there. It was obviously a drawing done by Tommy Cummings, a preliminary to the portrait in pastels.

Alberg turned to look at Hingle. "You know what it is, don't you?"

"He threw it out," said Alfred defensively.

Alberg moved closer to the sketch. The only light in the shed came from a high-watt bulb hanging on a long cord from the middle of the ceiling, above a long high table at which Alfred did his repair work. It left most of the rest of the place in shadow.

"He didn't want it," said Alfred. "There's no reason I shouldn't have it."

"Have you got a flashlight?"

Alfred didn't move for a moment. Then he got a flashlight from a built-in table in the corner, above which hung his tools. Silently, he handed it to Alberg, who shone it onto the sketch.

It was rough, uninteresting, lifeless; no wonder he'd thrown it away, thought Alberg. "Was this the only one you found?"

"There were lots of them. This is the only one I liked."

Her head was back; maybe she was supposed to be laughing. It was hard to tell. Alberg was left with an impression of listlessness.

He switched off the flashlight and handed it back to Alfred. "What the hell made you want to keep it?" he said.

Alfred flushed. "I told you. I liked it. Why? Do you think I'd be stupid enough to take it if I'd killed her? Put it up on my damn wall for anybody to see?"

Alberg hesitated. "I don't know, Alfred. Would you?"

CHAPTER 13

Two days later Alberg reached up to straighten Tommy Cummings' original portrait, which was hanging slightly askew from the pushpin which held it to his office wall. It looked incongruous against the pea-green paint, and hung too near the framed photograph of his daughters for his liking. Yet if he had put it anywhere else it wouldn't have been close enough for him to study, and he had come to think it important that he study it. Or maybe it was just a macabre point of focus for his mullings and musings, a lightning rod for his frustrations. It had become almost as familiar to him as was the photograph of Janey and Diana.

He had searched Alfred Hingle's house again, and the shed, too. He hadn't found anything. He hadn't expected to find anything.

Of course the sketch Hingle had filched from Cummings' trash could in itself be construed as evidence. But evidence of what? Of his already well-known habit of rummaging through other people's garbage, that was what.

Alberg got up and went to the window, which overlooked the hills beyond the town. He realized that in just a few more weeks it would be Christmas. He still hadn't taken all his annual leave, and headquarters was on his back about using up his days before the end of the year. Maybe he'd invite himself to his parents' home in Ontario. He would have preferred to spend the holidays with his daughters, but he knew they planned to stay in Calgary and have Christmas with their other grandparents. Maura, his ex-wife, would be there, too.

He went back to his desk and gazed at the photograph of his daughters, permitting himself a moment of self-pity. He had expected them to provide him with a new picture of themselves by now. Each time he looked at this one he felt foolish and bewildered, because he had been so dumbfounded by the changes in them when they'd come for the Labor Day weekend. Diana had let her short hair grow until it fell halfway down her back, and Janey had had her long mane cut; it curled feverishly all over her head now. At least neither of them had sported purple streaks or a shaven nape. At least he could be thankful for that.

He'd brought his daughters to his office while they were in Sechelt, of course, and their laughter had filled the small room when they saw their photograph on the wall. He had taken it himself, a few months before he and Maura separated. His daughters seemed to have forgotten all about it. Maybe they'd never even seen it before. You'd think, he told himself again, that they'd want an up-to-date representation of themselves hanging on the wall beside the desk.

He sat down in his squeaky swivel chair, flipped open the folder which lay in front of him and went through yet again the steadily thickening file marked HOMICIDE, JANE DOE.

She had been in her late thirties. She was well nourished, in good health. She had never been pregnant. She had not smoked. Muscle tone was very good; she had probably followed a regular exercise program. She had stood five feet five inches tall and weighed 120 pounds. There were no scars or other identifying marks. The fingernails were of medium length; most were broken, and earth and fragments of bark and moss and decaying leaves had been found beneath them. She had clawed at the branches that had entrapped her, but not, apparently, at her assailant.

Her legs and underarms had been recently shaved, her hair had been professionally bleached within three weeks prior to death. Her teeth were in excellent condition. The minimal dental work she had required could have been performed anywhere in North America. There was no evidence of sexual attack or of recent sexual activity.

On the third finger of her right hand she had worn a wide filigreed ring of 10-carat gold; on the fourth finger of the same hand was a 14-carat setting in the shape of a small, scooped wave which held a pearl. There was an inexpensive Timex digital watch on her left wrist, and 14-carat gold studs in her pierced ears. Her hair had apparently been held back at the sides by combs which could have been purchased in any drugstore or department store; they had been found in the tangle of logs where she was killed.

When she died she was wearing a brassiere and panties, a short-sleeved white T-shirt under a long-sleeved navy blue sweatshirt, jeans, heavy white knee-high socks with two dark blue horizontal stripes at the top, red plastic boots, and a red raincoat, also made of plastic. The brassiere had been washed so often that the label was indecipherable, but it was eventually identified by a Vancouver distributor as an American-manufactured item marketed in the tens of thousands over a period of several years in outlets across Canada. The panties, also well worn, could not be positively identified. The T-shirt was a small size in a common brand of men's underclothing. The sweatshirt was an international brand sold extensively throughout the country. So were the jeans.

The boots and the raincoat were new and had been traced to the Hudson's Bay Company, the exclusive distributors in British Columbia. There were no Bay stores on the Sunshine Coast, but there were a lot of them in the Lower Mainland—the area around metropolitan Vancouver—and several on Vancouver Island. Copies of the portrait were being shown to employees, but Alberg didn't expect anything to come of it.

The stone found in the raincoat pocket was smooth, creamy gray in color, and looked like a misshapen bird's egg. There was nothing special about it—it could have been picked up from any beach—except that it gave no evidence of ever having been touched. The stone was of a shape and texture that invited touching, stroking, rolling firmly in the hand. Yet either she had not touched it, or had touched it wearing gloves which had now disappeared, or the stone had been carefully wiped clean of fingerprints: by the killer?

There were some partial prints on the raincoat, but they were the victim's.

He had to have touched her raincoat. He was wearing gloves, then. Had he also touched the stone? Wiped it clean, placed it in her pocket? Alberg rubbed his temples wearily. That was no more peculiar than cleaning off her face and propping her up against a goddamn tree.

She had now been dead for almost six days.

Her description matched none of the missing persons reports available on the computer.

Alberg closed the file and pushed it away. He put his feet up on his desk and locked his hands behind his head.

She had bled to death from two slashes across her throat. The weapon was an extremely sharp knife with a thin, narrow blade. It could have been an expensive, well-cared-for kitchen knife, a tool used in woodworking, a fileting knife; the possibilities, thought Alberg, were legion.

The weapon had not been found.

The exhaustive search of the crime scene hadn't turned up a handbag, either.

There were severe defensive wounds on her hands, wrists, and forearms.

The portrait was already producing in communities up and down the Sunshine Coast pity for the victim, admiration for the artist, and horror at the thought of a murderer even now hiding among the populace. It was widely and firmly held that he could not possibly be a resident, and so unfamiliar faces were no longer smiled upon; strangers were treated with a suspicious coldness that bewildered them.

So far nobody had recognized her. Alberg struggled for patience. It was just a matter of time, he thought, before people began to come forward.

She had fled through the blackberries, across the clearing and into the woods; from the road, then. Nobody takes pleasure walks along a deserted, forest-bordered highway late on a wet, cold November evening. So she must have been in a car. Either her own, or one belonging to someone she knew. At least Alberg fervently hoped so. A check through the files had come up with only one unsolved homicide in the area over the past ten years; it was assumed that the victim, an eighteen-year-old girl, had been hitchhiking. But this victim was a woman in her thirties, unlikely to be hitchhiking unless she'd had car trouble. And no cars had broken down on the coast highway that night.

Alberg took the portrait down from the wall. He rested his finger against the curve of the cheek. He thought of the polite signs that request admirers not to touch works of art because the gentlest of touches, repeated thousands of times, has an erosive power as great as wind or rain. He held the painting farther away and marveled again at the sunlight that streamed in from the left, casting a golden glow upon one side of the woman's face, while the other was veiled in delicate shadow.

He knew that if the victim had been a resident of the Sunshine Coast it was just a matter of time before somebody reported her missing—family, friends, co-workers—or recognized her from the portrait.

But if she *hadn't* lived here . . . that was a whole different story.

Ferries churn the waters of Howe Sound from Langdale, at the southern end of the Sunshine Coast, to Horseshoe Bay, near Vancouver. At the northern end they cross Jervis Inlet from Earls Cove to Saltery Bay, which is about twenty miles south of Powell River. Still more ferries traverse the Strait of Georgia between Powell River and Comox, on Vancouver Island.

The highway that stretches along the Sunshine Coast between Langdale and Earls Cove, a distance of forty-five miles, reappears at Saltery Bay and leads to Powell River. It continues for twenty more miles and comes to an abrupt end at the town of Lund. Beyond it lies almost a thousand miles of British Columbia coastline cleft by countless inlets and channels, cluttered with small islands, accessible only by boat and, from the east, by occasional logging tracks and secondary roads.

If she hadn't lived on the Sunshine Coast, she must have arrived there by ferry from Horseshoe Bay, or from Vancouver Island via Powell River and Saltery Bay.

It was unlikely she would have come as a tourist in November, thought Alberg. So she must have had friends or family somewhere in the area, people who were expecting her. The canvass now under way was certain, he told himself, to eventually bring face-to-face with her portrait someone who had known her, someone who could identify her.

There was a knock on his office door and Sid Sokolowski came in. "We got something. Finally."

"The weapon?"

"A knapsack. And a kind of a purse thing. No wallet, no I.D. But there's a bit of this and a bit of that. Belonged to a woman, all right. Might be hers."

"Jesus." Alberg stood up and hurriedly shoved his shirttail more securely into his pants. "Where are they?"

"I've got the guys working on them."

"Who found them?"

"Guy owns that restaurant at Davis Bay. He went out to push his garbage bags into his trash can, saw them in the bottom. Good thing he looked. Usually you don't look, you just dump."

Alberg picked up the painting and tacked it back on the wall. Whenever he looked at it, she looked right back at him. He kept thinking there was something there for him to discover, something other than loveliness and melancholy. But her lips never moved, she never spoke to him, and all he saw in her eyes was the reflection of an out-of-sight window.

Maybe the knapsack, or the purse, would speak to him.

"Let's go," he said.

CHAPTER 14

"You'll find that she didn't come from around here," said Mrs. Mitchell decisively, the next day. She was small and round, with gray hair cut straight across at ear level, and straight across her forehead in bangs. She nodded knowingly at Cassandra, who was making her regular Sunday visit.

Cassandra knew at once who her mother was talking about.

Mrs. Mitchell irritated her daughter in several ways. She chewed gum and sometimes caused it to make cracking sounds. Although she was a well-fed woman, she picked at her food every Sunday evening, when Cassandra had prepared her meal. And instead of expressing opinions, Mrs. Mitchell made pronouncements.

"I don't know how you can possibly say such a thing," said Cassandra, more sharply than she had intended.

"If she were from Sechelt," said her mother, "or anywhere on the Sunshine Coast, for that matter, somebody would have reported her missing by now. Around here," she said comfortably, "we care about each other."

A shiver of rage passed through Cassandra's body. It originated within her rib cage and sliced straight down into someplace in the vaginal area, where it culminated in a tiny convulsion. She concentrated on roughly brushing crumbs from the tablecloth in front of her onto the floor.

"Though you can't tell, these days," Mrs. Mitchell went on. "These days people just up and disappear without a word to a soul. Margie Corcoran's husband did that last year. Of course, there was another woman. Everybody knew it." She shifted her bulk in the chair. "Let's get away from this table. I can't stand sitting here looking at dirty plates."

While her mother moved into the tiny living room of her Golden Arms apartment, Cassandra cleared the table, rinsed the dishes, and stacked them on the counter next to the sink.

It was surely inconceivable, she thought, that a woman found murdered near the highway outside Sechelt could be anyone Roger knew from Los Angeles.

"Don't bother with all that now," Mrs. Mitchell called out. "I hardly get to see you. I don't want to spend our visiting time with you out there in the kitchen."

It hadn't been a good three days, thought Cassandra. Roger was jumpy and irritable and snapped at her every time she brought up the subject of his friend. So she'd stopped bringing it up. He'd stopped asking to borrow her car, too, at least for the moment.

"Did you get out to Bingo this week?" she said, determined to put her mind to something else. She sat down in the only easy chair in the living room. Mrs. Mitchell occupied the sofa. Behind a screen at the back of the room was a three-quarter bed, a small chest of drawers, and a night table.

"I was supposed to go with Joan Nunn." Mrs. Mitchell had put on her glasses and pulled some needlework from a basket next to the sofa. She was working on a cushion cover. "Her son-in-law came over from Vancouver; he had some business in Gibsons, I guess. Anyway he took her out for dinner. So I stayed home."

"You could have gone with Margie," said Cassandra. "Or Olive Penner. Or the Willoughbys."

Sally. Her name was Sally. Cassandra was sure Roger hadn't mentioned her last name. If he had, she thought, I could call her myself.

"I am not one to invite myself places, Cassandra," her mother was saying. She sounded insulted.

For a moment, Cassandra looked at her blankly. Then, "You could have gone alone," she said. "Good God, Mother, it's just up the hill."

Mrs. Mitchell worked in silence, her head bent over the cushion cover. "My legs have been giving me a bit of trouble lately. I don't feel confident, walking alone. The humiliation, if I should fall, and not be able to get up again. Not to mention the possible damage."

As soon as she'd made the call, she'd tell Roger, of course. He might feel guilty for not having done it himself, and angry with Cassandra for her effrontery, but mostly she knew he'd be relieved.

Mrs. Mitchell looked around her: at the coffee table, the end table next to the sofa, on the floor by her feet. "I've left my coffee in the kitchen."

But how could she persuade him to tell her Sally's last name?

Cassandra got up. She refilled her mother's cup and placed it on the end table. She glanced out the window and saw that it was raining again.

"You know old Mrs. Abrams?" said her mother. "Lives alone over near Porpoise Bay?"

He'd been badly shaken when he saw the portrait. She'd gone over and over it in her mind. He'd stared at it so intently, and his face was so gray and drawn.

"Well," said Mrs. Mitchell. "Maud Abrams' son cleaned up her back yard for her last month. Raked up all the leaves, spread manure on the gardens. And he propped up a young cherry tree he'd planted for her in the spring. He should have done it then, of course, right when he planted it, but he was probably in too much of a hurry. He's a lawyer, you know. Peter Abrams."

Cassandra nodded.

He had tried to convince himself, and her, that this person, this murdered person, wasn't the woman he knew.

"Up in Powell River." Mrs. Mitchell stopped for another sip of coffee. "One thing about you, Cassandra. You make delicious coffee."

"Thanks, Mother."

But he wasn't convinced. That's why he hadn't called Sally, Cassandra realized. He was afraid to.

"Anyway," said Mrs. Mitchell, "last month he was cleaning up out there, and he saw that the cherry tree was listing, so he propped it up and strung guy wires around." She looked over at Cassandra. "And two weeks ago Maud was out there sprinkling food around for the birds, she tripped over one of those wires, landed on her head on a rock."

"Good heavens," said Cassandra absently.

What did he have against the police? He just didn't like them, she told herself. A lot of people didn't like them. She wasn't all that fond of them herself—except for Karl Alberg.

But what would Sally be doing up here? Would she have come in search of Roger, for some reason? What was between the two of them, anyway?

Mrs. Mitchell picked up the cushion cover and resumed her work. "She would have been all right if it hadn't been for the rock, Maud would've. What a rock that size was doing in the middle of the lawn I can't figure, since he'd supposedly cleaned up the yard. And why those wires didn't have red ribbons or something tied on them, I can't figure, either. So she smashed her head on the rock, poor Maud. Jaw just smashed right in."

Cassandra suddenly remembered the day soon after they met when she and Roger had gone cycling, on bikes rented from the hardware store. He was showing off, flying no-hands down the hill in front of the hospital, when he'd struck a rock and been thrown off. She remembered his paleness when he realized that he was bleeding, his fearfulness in the hospital's emergency room.

"She's still in the hospital," Mrs. Mitchell went on, "drinking through a straw. I was up there to see her Thursday. Or was it Wednesday?" She stopped to think. "No, it must have been Thursday."

"Have you got any wine or anything?" said Cassandra.

Her mother gave her an exasperated glance. "I think I have a bottle of something, somewhere."

"Do you mind if I have some?"

"Help yourself. If you must."

In a kitchen cupboard Cassandra found some Irish Cream, unopened, and a half-full bottle of vodka which she herself had put there several months earlier. She put ice in a glass, splashed in some vodka, and immediately felt stronger.

Nobody, she thought, who's squeamish at the sight of his own blood could possibly shed anybody else's.

"What's wrong with you, Cassandra?" said her mother when Cassandra had seated herself again in the living room.

"Nothing, Mother. Nothing at all," said Cassandra. She tried a smile. It didn't feel quite right. "Really. I'm a bit preoccupied, maybe. That's all."

Mrs. Mitchell put her needlework aside. "The police came here, you know," she said. "Asking if we'd seen anything. After they found that poor woman's body. Because it happened quite near here, you know. In that clearing down there by the highway. All that's between us and that clearing is a bunch of woods and Alfred Hingle's place."

My God, said Cassandra to herself. What have I been thinking that I didn't want to know about?

"Well?" she said to her mother. She drank some vodka. "Did anybody have anything interesting to tell them?"

"Good grief, Cassandra," said Mrs. Mitchell good-humoredly, "the whole bunch of us is either deaf, blind, lame, or fast becoming senile. Much good we could do them." She tucked her needlework back into its basket and picked up her cup and saucer. Slowly, deliberately, she took a sip. "What do you hear from your friend the staff sergeant? He must be involved in this, isn't he? What have they found out?"

"I don't see him much anymore, Mother."

Mrs. Mitchell studied her. "He was a nice-looking chap, I thought. Police work—that's steady. Around here it can't be very dangerous."

"I'm not looking for a husband, Mother." She took another drink.

"I'm told," said her mother casually, "that you've been seeing a lot of that actor. Hanna Galbraith's boy."

"That's true," said Cassandra steadily.

"Hanna says he'll be going back soon to wherever he came from. Los Angeles, is it?"

"Los Angeles. Yes."

"He's staying with his sister Stella, I hear."

"That's right, yes."

He's got to tell them, she thought with sudden conviction. It settled upon her implacably, a coldness around her heart. He's got to help them.

"Have you seen that picture of the dead woman they've got up all over the place?" said her mother.

"Yes, I have."

"They've even put one in the O.A.P. hall. People stand and stare at it. It's quite remarkable. Who did they get to draw it, do you know?"

Cassandra stood up. "Tommy Cummings from the school did it. He—they showed him the body, and he drew her face. Mother—"

Mrs. Mitchell was stupefied. "We thought—we just assumed—we thought they'd found a picture of her somewhere. In her purse, or somewhere."

Cassandra had picked up her raincoat from where she'd draped it over the back of a kitchen chair. She began edging toward the door. "Mother, I have to go. I'm sorry."

The woman was dead. Somebody had cut her damn throat.

"Cassandra," said her mother, shocked. "It's barely seven. You might have told me you wouldn't be able to stay."

Either you go to them, she'd say. Right now. Or I will.

"I'm sorry, Mother," she said again. She kissed Mrs. Mitchell's cheek, squeezed her hand, and hurried out into the rainy darkness to the parking lot behind Golden Arms.

It was the first Sunday that she'd left her mother's apartment without doing the dishes.

CHAPTER 15

It was almost midnight before she got him on the phone. She'd called every half hour. She didn't leave messages because she wasn't at all sure that he'd return them. Of course his sister must have recognized Cassandra's voice, but if she did, she didn't acknowledge it, for which Cassandra was grateful.

Finally, he answered the phone himself.

"Roger," she said. "It's me." She found herself speaking in a tone so low that it was almost a whisper. She was in bed by now, knees drawn up, wearing a flannel nightgown and an old chenille bathrobe. She couldn't seem to get warm enough, even though the electric blanket was turned up to high.

"Cassandra. What can I do for you?" He sounded courteous, civilized. She wondered if his sister was hovering somewhere in the room with him.

"Are you alone?" She realized that she was hunched tensely over the phone, which was wedged between her thighs and her stomach.

"In the house? No. In the kitchen? Yes."

"Roger, you've got to call them. The police. About the picture. You've got to."

She listened intently, and thought she heard him breathing, slowly and regularly.

"No, I don't, Cassandra," he said flatly.

"Yes. You do." She was staring hard at the bedspread that covered her knees. It was ivory colored, and becoming worn. She didn't know what it was made of, but it was washable. Maybe she washed it too often. Maybe that was making it wear out.

He sighed into the phone and said wearily, "Cassandra. You're like a dog with a goddamn bone. Put it out of your head. I have. Jesus Christ. You're irrational, do you know that?"

"If you don't talk to them," she said, "then I will."

He didn't say anything. She could hear the rain pattering ceaselessly outside the house. Her bedroom curtains were drawn. She couldn't see the rain and the black night, but she knew they were out there. She thought about the lawn behind her house that swept up to woodland. Deer lived there, and porcupines, and other pleasant, harmless things. But it had been in woods that someone had killed someone who looked like Roger's friend, too.

"Roger?"

"I heard you. If I don't go to the cops, you will. I heard you. I'm getting pretty damn pissed off about all this, Cassandra. I gotta tell you. I am. Pretty damn pissed off."

She just waited, instead of answering him. She didn't have anything more to say, anyway.

"Jesus H. Christ." She heard the scraping of a chair across the floor. "Look. I told you it was just a mistake. Just the way the light hit the fucking thing, or something."

Cassandra noticed that he had lowered his voice and wondered if he'd heard something—maybe his sister was getting up to go to the bathroom, or maybe his brother-in-law was going to come in and tell him to get off the phone so he could sleep.

"But okay," he went on softly. "So you can't believe that. You think it's her: Sally. Or you think it could be. Which is a load of crap. But that's not what's really on your mind. Is it? You're thinking, if this chick that got herself murdered is a friend of old Roger's, then maybe it was old Roger who did her in. That's what you're thinking. Isn't it?"

His voice was warm now, relaxed and amused. She reminded herself that he was an actor.

"Not necessarily," she said cautiously. "No, of course not," she said more firmly. "Don't be ridiculous."

"Now she got killed last Sunday night, right?" he said, as though she hadn't spoken.

"Right. Yes."

"And what was I doing last Sunday night?"

"I know, I know," said Cassandra. "You borrowed my car."

"And why did I borrow your car?"

"Don't you see?" said Cassandra desperately. "That's why you can go to the police. You can tell them that you *might*, you just *might* be able to identify her. And you don't have to worry about them suspecting you. Because you can tell them where you were! You've got an alibi!"

"Jesus God," he said evenly. "You can be so goddamn stupid."

Cassandra opened her mouth to protest. She wanted to feel outraged, indignant. If there was anything she wasn't, it was stupid. She was absolutely certain of that.

"I am not going to the goddamn cops," said Roger, and his anger came right through the telephone line and made her shudder. "You go if you want to. Go ahead. But you'd better do it fast. You'd better do your fucking civic duty first thing tomorrow. Because I'm getting out of this fucking place."

"Roger—"

"Jesus, Cassandra," he said, with a sob in his voice. "How can you think it? My God. . . ." He hung up.

Cassandra took the receiver from her ear and looked at it blankly. Then she hung it up, put the phone back on her bedside table, and turned out the light.

She lay on her side, facing the curtained window, curled up under the electric blanket, and thought about how cold she was, and wondered if Roger's sob had been genuine, and realized that she didn't actually know him at all.

CHAPTER 16

The handbag was old and worn but made of good leather. It contained a nail file, a small, flat tin of aspirin, a crumpled Kleenex, a brush with several strands of blonde hair caught among its plastic teeth, and a felt-tip pen.

The faded denim knapsack was empty.

Everything had been sent to the lab in Vancouver, and attempts were being made to trace the manufacturers and distributors of the bag and the knapsack.

Alberg, considering these facts on Monday morning, was frustrated and angry. The killer's disposal of this evidence was not, as Alberg had hoped, a panicky reaction to what he'd done. He had carefully gathered up his victim's belongings, scrupulously gone through them, and discarded in the restaurant trash can only those things which he'd decided wouldn't be of any help to the police.

What had he done with her wallet, her credit cards, her money—all the other things she must have been carrying around with her?

Alberg couldn't even know for certain that the handbag and the knapsack belonged to the woman in Tommy Cummings' portrait. But he was convinced that they had, and that comparison of the hairs in the brush with the dead woman's hair would prove it.

The killer would know that, too. He hadn't minded having those particular items connected with his victim; he'd already disposed in some other way of anything that might identify her.

When the phone on Alberg's desk buzzed, it was just past eight-thirty.

"What is it?" he snapped.

"Oh dearie me," said Isabella. "Testy, aren't we? It's Percy Harwood up in Powell River. Maybe I should tell him to call back when you're feeling happier."

"Don't be smart, Isabella," said Alberg coldly. "Put him through."

"You owe us one, buddy," said Harwood.

"Oh, Jesus," said Alberg. "You've got an I.D."

"Right bang on."

Alberg scrabbled around for pen and paper. "Give it to me."

"One Eleanor Sally Dublin. A hotel manager recognized the sketch. Also a waitress in the self-same joint. She checked in on Friday, November 1, off the ferry from Comox. She told the manager she was heading down the coast. Didn't say where to, or why. But she left the next morning. And she told the waitress she was hitchhiking."

"Jesus Christ."

"Yeah. Some of them, they never learn."

"What home address did she give the hotel? How did she pay?"

"Paid with an American Express card. Home address in Los Angeles."

"Jesus," said Alberg. "Okay. Let's have it."

When he'd finished talking to Harwood, he got up and went out into the reception area. "Isabella," he said.

She tossed her mane of unfashionably long hair over her shoulder. Today her bulky cardigan, worn over a black skirt and a white blouse, was bright red, with large many-colored flowers knitted across the top. "No apology," she said magnanimously, "is necessary."

"Where's Sid?"

She looked up at him. "It would have been nice, though. Especially since by rights I don't even have to be here today."

"Isabella. Please. I don't have time for this."

"He's in the interview room," she said distantly. "Talking to those environmentalists." There had been complaints from one of the logging companies that vandals had driven spikes into some of the great Douglas firs scheduled for harvesting.

"Please ask him to come to my office. And round up Sanducci, too." He put his hands on the edge of her desk and leaned close to her. "Now."

Isabella peered in astonishment at his sudden enormous smile. She nodded, and got up from her desk.

Three hours later, Alberg went to see Cassandra.

The library was closed; he'd forgotten about the Remembrance Day holiday.

He drove quickly to her house, trying not to entertain any of the horrendous possibilities that were flooding his mind.

When he drove up she was in her front yard, crouched near the house with her back to the road. She heard his car, looked to see who it was, and then looked away. He pulled into the driveway in front of her garage, turned off the motor, and just sat there for a moment, filled with relief. He noticed through the open garage door that the yellow Hornet was there, where it belonged.

He saw as he approached across the lawn that she was digging energetically in the earth next to the foundation.

"What are you doing?" he said.

Cassandra didn't turn around. "I've decided to make a flower bed along here," she said.

"In November?"

She was turning over the sod with hectic, furious thrusts of a small spade. Six-inch stakes equidistant from the house marked the perimeter of what was to be her garden.

Alberg stood behind her with his arms dangling at his sides. He put his hands in his pockets. All he could see was the back of her head, her faded denim jacket, the dirt-smeared gloves wielding the spade.

"Do you think you could stop that for a few minutes?" he said.

"It's going to rain again," said Cassandra. "I want to finish this before it rains."

"Cassandra. I have to talk to you."

She had dug up the grass halfway between the end of the house and the front steps. She hadn't even put in the stakes, yet, along the grass on the opposite side of the steps.

"I wouldn't bother you," he said, "if it wasn't important."

She paused and let the edge of her hand rest on her upraised knee. Then she tossed the spade to the ground and stood up, pulling off the gloves. She dropped them onto the grass and brushed vigorously at the grass-stained knees of her jeans. "Okay," she said, her hands on her hips. "What is it?"

Alberg on his way to her house had imagined them murmuring together, heads close. It was a confidence he would give her. She might be upset, he could even see a few tears in her eyes, on her cheeks, but he would wipe them away with his fingers; he would soothe her, return her life to normality; he would keep her safe.

He mustn't have been completely alert, when he allowed that fantasy to happen.

Still, he wanted to try. He knew that what she was showing him was not all there was. "Can we go inside?" he said. He wouldn't ask for it, under the circumstances, but maybe on her own she'd make them some coffee.

"Look, Karl." She nodded to the half-dug garden. "I told you, I want to get this finished before it rains. Say what you have to say and let me get on with it, will you?" She looked straight at him. She pushed her thick dark hair away from her face. He wished that she would smile at him, but saw that she was far too tense.

"Okay. I need to know where Roger Galbraith is staying. The address."

She looked up into the thick prickly branches of the monkey tree that grew halfway between her house and the road.

"What's his sister's name?" said Alberg.

"Get it from his mother."

"His mother?"

"She lives at Golden Arms. I thought you police officers would know a thing like that."

"I didn't know. Now that I'm here, why don't you tell me?"

"Why do you want to know?"

"I have to talk to him."

"What about?"

He looked at her. "Surely that's his business," he said gently. "Not yours."

She was standing directly in front of him, about four feet away, and she had a closed and wary look which was familiar to him, but which he had never expected to see on Cassandra's face.

Rain began to fall in small tentative drops upon his notebook. "Cassandra. What do you think I'm going to do? Beat him up?"

"It's been known to happen," she said defensively.

He looked right and left, as if for reinforcements. "I can't believe this."

Her face was flushed and her hands had clenched.

"Fuck it," he said, and shoved the notebook and the pen back into his pocket. He began walking swiftly to his car. "I'll find out from somebody else. I thought we might be able to keep it quiet for a while," he lied to her over his shoulder, "just between you and me and him, until he's had a chance to explain himself. But if you want it all over the goddamn town that the R.C.M.P. is looking for your friend Roger, fine." He got in the car, slammed the door, and started the motor with a roar.

He heard her call him, and sat looking out through the windshield at the Hornet until she had gotten around to his side of the car. Then he opened his window.

"Why are you looking for him?"

"Jesus." Alberg saw the rain falling on her hair, her face, her jacket. He was surprised at how hard his hands were gripping the steering wheel. "I can't tell you why I'm looking for him. It's none of your damn business. All I can tell you is to stay away from him. But you wouldn't listen to that."

"I think I know what this is about," said Cassandra.

"Good. Progress."

"He was—he was absolutely paralyzed with shock when he saw Tommy's picture."

"What the hell do you think you're doing?" said Alberg, furious. "This is a goddamn homicide investigation. Why the hell didn't he come and tell us he recognized her? What kind of a jerk is this guy, anyway?" He took a deep breath. "And when you knew he wasn't going to do it," he said evenly, "why didn't you?"

Cassandra stepped back from the car. "His sister's name is Stella Newman," she said dully. "Roberts Creek Road."

"Thanks," said Alberg. He backed less than carefully out of her driveway. Gravel spewed from the tires as he accelerated down the access road, heading back to the highway.

On Roberts Creek Road he found without difficulty the mailbox marked NEWMAN. He turned into a long driveway which led to a house with a small barn and a shed behind it and the remains of a large vegetable garden to one side. In a fenced pasture back of the barn two horses were grazing.

A big black Labrador with a gray muzzle emerged from under the steps as Alberg drove up. The dog stood quietly, its tail wagging, while Alberg parked and got out.

"Hi, fella," he said, stretching out his hand. The dog nosed his palm politely, then slowly and stiffly returned to his place beneath the steps.

Alberg knocked several times and heard no sounds from within the house. The rain pattered on his jacket, on the wooden porch. Curtains were drawn across the windows on either side of the front door. He knocked again and this time a voice called out, "Just a minute. I'm coming."

A minute later the door opened.

Roger Galbraith looked as though he'd just gotten up. His hair was flattened on one side, and his cheek was creased. He was wearing a pair of jeans and a V-necked sweatshirt that revealed curly black chest hair. He was barefoot.

"My name's Alberg. I'm with the R.C.M. Police. I have some questions for you."

Galbraith's pale face got paler. He looked beyond Alberg to the unmarked Oldsmobile. "I thought you'd be wearing a uniform and driving a cop car," he said. He had a deep, pleasant voice, but it was strained. He laughed and ran his fingers through his hair.

"I drive my own car most of the time. May I come in?"

"Yeah, sure." Galbraith stepped back and pulled the door open. "Uh, listen," he said as he closed the door behind Alberg. "My sister's not here. She left me a note. She's gone to have coffee with a friend, or something. What time is it?"

Alberg looked at his watch. "Almost noon."

Galbraith stared down at the linoleum that covered the hall floor. "Yeah, well, she'll be back any minute." He looked up at Alberg. "Is there any way—uh, could we go for a walk or something?"

"It's raining out there."

"I could lend you one of my brother-in-law's ponchos. He's got a boat, does a lot of fishing."

He was extremely nervous. But he looked steadily at Alberg when he spoke to him.

"I don't like that idea much," said Alberg. "How about coming down to the detachment, if you don't want to talk here?"

"Oh shit, Christ, no," said Galbraith. He took a step back, his bare toes clutching at the linoleum.

"Hey, take it easy," said Alberg, with some indignation.

"Look, man, I don't want to go to any cop shop, no way." He had raised his hands, palms out, and was shaking his head.

Alberg's eyes kept going to the gold ring the actor wore in his right ear. "We've got us a problem, here," he said. "I don't want to walk in the goddamn rain, and you don't want to sit down here, and you don't want to come to my office. But the fact of it is that I've got to talk to you, because of your friend who got herself killed up here, and that's not going to go away."

Galbraith looked at him wildly. Then he burst into sobs and covered his face with his hands.

Alberg stared at him. The man was shaking. Tears were spilling through his fingers. On the linoleum his bare feet looked embarrassingly vulnerable.

"Hey, hey," said Alberg clumsily.

"Oh shit," said Galbraith between sobs. "I tried to tell myself it wasn't her, it couldn't be her, I knew it couldn't be, but every time I looked at that fucking picture it hit me in the chest; I thought I was having a heart attack." His voice was pitched high, the words muffled by his crying. He pulled his hands from his face and shuffled down the hall away from Alberg, shoulders bent, moving like an arthritic old man.

Alberg followed him into the kitchen, where Galbraith tore a paper towel from a rack on the wall and blew his nose and wiped his eyes. "Jesus. Shit," he muttered. He splashed water on his face and dried it with a dish towel hanging inside the cupboard under the sink. "Okay," he said, lowering himself wearily into a chair at the kitchen table. "My sister's got to know about it sooner or later, anyway." He looked at Alberg with sudden curiosity. "So Cassandra really did it, huh? She set the cops on me." He shrugged. "She warned me she would. I don't think I believed her."

"I'm not here because of Cassandra," said Alberg.

But it was good to know that he might have been. Very good.

He sat across the table from Galbraith, pushing aside an old-fashioned toaster to make room for his notebook. "She was identified from the sketch. In Powell River. She told somebody there she was going to hitchhike down the coast."

Galbraith stopped breathing. "Oh Christ. Then somebody picked her up. Some psycho picked her up, and killed her."

Alberg flipped open the notebook. "No. I don't think so. She was on her way here, to Sechelt. To see you." He aimed a level gaze at Galbraith. "I don't think some psycho killed her. I think you did."

CHAPTER 17

"Oh, no, man. You've got it all wrong." His fingers clung to the edge of the table as if it were a raft. "What the hell makes you think she was coming to see me?"

"We talked to her agent. He's your agent, too, right? He says you two were pretty close."

"Look, she hadn't been in touch with me. I'm telling you. It's coincidence, that's all. It's pure coincidence."

Alberg gave him a slow grin and shook his head.

Galbraith slumped in his chair. He shook his head. Tears quivered in his eyes, spilled over upon his cheeks. "Shit," he said, wiping them away with his hands.

"Tell me about her," said Alberg.

"You said—she was hitching?"

"That's right."

"Shit. That's Sally, all right. You couldn't tell that broad a goddamn thing." He got up suddenly and went to the kitchen window. He slid his hands into his jeans pockets and stood there looking out at the rain falling upon the grazing horses.

Alberg pulled a five-by-seven-inch copy of the portrait from his inside jacket pocket. "This is her, right?"

Galbraith stiffened, then turned slowly around to face Alberg. He reached for the drawing. "As soon as I saw it," he said, "I knew." Tears sparkled again. His supply, thought Alberg unkindly, was inexhaustible. Roger nodded and thrust the portrait back at the staff sergeant. He went over to the stove and turned on the burner under a half full coffeepot. He got cups from the cupboard, and a bowl of sugar. "You want coffee?"

"Sure. Black. Was she a successful actress?"

Galbraith came back to the table. He gave Alberg an ironic look. "About as successful as I am. Which is to say no, not really. She got enough work to keep her busy. But she didn't need the money anyway."

"Why?"

He sat down, resting his arms on his knees, and looked unseeing at the floor, which was covered in the same linoleum as the hall. "She made a bundle a few years ago. It happens. You get hot for a while, the money pours in." He sat up. "Most people figure that's it, I've finally made it. As fast as we get it, we spend it. And then everything dries up and you're back where you started, dead broke. But not Sally." He grinned at Alberg. "She plowed it all into real estate. I thought I'd die laughing, Sally buying real estate. I tell you, I ain't laughing now." He looked quizzically at the staff sergeant. "What did you say your name was?"

"Alberg."

"What do I call you? Inspector? Or what?"

"Staff sergeant."

Galbraith raised his eyebrows. "Not very impressive."

Alberg looked stonily back at him.

"Sounds like the army," said Galbraith absently, his gaze moving to the window. "Shit, it rains a lot in this place." He heard the coffeepot begin to burble and got up to take it off the stove.

"If she was so well off," said Alberg, "why was she hitchhiking?"

"She hitchhikes everywhere." He brought two cups of black coffee to the table. It smelled strong and old. "She has a car, an old Volkswagen Beetle, but she hardly ever drives it." He stopped. "She *had* a car," he said, carefully. "Jesus." He looked bleakly at Alberg. "I can't believe this."

"Not a good habit to get into. Hitchhiking."

"Yeah, yeah," said Galbraith. "You think I didn't tell her that? Everybody told her that. She said if anything was going to happen to her it would have happened by now. She said she was too old to worry, now. Shit." He slumped and put a hand over his eyes.

Alberg waited. He drank some of the coffee, which tasted as foul as it smelled. Galbraith gave a shuddery sigh, pulled his hand away, and sat up straight again.

"Why did she come looking for you?" said Alberg. "What was so important that it couldn't wait until you got back? Or did she think maybe you weren't going back?"

Galbraith looked at him intently for a long moment. Alberg was aware of the rain drumming against the window, and the murmuring of the refrigerator. Outside the dog barked a few times, halfheartedly, then lapsed into silence.

"Okay," said Roger decisively. "Okay." He stood up. "Just give me a minute. I've gotta take a piss."

While he was gone Alberg got an ashtray from the counter, emptied it into a garbage bag under the sink, and lit a cigarette. He looked around the kitchen. The phone sat on a set of shelves, which also contained a few magazines and books and another dirty ashtray. There was a calendar on the wall above, with large squares around the dates. He could see scribblings in some of them, all in the same handwriting. There were two pairs of rubber boots sprawled on a rumpled mat beside the doorway which led outside.

"Weren't you afraid I'd try to escape?" said Roger, grinning, when he reappeared.

Alberg smiled at him. "Nope. The whole coast knows what you look like by now."

Roger's smile faltered. "Hey. Serious business."

"You betcha," said Alberg. He noticed that Galbraith had combed his hair and put on a pair of slippers.

"How come you don't wear a uniform?" said Galbraith. He rubbed his jaw and looked aimlessly around the kitchen. "My brother-in-law's with the ferries. I don't know what he does, exactly. He's got this uniform. . . ." He sat down. "My sister always was a sucker for a uniform." He glanced at Alberg and grinned. "You like to keep yourself outside the herd, huh?"

"Something like that," said Alberg. "Why'd she come all the way up here after you?"

"I don't know for sure. But I'll tell you what I can." Roger got up and emptied his coffee cup into the sink. He went back to the window and stared out for a minute. Finally he sat down again. "Sally used to get these airhead parts. And that was fine—she did them, no problem—because she *was* a little bit of an airhead. Then she bought this property and it turned out she was a businesswoman, too. Shocked the hell out of me, but there you are." He leaned toward Alberg. "She owns three apartment buildings and four dry-cleaning places now. Can you believe that?" He sat back. "Owned, I mean." He shook his head. "She parlayed her little stake into all that. Me, I spent mine. On cars, clothes, rent, coke—" He stopped.

"I don't care what you do for entertainment," said Alberg, "as long as you don't do it here."

Roger grinned at him. "Way to go, Constable."

Alberg looked at him thoughtfully.

"Okay, okay." He slumped back in his chair.

"What was she to you? Friend? Lover? What?"

"Friend. She used to be my—lover. Now, we're friends."

"How often did you see her?"

"Up until about a year ago, at least once a week. We had breakfast together every Saturday. Brunch. And we talked on the phone. She loved the goddamn telephone." He laughed. "If my phone rang in the middle of the night I knew it was going to be Sally."

"What happened a year ago?"

Roger hesitated. "Is this stuff on the record?" He pointed

to Alberg's notebook. "I don't see you writing much. Does that mean we're off the record?"

"You'll have to come down to the detachment and sign a statement. For the record."

Roger got up and paced the kitchen. "You're a cop, after all. I don't get a thrill out of spilling my guts to a cop."

"Your friend's dead. She got her throat cut. We're trying to find out who did it. That's all I'm interested in. I don't care what kind of shit you're mixed up in outside my jurisdiction. I only care about what went down right here."

"Yeah." Galbraith had stopped pacing. "Shit. Her throat cut." He sat down. "Right. Okay."

He was very still for a moment. Then he shuddered and looked at Alberg. "I do a little dope. Not much. But it was getting to be more. It was using up too much of my cash. So I started doing some dealing, to help with expenses. Only for people I knew. Friends. About a year ago, this was. Sally found out, and she let me know she didn't like it."

He looked away and up, into the corner of the ceiling. "Am I doing this?" He sounded astonished, disapproving. He put a hand on his heart. "Tell me, am I really telling the man all this shit?"

He looked back at Alberg. "So anyway I ignored her, of course, tried to jolly her out of it, but she'd have none of that. Very moral-type person, Sally." He was crying again. "Jesus," he said, and got up to rip off another paper towel.

"Okay," he said as she sat down. "So a few months ago I begin to get calls from total strangers wanting the stuff. Alarming. But they're all sent by people I know, so what the hell. Then, sometime in August it was, somebody calls, tries to put in an order for smack." He looked at Alberg wide-eyed, in mock horror. "Smack. Horse. Heroin."

"I know what it is," said Alberg.

Roger grinned. "You probably see a lot of it, around here."

"Get on with it," said Alberg.

"So anyway, this freaks me right out. I tell the guy no. I hang up the phone, I start to wonder what the fuck I'm doing. So of course I call Sally." He got up and opened the refrigerator, took out a jar of apple cider, and poured himself a glass. He drank it down and poured another and brought it to the table. "I told her what happened, I told her I was going away for a while. 'You in trouble with the cops?' she says. 'No no no,' I tell her. Then I think about it. 'Shit,' I said. 'You don't think that was a *cop* on the phone?'"

He was holding an invisible telephone to his ear, staring concentratedly at the tabletop. There was such incredulity in his voice that Alberg couldn't help but grin.

"Over the phone," said Roger, "I sort of heard her shrug, you know? 'No no no,' I told her. 'I'm just in trouble. Some kind of trouble. Not cops.' 'Well,' she says, 'what're you going to do, anyway?' 'I'm going to get clean,' I said. 'I don't know.' Then she says, 'Where are you going?' And I said, 'Maybe I'll go to where my sister is. And my mother. Sechelt. Up around Vancouver.'" He put down the imaginary receiver. He shrugged. "We were just talking. I could tell she was worried, trying to figure out if I was leaving stuff out."

"Were you?"

"No. That's all there was. I just wanted to get away from it for a while." He drank down the cider and got up to put the glass in the sink.

"You still haven't explained what she was doing up here."

Galbraith put the plug in the sink, squeezed some detergent over the dishes lying there, and turned on the water. "I should have called her. Told her I was okay. I knew she'd start to get upset if I didn't show up in a few weeks." He turned off the water and left the dishes to soak.

"Upset enough to come after you? Hitchhiking?" said Alberg skeptically.

"It's not the first time," said Roger, sitting down. "I get to feeling I'm up to here in dogshit," he said, his hand knifelike at his throat. "Every so often. So I take off."

"And she'd follow you?"

"A couple of times she did. When I went to Arizona. And once in Oregon. Didn't tell her much then, either. But she found me all the same. She should have been a cop."

"Did she follow all her friends," said Alberg dryly, "when they went off to get away from it all? Or just you?"

"Just me," said Roger evenly. "As far as I know."

"Why didn't you call her, let her know you were all right? Or did you want her to come after you?"

Roger struggled with himself for a minute. Then, "I didn't even think about her," he said heavily. "And that's the truth. I know it's hard to believe, but I haven't given her a single fucking thought since I left L.A."

Alberg pushed back his chair and stood up. The backs of his thighs tingled. He felt disheveled, grubby, and overweight. "Oh, I can believe it," he said.

Roger followed him down the hall.

"You'll have to come with me," said Alberg at the front door. "We want to know where you were last Sunday night. Among other things."

A car was turning off the road onto the driveway. "That's my sister," said Roger. "I'd like to tell her about it first." He rubbed his face. "And shave, too. Okay?"

"Sure," said Alberg. "I'll wait."

"Can we—uh, leave out the stuff about the coke?" said Roger, watching his sister's car as it slowly approached the house.

"We'll figure out something."

"Hey," said Roger with a laugh. "I'm not a suspect anymore, right?" The car pulled up beside Alberg's Oldsmobile. Roger waved as his sister got out and looked over at him inquiringly.

"Sure you are," said Alberg, smiling.

CHAPTER 18

"They've been grilling me, Cassandra. For hours. I feel like a fucking steak. Get me a drink, will you? Please?"

Cassandra brought him a drink. She was still in her gardening clothes, but she'd taken off her sneakers when she noticed that she was tracking bits of dirt and pieces of wet grass all over the house. She had continued to work outside even after the rain began, and her socks were wet when she took off her shoes, but she had hardly noticed. For hours she had been doing meaningless household tasks that she couldn't now remember. And waiting. It hadn't occurred to her to change her clothes.

"What happened?" She sat down in the living room, where he had dropped onto the sofa in an attitude of exhaustion.

"They think I did it. Christ, Cassandra. They really think it was me."

"Did they ask you if you had an alibi?" The words seemed awkward, almost clumsy. She imagined them written. That was much better.

"I told them—I mean, what was I going to tell them? I couldn't tell them." When he picked up his glass Cassandra saw that his hand was trembling. She hoped he'd be able to put it down again safely, without cracking the glass surface of the coffee table, and was relieved when he did.

"What *did* you tell them?" She noticed with admiration that her voice was calm.

Roger probed cautiously at his chest with two fingers. "I've got a pain," he said, "right here. Not really a pain. Kind of a heavy feeling. Like something big and unfriendly's sitting on my chest."

"Roger. What did you tell them?"

"I told them I was driving your car." He swung his feet

to the floor and stood up. "What the hell was I supposed to tell them? It's true, anyway."

"But Roger," she said patiently. "They're not going to believe that, if you don't tell them you went to see somebody who can confirm it."

"Christ," he said, his voice breaking. He covered his face with his hands. "I can't believe it. I can't fucking believe it."

She couldn't help but wonder if all this emotion was genuine. The man was a chameleon, after all. "Did you hear me?" she said, more sharply.

He took away his hands and she saw the tears on his face. "They searched my sister's house. Jesus. Looking for a weapon, probably." He glanced over at her. "They're going to search your car, too. I hope you haven't bled in it lately."

Cassandra sighed and discovered a tension in her body she hadn't known was there.

Roger was looking at the floor and shaking his head. "Christ, I've never heard of anything so stupid. Fucking cops." He stood up and went to the window. It was early evening, and the sky was almost completely dark.

"There were three of them," he said to Cassandra. "Your friend, that big blond guy. And another one, even bigger. And a smooth-looking young dude. I don't remember their names. Do you know you aren't even allowed a phone call in this fucking country? They kept saying I didn't need a lawyer, they weren't going to charge me with anything. And then the big guy says, 'Yet,' he says, so ominous I thought my teeth were going to fall out." He glanced at Cassandra, to see whether she would smile. "Over and over," he said, sliding his hands into the pockets of his jeans. "The same fucking questions. Jesus." He walked the length of the living room and back again. "I didn't know she was here. I swear it. Christ. Why the hell would I kill her? She was my friend. Practically the only one I've got." He was starting to weep again. He sat down and wiped at his eyes. "They told me not to leave. Can you believe it? I don't think they can do that. Jesus."

"I wish I'd gone with you that night," said Cassandra. She thought of Alberg and felt a surge of outrage. She wondered if there was any law that said she had to let the Mounties search her car.

Roger took a ragged breath and leaned back into the sofa. "Well," he said. "I want to talk to you about that." He rested his arms along the top of the sofa and turned his head so he could look directly at her.

"About what?" she said warily.

"You *might* have gone with me."

"I know. But I didn't."

He looked straight ahead of him for a minute, and then back at Cassandra.

She shook her head firmly, disbelievingly.

"You don't have to do it," said Roger quickly. "I wouldn't want you to do anything you didn't feel right about."

"I wouldn't feel right about it," said Cassandra. "I certainly wouldn't."

"The thing is," he said, "we both know I didn't do it. We both know I couldn't have done it, because I was someplace else, doing something else. But for obvious reasons I can't tell the cops about that."

"I know. You didn't do it. Somebody else did it. And there are going to be things that point to him, to that other person." She leaned forward, eager to reassure him. "The only thing that points to you is that you knew her. But whoever killed her—well, he must have made mistakes, left clues, things like that. As soon as the police find some of those things they'll stop suspecting you."

"Cassandra. You are so fucking naive."

She sat back.

"I mean, do you have any idea how many unsolved murders there are? Why the hell are you so sure this guy left any clues? If he'd left any fucking clues they would have found them by now, and they wouldn't be nosing around me."

He stood up and zipped his jacket closed. It was made of denim, with tan leather inserts. "They'll be around tonight or tomorrow morning to do a number on the Hornet."

"I don't care. I won't let them, probably."

"Then they'll get a warrant. Cassandra." He came and

stood in front of her. "They're serious. This is serious business. I am in deep shit." He pulled her to her feet. "I need your help. I've gotta have your help."

He looked exhausted. There were dark hollows beneath his eyes, and the lines from his nose to the corners of his mouth had grown deeper. Cassandra even thought there might be a little more gray in his hair than when he had first arrived in Sechelt.

His hands were digging into her shoulders.

"I can't give you that kind of help," she said.

He let go of her. "You're some kind of friend," he said bitterly.

"I'll drive you back to your sister's place." She picked up her denim jacket from the back of the sofa and put it on.

"Some kind of friend." There was ice in his voice. She refused to look at him.

"That's not the sort of thing you ask a friend to do," she said. She went to the front door and opened it. "Come on," she said, and looked back to see if he was following, but he wasn't. He was just standing there, staring at her, and fury had narrowed his eyes and mottled his face. Cassandra couldn't move for a moment. She looked back at him, her hand frozen on the doorknob, and felt coldness climbing up her legs, her thighs, clutching at her chest.

Then he seemed to take hold of himself. The tension left his body; his face smoothed itself, regained its proper color. He went to her and took her in his arms. "It's all right," he said, rubbing her back. He made soothing sounds. "Don't think about it right now."

They went out onto the porch and Cassandra closed the door. She felt the cold wet concrete under her feet and remembered that she had no shoes on. She didn't bother to go back for them.

"I couldn't do it," she said, padding next to Roger through puddles on the way to her car.

His arm was around her shoulders. "I know," he said. "Maybe you can't. Just think about it. That's all I'm asking. Once you're back home and in bed. Think about it then."

CHAPTER 19

When she got back, the police were waiting outside her house. She recognized Alberg's white Oldsmobile at once. She drove the Hornet into the garage, and when she'd turned off the motor and climbed out, she heard the door of the Oldsmobile open and close, and the crunching of feet upon the gravel of her driveway.

The rain had turned to drizzle, and a wind was blowing cold from the ocean.

She forced herself to turn around slowly, deliberately, and watched Alberg and a uniformed officer approach. She'd left her porch light on, and in the spill of it the two men seemed to be moving in on her in a calculating, almost threatening manner. But when they got close she had to admit that this was illusion; Alberg looked haggard and unhappy and the other man, who was much younger, removed his hat as he neared her, and when he stopped gave her a slight, almost courtly nod.

"We have to take the Hornet, Cassandra," said Alberg.

It was interesting, she thought, that he didn't turn into another person when he addressed her as a cop. He sounded official, all right: detached and determined. But there was nothing in his conduct that attempted to deny whatever relationship it was that existed between them. She could almost have felt relieved, protected, by his largeness, his sureness.

"Are you going to arrest him?" she said.

The other man moved his feet a little, rasping the gravel beneath his shoes, and she looked at him sharply. He made a small gesture of apology.

"You'll have it back tomorrow," said Alberg. "I'll get someone to drive you to work."

"No, thank you," said Cassandra quickly.

"Then I'll do it myself. Would you give Corporal Sanducci your keys, please?"

She was holding them. She hadn't taken her purse, when she'd driven Roger home. She realized that she hadn't, therefore, had her driver's license with her and felt a second of panic, wondering if they'd think of that and charge her for it. She worked the car keys off the ring and handed them to Sanducci.

"Thank you, ma'am," he said.

"I have to ask you some questions," said Alberg. He wasn't the least bit embarrassed. "Do you mind if we do it now?"

Cassandra shrugged and walked toward her front porch. She listened for the sound of the Hornet's door being opened but heard nothing except Alberg's footsteps behind her and the wind in the woods that embraced her house on two sides.

Inside, she took off her jacket and hung it in the hall closet and went into the living room, where she turned on lamps and sat down in the chair by the window, her knees together, her hands in her lap. Alberg settled himself on the sofa and got out a notebook and a pen.

"The victim has been identified as Eleanor Sally Dublin," he said. "American. Los Angeles. She was an actress, a friend of Roger Galbraith's. We don't know her purpose in coming to the Sunshine Coast, but she knew that he was here and apparently had reason to be concerned about him."

Outside the corporal had started the Hornet and was backing it slowly down the driveway.

"Why didn't she just call him, then?" said Cassandra. She was dismayed to think that someone had been "concerned" about him. What was there to be concerned about? She felt guilty, not having noticed anything. Was he sick?

She heard her car being driven away. She wondered what they would do to it. She tried to remember exactly what was in it: in the trunk, and the glove compartment, and lying on the back seat, and on the floor. It was disquieting to think of cops poking around in her car. She wondered if they'd want to poke around in her house, too. The thought of this made her very angry.

Alberg was staring at her feet, and she became aware of how cold they were. He looked up at her face, then down again, at her wet, dirty socks, once white. She made a determined effort not to squiggle her toes, to keep her feet flat upon the floor, while she looked him squarely in the eyes.

"I don't know," said Alberg finally. "It's a good question. She was impulsive." He shook his head, wearily. "I don't know."

"Then you don't know that it was because of him that she showed up here."

"No," he said. "We don't know that. But for the moment, that's what we're assuming."

Cassandra made a sound of contempt, and put her hands on the arms of her chair.

"He says you loaned him your car, the night she was killed."

"That's right."

"He says he went driving."

She nodded.

"Did he tell you where?"

"Did he tell *you* where?"

He sighed, and put the notebook and the pen carefully on the coffee table. He leaned forward, arms on his knees, and looked for a while at the carpet. "Cassandra. I want you to understand something," he said to the carpet. Then he looked up. "My purpose is not to harass your boyfriend."

She felt her face flush. "I am not an adolescent," she said coldly. "He is not my 'boyfriend.'"

"I'm sorry. Anyway, I'm not out to get him, whatever he is. If he didn't do it, he's got nothing to worry about." He sat back and rested one arm along the back of the sofa. "See, 'driving around'; that's not good enough. We need some corroboration."

"An alibi, you mean."

He looked at her. "Yeah. He needs an alibi. That's right."

"What happens to him if he doesn't have one?"

"We probably arrest him."

"Do you have any evidence?"

"We don't need any."

"You mean you can just go around arresting people, just like that?" said Cassandra. She was incredulous.

"The fact that he knew the victim," said Alberg patiently, "and that he was apparently the only person around here who did, gives us reasonable probable grounds to lock him up for twenty-four hours."

"And then what?"

He shook his head. "The point is, either he did it or he didn't. If he didn't, the more information we get, the better off he is." He paused. "If he did," said the staff sergeant quietly, "then I don't think it's something you'd want him to get away with. Is it?"

Cassandra rubbed her hands on the arms of her chair. "Are you looking anyplace else? Or are you only looking at him?"

"We're looking at everything there is to look at."

"What do you want from me?"

"Do you know where he went, what he did, when he borrowed your car that night?"

She had known she wouldn't be able to go on avoiding it. She glanced at Alberg, who was watching her closely, his face infuriatingly unreadable. She knew that her own was revealing all sorts of things.

"I only know what he told me," she said. "And I think he ought to make his own explanations." She felt immediately relieved. "I've been trying to persuade him to tell you. I'll go on trying to persuade him. That's all I can do."

Alberg nodded slowly, still watching her. "You were with him when he recognized the portrait, right?"

"Yes. I guess so. Yes."

"How did he react?"

"He was very upset," she said quickly, eagerly. "He got pale and shaky. It was a shock, a genuine shock to him."

"Did he tell you that he knew her?"

"No. I don't think he wanted to believe it. He said it just looked like her, that it gave him a start because it looked like her, but that it couldn't actually *be* her."

"Why?"

"Well, because it was just so unlikely, I guess."

Alberg had retrieved the notebook and was writing in it, which made Cassandra uneasy.

"Had he ever mentioned her to you before?" he said.

"No."

"What did he actually say, when he saw the portrait?"

"At first he just exclaimed a lot," said Cassandra carefully. "He was so upset that I asked him if he'd recognized it. After a while he said no, that it just reminded him of somebody, a friend in Los Angeles. That's all he said."

"Has he borrowed your car on other occasions?"

"Yes. Several times. Sometimes he uses his sister's."

"Has he ever asked you to keep anything for him? Here, or at the library?"

"You mean, like a knife?" said Cassandra bitterly. She shook her head. "No. Nothing."

"Do you know whether he uses drugs?"

"Good God," Cassandra burst out. "Why the hell don't you ask *him* these things?"

"We have," said Alberg calmly. "Of course. Now I'm asking you."

"I don't live with the man. I'm not his only friend around here," she said, red-faced and agitated.

"I know," said Alberg. "You're not the only person we'll be talking to about him, either. But you're the one I'm talking to now. Do you know whether he uses drugs?"

"No," said Cassandra angrily. "I don't know whether he does or not. And I don't care."

Alberg nodded. "Okay." He put the notebook and the pen in an inside pocket of his jacket and stood up to leave.

I should have offered him some coffee, thought Cassandra. No, I shouldn't have. This wasn't a goddamn social call.

"Thank you for your cooperation," said Alberg formally. "What time will you be leaving for work in the morning?"

"Why?"

"I'd like to give you a lift. To make up for the inconvenience."

She followed him to the front door. "What are you going to do to my car, anyway?"

"Oh, just take a look at it," he said vaguely. "When you get it back, you'll never know we had it. What time?"

"I'll get a ride from the volunteer," said Cassandra, holding the door open. "Thanks anyway," she added grudgingly.

"Whatever you like," said Alberg. "We'll return the Hornet sometime tomorrow and put the keys through the mail slot. Okay?"

"Okay."

He turned on the step to smile at her. "If there's anything you think he should tell us," he said softly, "I sure hope you can convince him to do it. Otherwise, I'm afraid he's in a lot of trouble."

He walked off across her front lawn to his car, which was parked in front of the house. She closed the door quickly, locked it, took the phone off the hook, undressed, got into bed, and, shivering with cold, turned up her electric blanket.

CHAPTER 20

The sun, which had come out of hiding Tuesday morning, was still shining on Saturday, Alberg's day off. The tops of the mountains had reappeared covered in snow, as if the clouds before they retreated had pressed themselves hard against that part of the earth within their grasp. The air was so clear that Alberg thought his vision must have unaccountably improved; this, he felt, must have been the way of his seeing when he was a child. Each tree on the mountains surrounding Sechelt had been individually whitened and stood in relief; behind each hid a slim dark shadow.

The snowline was drawn abruptly about a thousand feet down the mountainsides. Below, it was as though spring had come three months early, or summer had returned.

The sunshine was the first thing Alberg noticed when he awakened that morning. The second thing was the pile of books on the table beside his bed. It was the books that made him decide to pay a call on Tommy Cummings.

Alberg drove northwest along the highway from Gibsons, where he lived, to Sechelt with his car window open, and he saw from time to time smoke drifting into the limpid air from small fires in which the final yard-clearings of the year were being burned. He was troubled and preoccupied, but the day soothed his soul and reminded him why he had so swiftly grown to love the Sunshine Coast.

Two girls riding bareback on stolid, barrel-shaped mares waved at him. So did a motorcyclist who passed him with a roar. None of them knew him; it was just that kind of a day. He waved back and felt better for it.

In Sechelt he first drove slowly past the library. He made it a point to check on Cassandra every day, because Galbraith still hadn't provided himself with an alibi.

When the actor told his interrogators about all the women he regularly visited, a horrified Sokolowski had wanted to warn every single one of them. He had pulled Alberg aside in the middle of the interview. "My wife met him a few times," he said. "In the library, the supermarket—like that. This guy is genuinely dangerous, Karl," the sergeant had said urgently. "Once she introduced me to him. We were out at a movie, there he was in the popcorn lineup. Elsie says to me, 'There he is, that actor from Los Angeles I told you about.' And he hears her, and turns around, and grins at her. Then he comes over. He sticks out his paw at me. 'Hi,' he says. 'I'm Roger.' Like it was an adjective. Jesus, the ego. We gotta get the word out to the women about this guy, Karl."

Alberg hadn't been able to figure out a way to do that. He'd settled, guiltily, for keeping an eye on Cassandra.

He saw the Hornet parked in front of the library, and through the floor-to-ceiling windows he spotted Cassandra talking to her friend Phyllis Dempter, the dentist's wife. Relieved, he speeded up and drove on.

He parked in front of the hardware store, got out, and locked his car. When he turned around an elderly woman was staring at him. She wore a gray coat and a gray hat and had very thick eyeglasses. A big, square, black handbag was hung over one wrist. Her hands, encased in purple woolen gloves, clutched a book. She mumbled something at him. Alberg leaned closer, to hear. "I beg your pardon?" he said.

She mumbled again.

"I'm sorry," said Alberg. "I didn't hear you."

"I said, God's word will save you," she said loudly. She waved the Bible in his face. "The Lord God will save you. His word is thy salvation."

Alberg stepped back quickly. "Ah," he said, and edged toward the stairway beside the hardware store that led up to Tommy's apartment.

Her wrinkled face had become red with exertion. "Blasphemy is forbidden," she said incongruously.

"Right," said Alberg, with a foot on the first step.

"He isn't there," said the old woman.

"I agree," said Alberg. He smiled, nodded, and took another step up.

"Why are you doing that?" she said irritably. "I just told you. He isn't there."

Alberg stopped. "What? Who? Tommy?"

"He's doing it on the beach again," said the old woman. Her eyes wandered from his face and fixed on something up the street.

"He's doing *what* on the beach?" said Alberg, alarmed.

"There," she said, and walked rapidly away.

Alberg returned to the sidewalk and watched as she approached a young woman with a baby in a backpack. He heard the old woman mutter something. "Hi, Muriel," said the young woman pleasantly, and without breaking stride she swept past and into the hardware store.

Alberg set off in the other direction, toward the sea, three blocks away.

He stood on the rocky beach with his hands in his pockets, breathing and smiling. The ocean was blue again. He listened to the waves and thought the sea was languid and sensual. After a few minutes of this he looked around him. There were several people on the beach, walking slowly, gazing out toward Vancouver Island sprawled across the horizon. The range of mountains that ran the length of the Island like a spine glinted white in the sunlight. To his left Alberg saw the restaurant where he had first met Cassandra; he allowed himself a wistful moment, thinking about that. To his right, about five hundred yards away, he spotted Tommy sitting cross-legged on a huge log, holding a sketchbook in his lap.

Tommy was too concentrated to notice as Alberg drew near. The staff sergeant enjoyed the sight of him, wearing jeans and a sweater, relaxed, absorbed in his work. He was humming to himself over the sound of the sea as he sketched. When Alberg's shadow fell across the paper Tommy turned, a hand shading his eyes.

"What are you drawing?" said Alberg with a smile.

"That piece of driftwood," said Tommy.

Alberg squatted down and examined it—a gray, weathered, satiny-looking chunk of a tree branch, or a slim-trunked log. He was curious to see the artist's sketch, but thought it would be rude to peer at it and indelicate to ask permission.

"I want to pick your brain," he said.

Tommy squinted at him, startled.

"I came to ask you some questions about painting."

"Really? Why?"

Alberg shrugged. "I don't know, exactly." He laughed. "I often let myself wander up little paths that go nowhere."

The art teacher hesitated. Then he flipped the sketchbook closed, gathered up his pencils, and put them in his pocket.

"Hey," said Alberg. "Look, I'm really sorry that I interrupted you. I know you don't get a lot of time to do this."

"It's all right. Really. I was just about finished. Come on back to my place. I'll make us some coffee."

This time either Alberg noticed more in Cummings' apartment or what he saw made more sense to him. The big drafting board in the corner; a row of jars containing brushes of various shapes and sizes; the oversized shelf in the bookcase, stuffed with oversized books. Alberg nodded in satisfaction as he looked around. Light from the north, the west, and the skylight in the ceiling. In a glass-doored cupboard, tubes of oil paints and probably, he said knowledgeably to himself, acrylics, too; also boxes of charcoal and pastels. On a shelf beside the drafting board, a pile of sketchbooks. On another, an elegantly shaped piece of driftwood, a pile of stones, some shells.

"I've been doing some reading," said Alberg. "About portraits."

"That's interesting," said Tommy politely. He folded his arms and looked as though he couldn't decide whether Alberg was serious.

"I went to the library. Got some books."

"Why?" said Tommy.

"Not sure, exactly. I guess I was curious about how you did it. How you got that woman to look alive."

"There's no trick to it," said Tommy. He went into the kitchen and busied himself with the automatic drip coffeepot. "How did you know where I was, by the way?"

Alberg told him about the old woman with the Bible.

Tommy laughed. "That's Muriel. She's very worried about people's souls. She's particularly worried about mine."

"Why?"

"She knows that I paint. She thinks it's got something to do with the devil." He went around the counter to rejoin Alberg in the living room. "Sit down, sit down." He gestured to the sofa, and Alberg sat.

"I read about light, and color, and all that," said the staff sergeant. "And I looked at some books of portraits. It wasn't much help."

Tommy sat in a chair across from him, hands on his knees.

"She's been identified," said Alberg. "I guess you know that. It's been in the papers."

"Really? No, I didn't know."

"She was an actress from California."

Tommy's eyes widened. "There's an actor—" he began. "He visited the school. The elementary school. He's from Los Angeles. Did she—was she acquainted with . . . Excuse me." He let go of his eagerness, disparaging it. "It's none of my business."

"I think your curiosity is understandable," said Alberg easily, "under the circumstances. Yeah, they were acquainted." He got up and wandered over to the bookshelves. He peered at the titles, then glanced back at Tommy. "Do you mind?"

"No, no. Help yourself."

Alberg pulled out a book about Matisse, flipped through the pages, put it back, went on to Georgia O'Keeffe. "It's been thought of as a kind of magic, hasn't it," he said. "Portrait-painting." He grinned at the art teacher. "At least, that's what the books tell me."

Cummings looked at him intently. He didn't smile back. "That's right," he said, after a moment.

"In parts of Europe," said Alberg, "people believed that portraits had miraculous powers. Isn't that right?"

"Yes," said Cummings remotely. "And in Egypt, a dead person's soul was supposed to be able to return to any likeness which might have been made of him."

Alberg returned the book to the shelf and went to the north window. "Just look at those mountains," he said. "It's like the trees have been painted on them, in snow." He turned and shoved his hands in his pockets. "I've been looking at too damn many books."

"That's unusual, isn't it?" said Tommy. "I mean, for a policeman."

"Why do you say that?" Alberg sat down again and looked curiously at him. "Have you had many experiences with the police?"

"No no no. I just meant—" He raised his hands in surrender and smiled. "Clichés. I was thinking in clichés." He got up and went to get the coffee.

"Your painting is more real than a photograph," said Alberg. He felt physically tense, with an excitement he couldn't explain. "It's not perfect," he said. "I can see the sketch marks; her hair kind of dissolves into the paper; I don't think you got the chin quite right."

"Oh, really?" said Tommy coolly, from the kitchen. "Don't you?"

"But there's a real person there. Somehow you managed to create a real, living person from a corpse."

"And?"

"And I want to know how you did it."

Tommy brought in the coffee and gave Alberg a dry glance. "Have you ever had somebody do this for you before? How many times have you seen a portrait which you knew was painted from sketches made of a dead face?" He shrugged. "It's fascinating, isn't it?" he said, detached. "It isn't particularly unusual to do a painting of a person after he's dead. The difference here is only that normally you'd use photographs taken while she was alive. But we didn't have any." He hesitated.

Alberg watched him get up and go over to the bookcase. He looked along the middle shelf until he'd found what he wanted. He pulled out a large thick volume and brought it over to the sofa.

"Can I show you something?" said Tommy.

"Sure," said Alberg.

Tommy sat beside him and leafed through the book. "Here," he said, pushing it across his knees so that it was angled toward Alberg. "This one. It's an El Greco. Tell me what you see."

It was a familiar painting of a woman wearing white fur. Alberg saw the roundness of her forehead, cheeks, nose, lips; he thought he could smell the fur.

He concentrated obediently on her face. "She looks cautious," he said after a while. "Wary. As if she's about to run away."

Tommy pulled the book toward him so that he could read it. "This man, the man who wrote the text, refers to her 'twisted, unhappy smile.'"

Alberg craned his head to look again at the painting. He couldn't see any twisted, unhappy smile.

Tommy found another one and showed it to him. "What about this one?"

"It's the *Mona Lisa*."

"Good," said Tommy, with gentle mockery.

Alberg concentrated. "It's a private smile. She looks like she's humoring him: da Vinci. There's dignity in her face."

Again Tommy referred to the text. "He says she's wearing a look of 'mirthless amusement.' One more." He thumbed through the book, then showed a third portrait to Alberg.

It was Andrea del Sarto's *Portrait of an Architect*. Alberg said the architect looked startled and suspicious. The book's author called the painting "abstracted . . . [and] dreamy."

Alberg shook his head.

"You see?" said Tommy. "Everything is in the eye of the beholder." He closed the book. "That actor, her friend: he sees things in the portrait that he knows existed in her. People who didn't know her, like you, they see all kinds of things there. Depending on what you're thinking, how you're feeling, what you're looking for."

Alberg sighed. "Okay. I give up." He reached for his coffee mug. "Anyway, I appreciate your time."

"Oh, it's my pleasure."

Alberg looked across the room at the paintings on the walls. "I still can't figure why you don't do more portraits, when you're so good at it."

"Oh, I don't know. It's hard to explain." He rubbed at the scar on his forehead.

"Does that hurt?" said Alberg.

"What? This?" He pulled his hand away. "Oh no."

"How long have you been here, Tommy? May I call you Tommy?"

The art teacher flushed. "Oh yes," he said. "Sure."

"And I'm Karl."

"I've been here—oh, since the end of June, I guess it is. Yes. I moved in at the end of the school year. Before that I lived in a house, a small house. But this has got such wonderful light, you see." He gestured toward the skylight.

"When did you come to Sechelt?"

"Oh, well, I came to Sechelt—it was 1972, I think. Or maybe 1973." He gave Alberg a dazzling smile. "I came to Sechelt for the light, too. It's different, close to the sea. And I couldn't afford to live close to the sea in Vancouver. Besides, the beaches there aren't the same. Too many people."

Alberg finished his coffee and stood up. "Listen. Thanks again."

"Have you heard about my show?" said Tommy at the door.

"Your what? No. You mean, a display of your work?"

"Yes. At the arts center." He was smiling again.

"When?"

"A week from today." His smile faded. "You know, I think it's because of the portrait. That upsets me."

"It shouldn't," said Alberg, although he was privately dismayed. "That's a beautiful piece of work. You should be proud of it."

"Oh, I am," said Tommy softly. "I am."

Alberg started down the steps. "Thanks for the coffee," he called from halfway down.

"You're welcome," said Tommy. "Are you coming to the show?"

Alberg turned and looked at him appraisingly. "I wouldn't miss it for the world," he said.

He felt restless and dissatisfied as he drove home. Melancholy. Which was a hell of a way to react to sunshine.

He was convinced that there was something in the portraits he'd been shown—or in the conversation—that he'd missed.

CHAPTER 21

On his way up the walk to the front door of his house, Alberg turned to look at the slopes of the coastal mountains. The snowline had not, as he had half expected, melted away in the warmth of the autumn afternoon. It was always disconcerting, when the mountains whitened. There were no perpetually white peaks near Sechelt, like the ones which thrust themselves into view behind the lower mountaintops around Vancouver. He thought of the mountains on the Sunshine Coast as precipitous hills, and it was a shock to see how far into snow clouds they had penetrated.

He went inside and played for a while in the sun porch with the kitten. She was black with white front paws and a white splotch on her chest and another one smeared across her mouth; she looked like she had been interrupted while eating a marshmallow. He dangled a ball of foil attached to a long piece of string and watched as the kitten batted at it with her front paws, occasionally falling over in her careless excitement. The cat, her mother, sat nearby, cleaning herself, ignoring them. But when the kitten made an exasperated mewling sound the cat froze, eyes suddenly fixed on her offspring.

"It's all right, cat," said Alberg.

The kitten sat down, front paws primly together, and yawned, showing her teeth. The cat resumed her grooming.

Alberg got himself a beer and wandered into the living room, where he dropped into the wingback chair by the window and put his feet up on the hassock, which the kitten had begun using as a scratching post. Outside, the hydrangea bushes massed along the fence were covered with enormous blossoms that had gradually changed their color over the summer and fall from brilliant blue to a deep shade that was partly purple and partly rust. They would soon become a papery brown; he wouldn't cut off the dead blossoms until spring; he'd read somewhere that that was the thing to do, or else somebody had told him about it.

He opened his notebook and flipped through the pages, stopping to reread the sections that caught his eye. There weren't many of them.

The reports they'd gotten back from California didn't do Galbraith any harm. He wasn't on anybody's sheet. Alberg figured the man had exaggerated the extent of his activities. He might have thought he was in trouble, but he needn't have worried; to the Los Angeles police, his insignificance was immeasurable. They'd never heard of him.

Alberg didn't intend to tell him that.

The victim was also clean.

Alberg had talked briefly the day she was identified to Sally Dublin's agent; they had learned her profession from American Express and had gotten the name of her agent from the Screen Actors Guild. He was a gravel-voiced man named Bermas, who had insisted on taking Alberg's number and calling him back—collect—in order to confirm his identity. Bermas seemed more than politely grieved by Sally Dublin's death and was certainly horrified when told the manner of it. He said that he had not been aware that she was in British Columbia. When asked, he had admitted that he knew Roger Galbraith—was in fact his agent, too—and that Galbraith and the victim were acquainted.

Sally Dublin's closest relative was a brother who lived in Massachusetts. Bermas had given Alberg his name and address and that of Sally's lawyer. Sid Sokolowski had contacted the brother and gotten from him instructions about where to send the body. Sokolowski had also spoken to the lawyer, who said that although she had made a will, leaving half her sizable estate to the brother and half to the Screen Actors Guild, she had not made any arrangements for her burial or cremation.

Sally Dublin, Bermas had said, could be impulsive to the point of recklessness. He had confirmed her habitual hitchhiking.

Alberg gazed, unseeing, through his living room window.

After a while he put in a call to Los Angeles.

Bermas wasn't in his office, but Alberg reached him at his home.

"I have to assume," said Alberg when they'd gotten through the preliminaries, "that he's the reason she came up here. What do you know about their relationship?"

"You got him in the slammer, or what?" said Bermas.

"We're talking to him," said Alberg carefully. "That's all."

"I can't see it," said Bermas. "Roger as a killer. Shit, I don't think I could even get him *cast* as a killer." He hesitated.

Alberg waited.

Finally, "They had a big thing going, Sally and Roger," the agent said reluctantly. "A long time ago, now. I remember when they split up—Sally moved in with a guy, I think he worked for one of the record companies. Lasted about two weeks, total. He had this dog, a German shepherd. She caught them in flagrante delicto."

"What, the record guy and the dog?" said Alberg.

"Yeah. Hey, we got all kinds, fella. You oughta come down here, take a look."

"We've got the same kinds up here, thanks. Fella."

"Well, anyhow, she'd given up her apartment, see? For this pukehead. As it turned out. So she storms out of his place and she lies to a couple of banks, mortgages herself up to the hilt, buys herself a little house. This was before computers took over the world, you understand. No more moving in with guys, she tells me. And she never did. Made herself some good bread maybe a year or so later, did some good investing. She had a sharp head on her, Sally."

"What about Galbraith?"

"Roger, he's not so sharp," said Bermas with a honking laugh. "They made quite a pair, those two. Rog dressed to the nines all the time, like any minute somebody's going to discover him, never mind it's way too late for that. And Sally stomping around in jeans and no makeup. But they were good friends, you know?"

"Lately?"

"Oh yeah. Sally was always on my case, trying to get him work. I get him work. Not as much as she wanted, but enough."

"Why do you think he didn't bother to tell you he was coming up here?"

"Roger never tells me nothin'. That's one of his problems. Doesn't call me enough. Bug me. He doesn't want to look like he needs the work, you know? Jesus, I'd probably forget all about him if it wasn't for Sally and my secretary. My secretary admires him. He's good, no question about it. Just never quite made it. Them's the breaks."

"Did you ever see them fight? Argue?"

"Shit, Sally wouldn't fight with anybody. Even when she ought to. Even the record guy, no ranting and raving, she just turned right around and walked out on him."

"What about Roger?"

"She didn't walk out on Roger," Bermas assured him. "He didn't walk out on her, either. They just split up. Easy like. I told you, they're good friends. Were. It was nice to see."

Alberg thanked him, and they hung up. He drained his can of beer and went to the kitchen for another one.

"Shit," he said, sitting down with his notebook again, this time at the big round oak table in the dining area part of his living room.

If Sally Dublin had been killed because of who she was, Galbraith was the only possible suspect. They'd have to put more pressure on him, Alberg decided.

He thought about the ten-year-old homicide of the hitchhiker. He hadn't been inclined at first to connect it with Sally Dublin's killing, because so much time had elapsed between the incidents.

But he couldn't deny that there were similarities.

Both victims were attractive women. Both were apparently hitchhiking. And neither had been sexually assaulted. He'd have to study the file of the old case more closely, just to make sure there was nothing else that might tie the two deaths together. And they'd have to widen their inquiries to the mainland and Vancouver Island, in case they had similar unsolved homicides. And, although it was a long shot, Galbraith's whereabouts at the time of the first homicide would have to be checked out. For a moment Alberg allowed himself to fantasize that the actor had been visiting his B.C. relatives then, too.

The sun was now low on the horizon, slanting directly through his window onto the hardwood floor. He figured it must be about four o'clock, checked his watch: four-seventeen.

Then there was Alfred Hingle. There was nothing but the discovery of the corpse to tie him to the murder, except for the comparative proximity of his house to the scene of the crime.

And his record.

And, of course, the sketch. That strangely inept preliminary sketch, which Alfred had found, retrieved, and for some inexplicable reason tacked up on the wall of his shed.

Alberg closed the notebook and pushed it aside.

Not even four-thirty yet. With a brief sense of panic that he quickly smothered, he wondered what to do with the rest of the day, and the evening. He needed to talk to somebody. But his daughters in Calgary had part-time jobs and he knew they wouldn't be home yet. Sid's mother was visiting the Sokolowskis and they'd all gone to Vancouver for the day. And Cassandra . . .

He stood up and went purposefully to the bedroom. He'd shower, change, have dinner someplace, and whatever was playing at the movie theater in Gibsons, he'd go to see the damn thing.

CHAPTER 22

Roger showed up at Cassandra's door shortly after noon on Sunday.

His denim shirt was wrinkled in the back and under the arms, he wore just plain ordinary blue jeans, and his face looked shriveled with apprehension.

Cassandra was appalled. She hadn't seen him since the previous Monday, the day of his interrogation.

"Can I come in?" he said, as his sister backed her car out of the driveway and turned onto the highway.

"Of course you can come in," said Cassandra. She had to resist putting an arm around him and leading him inside, slowly, tenderly, as if he were an invalid.

He walked back and forth, back and forth across her living room, rubbing his hands, running his fingers through his hair until he looked like a wild man.

He had called her every day, at the library. "Have you thought about it?" he'd say, and she would reply, "Yes, I have. I can't do it." And he'd said, "Please think about it some more," and then he'd hang up without another word.

Now he said, "You mean it, don't you? You won't do it."

"No, Roger. I'm sorry."

He went to the end of the living room and looked out the glass doors at the lawn that swept across a slight rise and into the woods behind the house.

"They've had me back there, you know," he said tonelessly. "Did you know that?"

"Back where? To the police station?" She was still standing, gripping the sides of her full cotton skirt with both hands. It occurred to her that this would crease it, so she let go and smoothed the fabric with the palms of her hands.

"They just ask me the same fucking questions. That's all. And then they tell me again, don't leave Sechelt." He turned around. "Jesus Christ, am I going to be stuck here the rest of my life, having useless conversations with these fucking cops?" He walked toward her and Cassandra's heart stuttered, he looked so angry. But he let himself fall onto the sofa and stared morosely in front of him. "They've got that picture splattered all over the goddamn peninsula. Every time I turn around, there she is. And what good's it doing, for Christ's sake?" He got up and started pacing again. Cassandra sat down, not wanting to get in his way. "It's driving me fucking crazy. I can't go into the post office, I can't go to the liquor store, I can't go any fucking place in town but there she is, staring at me." Suddenly he bent over and covered his face with his hands.

"Roger." Cassandra got up and went to him. She touched his shoulder and he turned to her swiftly, weeping. She embraced him and felt him cling to her. "Roger, this is ridiculous. It's silly. You've got to tell them where you were."

"Christ, I can just see it," he said huskily. "Clapped in the slammer in goddamn Sechelt, B.C., for some goddamn coke."

"They're not going to put you in jail," said Cassandra firmly, although she wasn't at all sure they wouldn't. "They're interested in who killed your friend, not in the fact that you use dope."

"Shit," he said.

She pulled away and looked at his face. He seemed slightly less anxious, although maybe that was just the calming effect of the tears.

"Yeah, yeah," he said. "Okay." He let go of her and wiped his face with the backs of his hands. "That fucking jerk will deny it, of course. But you're right. I'm gonna have to do it."

"I'll drive you over there."

"Not today. It's Sunday. I only want to talk to Alberg." He went into the kitchen and came back with a piece of paper towel into which he blew his nose. "The big Polack gives me the creeps," said Roger bitterly. "He always looks like he's ready to flatten me. The other one, the young dude—shit on him." He went back to the kitchen and she heard him toss the paper towel into the garbage bag under the sink. "Alberg won't be there on a Sunday," he said when he came back. "He's the guy in charge. People in charge never work on Sundays."

"I think policemen do, sometimes," said Cassandra with a tentative smile. "We could call him and tell him you want to see him. I'm sure he'd come."

"No," said Roger sharply. He sat down. "Okay, okay, I've made my decision. I'll do it. I'll fink on the son-of-a-bitch if you won't help me, if it's the only way I can get out of this place." He glared up at her reproachfully. "But I need time to get used to the idea. I'll do it tomorrow morning."

Cassandra went to the kitchen and got them some coffee.

"Tell me about the guy who did the picture," said Roger, brooding.

"I told you. He's an art teacher. At the high school. That's really all I know about him."

"Have you seen anything else he's done?"

"Some things in the new Bank of Montreal," said Cassandra. "And a couple of days ago he came into the library and I asked him if he had some things we could hang on that big wall at the back, behind the reading area."

Roger swiveled his head to look at her.

"Well, there's been such a lot of talk," she said apologetically, "about the portrait. People admire it. And so of course there's a lot of interest in the painter."

"So?" said Roger coldly. "What happened?"

"Friday after school he brought in three paintings," said Cassandra, trying to sound businesslike.

"And you're going to put them up?"

She nodded.

Roger groaned. "Shit." He sighed. "What kinds of things are they?"

"There's a seascape, in oils. A watercolor—it's an arrangement of rocks and driftwood. And something he's done in acrylics, I think—a seagull in flight."

"No portraits?"

"Not unless you count the seagull," said Cassandra with a grin.

"Thank Christ for that, anyway." Roger sat up. He started tapping the heel of his sneaker soundlessly against the carpeted floor; his knee rose and fell, jerkily, keeping time.

He had to leave. Cassandra could see that. He had to get back to L.A. There she thought he'd be able to truly grieve for Sally. And there his real life waited for him. The life he'd been living in Sechelt wasn't real to him. None of it. Not even her. She watched his distress, his agitation, and she knew this.

"As soon as you tell Karl where you were," she said, "everything will be all right. They'll let you go. You can go home then."

His fingers rubbed again at his black curls. "Yeah, I can hardly wait. 'I was just buying some dope from this guy, Officer. Here, let me give you his name, check it out; he'll tell you.'"

"You don't even have to tell them you were buying dope," said Cassandra, getting exasperated. "Just tell them you were *with* him, for God's sake."

"What else would I be doing with a turd like that? Don't you think the cops know all about him? Shit," he said, striding once more back and forth across her living room, "I just mention the guy's name and they'll know what I was doing with him. Then the jerk's up to his ass in trouble and it's my fault. He'll probably come after me before I can get onto the goddamn ferry."

She didn't know whether to laugh at him or throw him out of her house.

It depended—and the thought entered her head with no warning—on whether she believed him.

Had he been buying dope the night Sally Dublin was murdered? If he hadn't, if he'd lied to her, no wonder he had been so anxious that she should provide him with an alibi.

Cassandra got slowly to her feet. "I think," she said carefully, "that we ought to get outside into the sunshine. You may not have noticed," she called back to him as she hurried into the bedroom for her purse, "but the sun's been shining for almost a whole week." When she returned to the living room he was looking at her curiously, his hands shoved into the pockets of his jeans. "I'm going to take you out for a late lunch," said Cassandra firmly. "Or an early dinner. Whatever. At that place by the water, where you can see Vancouver Island across the strait."

At first she thought he was going to argue, but then he shrugged and walked to the door.

"You'll have to give me a ride back to my sister's, though," he said.

"Sure," said Cassandra.

"Maybe I'll sing you a song," said Roger as they made their way to her car. "In the restaurant. A nice Scottish song."

"Yeah," said Cassandra. "Like 'Auld Lang Syne.'" She heard her voice break and was humiliated.

CHAPTER 23

Late Monday evening from a bluff above the ocean a man could be seen walking along the beach. His hands were in his pockets and he looked down as he walked, at the rocks. He walked slowly, his shoulders slightly bent, oblivious to the sound of the waves and to the sky pricked brilliantly with cold stars.

The dog watched him for a few minutes, then ran down from the bluff and padded up beside him. The man stopped. He reached down to rub behind the dog's ears.

The moon shone upon the stony beach, the sleeping sea. A breeze passed through the trees that grew upon the bluff. There was no one around except the man and the dog, hopefully wagging its tail.

The man began walking again. The dog watched him, then trotted to the foot of the bluff and found a stick. It ran to the man with the stick in its mouth and dropped it at the man's feet.

The man hesitated, then picked up the stick and threw it into the brush at the bottom of the bluff. As the dog chased after it, the man took something slowly from his pocket, then changed his mind and thrust it away again. He started walking more quickly up the beach.

But the dog ran up behind him with the stick, and dropped it, and barked happily.

Again the man threw the stick; again the dog ran to fetch it. Again the man took the knife from his pocket, and this time he followed the dog into the brush, and when the dog found the stick and turned to take it to him, he was already there.

The bushes reached to the man's thighs and were bare of leaves. The moon was bright and it drained the world of color.

The dog looked at him inquiringly, the stick still in his mouth. He took the stick away and laid it on the ground. The dog nudged the stick with its nose, stood back, and looked at him imperiously.

"Sit," said the man, gently.

The dog stopped wagging its tail and seemed to give a sigh. It sat, reluctantly, right in front of him.

The man bent toward the dog, his left hand on the back of its neck. He looked into the dog's eyes and stretched his right hand slowly behind him and brought the knife forward swiftly, savagely.

When it was over he sat on the ground next to the dog and stroked its head and softly sang to it, and the man wept, and knew that he was lost.

CHAPTER 24

The light had faded long ago; the November days were short. Outside there was a moon, and stars. Alberg that Monday night stood in the doorway of his sun porch looking down the hillside at the town of Gibsons and the small harbor where he hoped next summer he would be able to pick out the mast of his own sailboat.

It was hard, he thought, for a police officer to make friends outside the force. That's what he missed most about his family; they had been his friends. His daughters still were, but the distance between him and them seemed colossal.

He looked eastward, the view cut off abruptly by a nearby mountain, a black shape against the stars. And he imagined the thousands and thousands of mountains that separated him from them, the vast ranges of the Coastal Mountains, the Columbias, the Rockies; these divided into the smaller ranges of the Pacific, the Cariboo, the Monashee, the Selkirk, the Purcell. There were immense plateaus and valleys among the jagged reefs of the mountains, unimaginably high; so many more miles to walk than if flat prairie were what stretched from Alberg to his daughters in Calgary.

He missed his wife, too. He had no desire to live with her again. He didn't even think he loved her any longer. But he missed her.

Actually, he was usually happy living alone, he thought, stepping back inside the sun porch and closing the door; it was cold out there, now that the sun had set. He missed having good friends, that was all. Friends with whom he could be whatever he felt at the moment. Sharing himself with nobody at all got tiresome, boring. That's all it was.

He fixed himself a drink and wandered through the

house to the living room. There wasn't a thing he could think of to do.

He got the portrait and sat in the wingback chair and turned on the lamp.

She had become his silent companion, as much a part of his life as were the photographs of his family that he kept in albums, in frames on his dresser, on his office wall.

All kinds of things he saw in this dead woman's face. He knew why he saw some of them: a propensity for laughter was drawn for him in the delicate lines that radiated from her eyes and in the faint, shallow clefts at the sides of her mouth; self-possession in the direct blue gaze, the erect carriage of the head upon her neck and shoulders; her age, in the slight slackness of her skin, the suggestion of creases in her forehead.

He thought of the sketch hanging on the wall of Alfred Hingle's shed, and he wondered how many sketches Cummings had discarded before he got the one that resulted in the portrait Alberg now held in his hand. He'd sure finally managed to get it right, anyway.

But it still had not been satisfactorily explained why, as he looked at the portrait, Alberg was so certain of her compassion, her trenchant melancholy. Surely the artist's patience and the eventual freeing of his skill couldn't account entirely for this?

Cummings was probably right. It was all in the eye of the beholder. Galbraith saw whatever he saw in the portrait because he had known Sally Dublin. Alberg felt compassion for her because she was a beautiful woman who'd been senselessly slaughtered. He felt melancholy because he was feeling lonely, these days. He was transferring his own moods onto the portrait of somebody who had no choice but to accept them as her own. He put the portrait aside, disgusted with himself.

When the phone rang he was making himself a tuna sandwich. His first thought was that maybe somebody was calling to invite him to dinner. But he knew how unlikely that was.

I've got a right, he thought, to feel sorry for myself.

Suddenly, inexplicably, he was furious. He knew what

that son-of-a-bitch had been up to that night. Either he'd been buying coke, probably from Lazarus down in Gibsons, or else he'd been carving up his girlfriend.

And by Christ, thought Alberg, reaching for the phone, one way or another he was going to find out which and he didn't mind admitting that he was pulling for the homicide.

"Oh Mr. Alberg it's Norma Hingle, please come I don't know what to do." Her voice was stuffed with hysteria, clotted with sobs.

"What is it? What's the matter?"

"I don't know what to do," she said, "oh God all the way from the beach, there's blood all over his sweater."

Jesus Christ, thought Alberg, and his skin went cold.

"What's the matter?" he said sharply. "I don't know what you're saying."

"I just got home from work, it's Clyde, Clyde's been murdered he says, oh dear God, Alfred—I don't know what to do! He's crying and shouting, he says he's going to kill him!"

"Mrs. Hingle." He made himself speak slowly, calmly. "Norma. Please. Who's he going to kill? Where's Alfred now?"

"Out in the shed. He's with Clyde. He wouldn't let me see him. Oh my God, poor Alfred, oh it'll kill him."

"Did the dog get hit by a car?" said Alberg gently.

"No no," said Norma, her voice rising again. He heard her take several ragged breaths. "He found him on the beach," she said. "He says somebody stabbed him. He carried him all the way home. He put him in the shed and then he came in and he was crying, Mr. Alberg, crying, I've never in my life seen Alfred cry, and he was shouting and pounding at the walls. Oh please, come quickly, I don't know what to do!"

"Does he know who did it?"

"He says—he says he'll know him when he sees him. Oh dear God what does that mean? What am I going to do?"

"Try to keep him there," said Alberg. "I'll be over as soon as I can."

He called the dispatcher, who wanted to send somebody who was already on duty. But Alberg said no.

* * *

Norma Hingle must have been watching for him from the window. The outside light was on and she came out onto the porch as he drove from the access road along the ruts and across the circle so he could park at an angle in front of Alfred's pickup.

"Is he still in the shed?" he asked when he got out of the car.

"Yes." She looked drained, desperate.

Alberg went across the yard and knocked on the door of the shed. "Alfred?" he called. From inside the shed he heard a low, keening sound. "Alfred," he said more loudly, and the singing stopped.

Alberg heard quick hard footsteps and the door was flung open.

Alfred Hingle, thought Alberg, looking at him, was a broad and powerful man. He was holding a cloth that dripped pink drops upon the floor.

"I figured she'd call on you," he said. He went back to the table upon which he had placed the body of his dog, and Alberg followed.

"Jesus Christ," he said, staring down at Clyde. His throat had been cut. Alfred had cleaned the dog thoroughly, using the cloth in his hand and a bucket of water on the floor at his feet. The wounds were still oozing blood.

"I was taking him for a walk," said Alfred dully. "He ran off. He sometimes does. I called him and called him. Then I went looking for him." He swiveled his head to look at Alberg. "You talked to my wife about formalities," he said, "the last time you were here." He wrung out the cloth, sloshed it in the reddened water in the pail, and leaned over the dog's body, wiping gently, slowly.

Alberg went around to the other side of the table and put his hand on the side of Clyde's head, under his ear.

"There's no pulse," said Alfred. He stepped back and dropped the cloth in the bucket of water. "There was no pulse when I found him, and there's no pulse now."

"I'm sorry, Alfred."

"The last time you were here," said Hingle, "you had to speak to me about that woman I found murdered. Because of formalities, you said. Well I know all about that kind of formalities. Now I want a formality from you." He looked down at the dog and his face seemed to spasm. When he looked up again his eyes were dark and glittery. "This is a murder," said Alfred, pointing to Clyde. "This dog was killed by somebody. There's no accident that could happen to a dog that looks like this."

Alberg nodded.

"So I want this murder investigated. Just like the other one. I want you to do an autopsy, and look for clues, and hunt down the son-of-a-bitch that did this." He put his hand on the dog's flank. "I was going to do it myself."

Alberg nodded again.

"I know who it was," Alfred said darkly. "It had to be that actor. The one that killed the woman. There can't be two people going around here slitting throats. I saw him today. I saw him in Sechelt, it's Monday, I was doing my rounds in the town. I saw him, just driving around in that car of his sister's like he didn't have a care in the world. A man who'd kill a woman—he'd kill a dog without blinking an eye. I decided to go after him. But I changed my mind."

"Good," said Alberg.

"I want you to do your duty," said Alfred. "You're supposed to be trained in this kind of thing. It shouldn't make a tinker's damn bit of difference if it's a person or a dog. Murder's murder." He watched Alberg intently.

The staff sergeant got out his notebook. "Have you got a heater in here?"

Alfred stared at him.

"I've got to ask you some questions. I'd like to be a little warmer."

Alfred went slowly to the shelving on the long, windowless wall and found a small space heater which he plugged in and set near the two chairs in front of the Franklin stove. "I could light a fire," he said.

"Don't bother. This is fine." Alberg sat down. "Okay. Where and when did you find him?"

After a moment Alfred sat, too, with his feet wide apart, his hands on his thighs. The front of his Cowichan sweater was stained with blood.

CHAPTER 25

The next afternoon Alberg was at the place where Sally Dublin had died, wondering what he was doing there.

He'd driven north along the highway from Sechelt for no particular reason, unless it was a vague hope that getting away from his desk and into the continuing fair weather might sharpen his thinking. He had passed the clearing and at the next opportunity turned his car around.

As he headed back he tried to conjure up a dark, cold, rainy night; tried to imagine what explanation the driver of the car in which Sally must have been riding might have given her for pulling off the road.

Alberg drove off the highway next to the clearing and got out of the car. The grass and the spindly, leafless weeds were spongy beneath his feet, still retaining moisture from the recent rains.

He wondered as he stood there if she had run first toward the road, hoping for rescue. Maybe the guy hadn't originally stopped at the clearing at all, thought Alberg. Maybe he'd pulled over farther up the highway, and she had leapt out and run along the road and the car had followed her. Why hadn't she veered across the highway and struck out into the woods on the other side? Not that it would have made any difference, Alberg told himself, walking toward the brush that edged the clearing. There were no nearby houses over there, either.

The bushes crackled and rustled as he pushed through

them, and he heard the swift thrumming sound of wings and thought it was probably a grouse. It was early afternoon and the sun was warm upon his head and shoulders until he had made his way through the brush and into a stand of enormous cedars.

Beneath the canopy of distant branches the ground was cushioned by fallen needles; he walked across the clearing almost inaudibly, passing the tree trunk against which her body had been propped.

There was the place where the salal had been broken and trampled. Alberg went through to look at the snarl of logs and branches where she had gotten entangled, where she had been killed. Some of the fallen trees were four and five feet across, their broken boughs hung with brown withered lace. He leaned against a tree trunk. There wasn't any more to see than there'd been the night she'd died here. Everything of any possible significance had been removed, studied, and found to be devoid of any significance whatsoever.

Through her credit card, and with the help of Tommy Cummings' portrait, her movements had been traced from Los Angeles to Madeira Park, twenty miles north of Sechelt. She had arrived in Vancouver on October 23, stayed two nights, then gone by ferry to Victoria. She took bus tours in both cities. (Sokolowski, when he learned this, had exclaimed, flabbergasted, "Sightseeing! This broad was sightseeing." As though she ought to have known she was going to be murdered, and been less carefree.)

A real estate salesman named Homer Funk had given her a ride from Victoria to Nanaimo, where she had stayed in a motel at the edge of town.

They didn't know how she'd gotten from there to Comox, where she'd taken the ferry across the strait to Powell River.

They didn't know who'd picked her up in Powell River, either.

The last sighting of her was Sunday, November 3, the day of her death, when the only bag lady on the Sunshine Coast had seen her in Madeira Park. Maisie was a woman of indeterminate age who lived a relatively luxurious life in Garden Bay, which was across a narrow inlet from Madeira Park. She was universally disapproved of in Garden Bay, where she stole more fruits and vegetables from people's gardens than the deer. She swiped salmon, too, from unwary fishermen, usually tourists, when they left their catches even briefly unguarded. Maisie lived in a dilapidated old tug that had been beached years before. She told the officer who more to amuse himself than anything else showed her Sally Dublin's picture that she had indeed seen the dead woman.

She knew, of course, how Garden Bay felt about her. So on those few occasions when she spent money, she spent it in Madeira Park. That's where she was the day she saw Sally: buying, inexplicably, shoe polish and mouthwash at a small family grocery store that stayed open twelve hours a day, seven days a week. She liked the East Indians who ran the place, possibly because they felt as ostracized from the life of their community as she did from hers.

Alberg had driven up to Garden Bay. She refused to talk to him in her tugboat. She'd insisted that he take her to a coffee shop, where she thoroughly enjoyed the curious stares of the staff and the other customers, beaming at them triumphantly from time to time as she told her tale.

"She was a strange one," said Maisie. She was wearing a glossy auburn wig which she frequently washed but seldom brushed. "Stopped me on the street, she did. All burbling, she was." She asked Alberg if she could have a doughnut and without waiting for a reply signaled regally to the waitress and ordered two of them: chocolate, with chocolate icing and coconut flakes.

"What do you mean, 'burbling'?" said Alberg. "What was she burbling about?"

"She was going on about how beautiful it was." Maisie pronounced it "beeyoutifull," screwing up her face as if the word tasted bad. "Started to laugh, she did, told me she'd stopped somebody else and asked them how to get downtown. Well she was standing in it, wasn't she. Downtown. So she said she felt like a fool then for a bit, and I said no wonder. She told me she'd come up here from California to see a friend.

An actor, she said he was. Well I told her, all the actors we've got around here you can find them around Gibsons, where they do that TV program. But no, he was in Sechelt, she said. Well, I doubted that."

Sally had told Maisie that she'd gotten a ride from Earls Cove with the Madeira Park postmistress, who'd been to Powell River to visit her nephew. They'd met on the ferry, said Maisie, and this was later confirmed by the postmistress.

The last Maisie saw of Sally Dublin she was trotting down the street toward the highway, wearing a red raincoat with a hood, and there was a knapsack on her back.

Alberg heard the whisperings of a breeze in the cedar boughs, the soft clattering of the brush, the whisking sounds of giant ferns brushing against one another. Birds were chattering somewhere, and occasionally—it seemed very far away—he could hear a vehicle pass by on the highway. The sun poked curiously through the trees, casting shifting beams of light into the forest.

She had run through the woods, she had been followed by her killer, and later by a dozen police officers who had removed chunks of turf, sawed away pieces of the branches that had trapped her. Yet already the forest was beginning to recover from the invasion. Trampled bushes were slowly regaining their upright positions; broken twigs were becoming part of the forest floor; the snare of fallen logs had begun to fall in upon itself, creating a new pattern. By spring, thought Alberg, there would be no trace at all of what had happened here.

He made his way back to the level needle-carpeted area beneath the cedars. The earth had been removed from beneath and around the tree that had supported the body. There was, again, nothing to see.

But Alberg still couldn't figure out why she'd been propped up like that. It bothered him a great deal. And so he got down on his haunches and stared at the trunk of the cedar. Eventually he thought he saw a blonde hair caught in the rough bark. But nothing else.

Finally he went back to his car. He had to roll the window

down, because the sun had heated the interior air to a summer-like intensity.

He'd asked the local vet to do an autopsy on the dog. Clyde had apparently sat still for the slash across his throat, which indicated he'd been killed by someone he knew. But Alberg had already concluded that much for himself, and he knew Alfred Hingle had, too. Alberg had decided to put Sanducci on it. He figured they owed it to Hingle to at least make an effort to find out who'd killed his dog.

Sanducci was also gathering information from Lower Mainland and Vancouver Island police forces about unsolved homicides in which the victims were presumed to have been hitchhikers.

Alberg sat in the car for several minutes, enjoying the heat inside and the cool breeze that came in the open window.

Roger Galbraith had come up with an alibi. Sokolowski was still trying to track down Corkindale, the drug dealer who lived in the bush somewhere near Halfmoon Bay.

Up and down the coast, men were still trudging door to door with copies of the portrait of Sally Dublin, and the newspapers had been persuaded to run the picture for the third time.

Beyond this, there didn't seem to be a damn thing Alberg could do.

He started the car, pulled out onto the highway, and headed back to Sechelt.

He didn't like to admit it, but of course if Hingle had killed Sally Dublin, he might have killed his dog, too, in the hope that science would unequivocally conclude that both were dispatched with the same knife. Everybody in Sechelt knew how much Alfred loved his dog. Nobody would believe him capable of murdering Clyde.

Nobody, thought Alberg gloomily, but a cop.

CHAPTER 26

It was Wednesday morning, and Norma Hingle was vigorously polishing the bulbous brass base of a lamp which she considered one of the more successful results of her husband's scavengings.

She refused to let Alfred's propensity for collecting things overwhelm the house, but certain objects, once repaired and repainted, she had accepted willingly, even delightedly. The lamp, for one, and the small desk and chair in the corner of the kitchen, too. Here she kept grocery coupons and paper and pencils in a drawer; here she sat drawing up the weekly dinner menus, preparing the shopping list.

As she gave the lamp a final burnishing she admitted that she also appreciated the old-fashioned end table upon which it sat; there was a shelf underneath and a compartment at each end for magazines.

She put the Brasso back in the cupboard and dropped the cleaning cloths in the laundry hamper, and wondered if she ought to take some coffee out to Alfred, who was in the shed. His grief was all-consuming. She was beginning to worry about him.

He had called his boss Tuesday morning to say he wouldn't be in to work for a while. His boss had asked why and Alfred had told him. "My dog," he had announced heavily. "He's been murdered." Well God only knew what the man had thought of that.

Still, said Norma to herself, rummaging around in the cleaning cupboard for a dustcloth; still, he'd been honest about it. He couldn't be faulted for that. And he hardly ever took a day off work, even when he had a bad cold or the flu.

She began to dust in the living room. She wished she'd been able to persuade Alfred to go for a walk with her after breakfast. It wasn't good for him to shut himself away in the shed like that.

But he had refused, so she had gone alone. She found a clump of winter crocuses blooming at the edge of the woods, and some raucous Steller's jays had screeched at her, looking like pieces of the clear sky stuck in the tree branches. There were always things to see, and hear, and think about, when she went walking. But she enjoyed it much more when Alfred went with her.

She didn't mind the orderly clutter in the yard surrounding the house, mostly because nothing out there looked abandoned, even when in the summer weeds and wildflowers grew over the drainage pipes, and tall grasses hid the plastic flamingos. It was rather like a stock room in the back of some kind of store, she thought, with things waiting patiently for their day of usefulness.

She suddenly remembered the oaken barrels, and how the grass around them was yellowed, dead, because they'd been Clyde's favorite things to pee upon. She remembered the concentrated look on the dog's face as he lifted his leg. And this brought to her mind a flood of memories, bits and pieces of things, the way when Alfred threw the Frisbee for him Clyde would fling his entire body into the air, as if convinced that he could fly; the silly look of excitement he'd get when Alfred told him they were going in the truck; the way he stood so close to Alfred, almost leaning against him, every chance he got.

Norma had to put down the dustcloth and get a Kleenex and wipe her eyes. She'd been so fixed on Alfred's distress, she hadn't even thought about her own. She'd never considered Clyde in any way her dog, even when Alfred first brought him home as a puppy, yet of course she had loved him, too.

She blew her nose and washed her hands and wondered whether she would have the courage, eventually, to get Alfred another dog, as a surprise. She thought not.

She started when she heard the knock.

"I'm sorry to bother you," said Tommy Cummings, when she opened the door. "I probably should have phoned."

"Oh no," said Norma quickly. "That's all right. It's nice to see you," she added awkwardly, for he'd never come to the house before, even though they'd met dozens of times, usually when she and Alfred were out walking Clyde. "But why aren't you in school, then?"

"I don't have a class until ten," said Tommy. "I've brought something for your husband," he said, and she noticed a parcel under his arm.

"Well, that's very kind of you, I'm sure," said Norma. "Come in, Mr. Cummings."

"I heard about his dog," said Tommy, when they got to the kitchen.

"It's a terrible thing," said Norma, filling the kettle. "Alfred's in his shed. I'll just put this on to boil, and go and fetch him."

She found Alfred sitting in front of the Franklin stove. He hadn't lit a fire.

"What does he want?" said Alfred, when she'd told him about Tommy Cummings.

"He's brought you something."

He turned away from her to stare again into the small blackened cave. "I don't want it."

"You don't even know what it is."

"I don't want it."

Norma took a deep breath. "Alfred, I have to speak my mind. I respect your sorrow. And I feel my own grief about Clyde. It's a terrible, terrible thing. But this person in my kitchen has come to see you, not me. If you don't want to see him then you're going to have to tell him so yourself."

He turned slowly around to look up at her. His eyes behind his glasses were puffy. He didn't say anything. After a minute he stood up, pressing down on his thighs. He shuffled past Norma to the door of the shed.

In the kitchen the kettle was whistling, and Tommy Cummings stood as they came in. Norma hurried to make the tea.

"I heard about Clyde," said Tommy. "I'm terribly sorry. He was a fine dog. I know how you must miss him."

He looked small and slight next to Alfred.

"Sit down, the both of you," said Norma. She got out cups and saucers, cream and sugar.

Alfred's chair groaned, as usual, as he reluctantly sat down. Tommy Cummings perched on the edge of another chair as if any minute something was going to frighten him away. The flat parcel was on the table in front of him.

"The same fellow did it," said Alfred ominously, "as killed that woman."

Tommy looked startled but didn't say anything.

"I don't know it for a fact," said Alfred. "But it stands to reason."

Norma, embarrassed, pushed Tommy's parcel aside in order to make room for the tea things. "Not necessarily, Alfred," she felt obliged to say.

"I understood that it was some kind of accident," said Tommy hesitantly.

"You understood wrong," said Alfred.

Norma poured the tea. There was silence while the three of them creamed, sugared, stirred.

This whole business had put the actress from California right back into Norma's mind again. She had seen a lot of dead people in her time, but none of them had been murdered. Sometimes as she lay next to Alfred on sleepless nights—which were becoming more frequent, she had noticed, as she grew older—she had worried about the wearing away of her compassion. It had become perhaps too easy to distance herself from the sufferings of her patients. And when they died, she felt only momentary regret, and even this she thought was more a sop to civility than genuine emotion. But the shock and sorrow she had felt drawing the bedcovers up over the body of a young woman who had died of murder—that, she knew, had been genuine enough.

She was sure that Mr. Alberg didn't suspect Alfred. Not really. He was just carrying through with the formalities that he talked about, and they seemed to make him uncomfortable, too, as well they might.

"I guess they'll get him," said Tommy. "Soon enough."

It outraged Norma, angered her, even, the violence done upon that poor woman. At least, she thought, picking up her teacup, at least she hadn't been sexually attacked.

She remained immobile for several seconds, thinking about this, and about how grateful she was for it. Then she took a sip of her tea and put the cup carefully back on the saucer.

Alfred grunted. "They'd better move fast," he said to Tommy, "or he'll be out of the country."

The art teacher looked at him with fascination.

Alfred nodded, slowly. "It's got to be him. That actor fellow. That's the only person she knew around here, so I hear." He looked down at his tea. "Why he took it into his head to kill my dog, though . . . that I'll never understand."

A wave of heat rushed through Norma and pounded in her head. "That's slander," she said to Alfred. "That's out and out slander. You've got no right."

Tommy Cummings fumbled with the package on the table. Hurriedly he unwrapped it. He thrust it clumsily at Alfred. "Here. Please. I thought you might like to have this."

Alfred's furious gaze moved from Norma to the thing he had inadvertently taken hold of. She watched him, her heart still beating fast with fury. She saw him turn it around, grasp it with both hands, stare at it, and burst into sobs.

Instantly she was on her feet and around the table. She put her hands on his shoulders and looked down at the painting Tommy Cummings had made of Clyde.

It was like a blow to her chest. One hand flew to her mouth, the other clung to Alfred as though his flesh might suddenly dematerialize.

Clyde wore an expression she had seen hundreds of times, when Alfred stood up from the table or the sofa or his workbench in the shed; in the seconds in which it was not clear to Clyde what Alfred was going to do next, the dog wore that expression. It was eager anticipation, as if whatever Alfred decided to do would be fine with Clyde, but he was sure hoping it would be a few flings of the Frisbee or a walk along the beach.

Norma looked at Tommy Cummings in awe. She was aware of tears on her cheeks.

Tommy ducked his head and began carefully folding up the brown paper in which the painting had been wrapped. "I'm sorry it isn't framed," he said, to Norma.

"I'll get it framed," she said. "Right away, I'll do it."

Alfred was still clutching the painting with both hands, still sobbing. Norma got him some Kleenexes from the box on the counter, and finally he took them and removed his glasses and mopped at his face. He took a deep, shuddery breath. "I thank you. I do thank you." He stood and held out his hand to Tommy. "It was—it was very kind. Very kind. I don't know how I can ever repay you."

"You've already repaid me," said Tommy with a smile.

Alfred sat down and picked up the painting again. Norma went with Tommy Cummings to the door and there, before he went out to his car, she hugged him. He was touched by this, she could tell, because she could see a dampness gleaming in his eyes.

CHAPTER 27

"Isabella!"

When she poked her head in, Alberg was slouched in his chair with his feet up on the desk and his hands linked behind his head. He gave her a beatific smile. "Do you have any doughnuts, by any chance?"

She shook her head.

"Cookies?"

"Nope."

"Would it be possible for you to arrange to get some? Doughnuts, cookies, brownies—anything would do. For the conference. We're having a conference in here: Sokolowski, Sanducci, and me. Some refreshments would be nice."

"Nope."

He dropped his hands and sat up straighter. "What do you mean," he said coldly, "by 'nope'?"

"I mean no, it isn't possible. I've got better things to do than run around gathering up junk food for you to poison yourself with. You want poison," she said, retreating, "get your own."

He stalked out to the coffee machine, filled his mug, and added cream and sugar with an ostentation lost upon Isabella, who was banging the keys of her typewriter furiously.

"Sid!" he shouted. "Sanducci! Let's get to it."

They arrived in his office a couple of minutes later, Sanducci dragging behind him a collapsible metal chair, which he set up between Alberg's desk and the door. Sokolowski lowered himself into the black leather chair, planted his feet, laid a file folder upon his thighs, and opened it.

"Anything more on the actor?" said Alberg to Sokolowski.

"Corkindale says Galbraith was with him the night of the homicide," said the sergeant. "Just a friendly visit, of course. Doesn't know anything about any dope. He says Galbraith left about ten P.M. The guy could've got back down here in time to snuff his lady friend, I guess. Doesn't seem likely, though. The actor's probably clear. That is, if you're gonna believe Corkindale. Who hasn't said a word of truth in thirty-six years."

Alberg drank some coffee and pushed the mug away in disgust. "What about you?" he said to Sanducci.

"I heard from the mainland," said the corporal, flipping open his notebook. "They've had a few, over the last ten years. Young women, probably hitchhiking. Usually there was sexual assault, sometimes not. One was bashed on the head, another very messily stabbed with something that wasn't a blade, two were shot, one with a rifle, the other with a revolver. And no pattern in the locations, either. Hope, Chilliwack, Coquitlam, Squamish, Mission." He shrugged. "And then there's ours. From before. She lived in Roberts Creek. Stabbed. Direct hit to the heart. No sexual assault."

Alberg was looking at the portrait tacked on the wall near his desk. "What about the Island?" he said.

"Only one. Five years ago. That was a stabbing too. The girl was nineteen, lived in Courtenay. She was hitching to Nanaimo, where she was going to catch the ferry to Vancouver. Never got there."

"Anything else?" said Alberg, frowning at the portrait.

"It's the goddamn actor," said Sokolowski. "It's gotta be. He's the only person she knew around here. She was on her way to see him, for Christ's sake."

"We found nothing," said Alberg. "Not in his sister's house, or in her car, or in Cassandra's car. We've got zilch. And Mr. Galbraith's got an alibi now."

Sokolowski gave a contemptuous snort.

"He could have gotten out of town after he did it," said Sanducci. "Caught the first ferry in the morning and been long gone. Why didn't he?"

"He knew she was gonna be found," said the sergeant. "And he figured she was gonna be identified, sooner or later. Which she was. And then we'd find out that he knew her. Which we did. Things would look real bad for him then, if he'd skipped. We'd be on to the L.A.P.D. toot sweet." He stretched, reaching enormous arms toward the ceiling. "He's no dummy, this guy."

Alberg was straightening paper clips. He had a row of them now, on the top of his desk. He'd left the jog in the middle, and they looked like small brassy lightning bolts. "He cared about her," he said.

"Staff," said Sanducci patiently. "The guy's an actor."

"All right, all right," said Alberg irritably. "I know he's a goddamn actor."

"And Hingle," said Sokolowski, shifting his feet. "Hingle's still gotta be a viable suspect, too."

"A viable suspect," said Alberg. He swept the paper clips into his hand and dropped them into the wastebasket under the desk. "Christ. Yeah, okay. I read the file. Aggravated sexual assault, brandished a knife he didn't use. The guy served his time, for Christ's sake. He was clean before, he's been suspected of every goddamn thing that happened to a woman anywhere on this coast for the last twenty-five years. And not once has there been any evidence, not once has he been charged."

In the silence he tried the coffee again. He wondered if he could get used to drinking tea. Or fruit juice.

"You want to hear about the dog?" said Sanducci.

"Yeah. Sure. Let's hear about the dog," said Alberg with a sigh.

"Time of death between nine P.M. and midnight Monday. You said Hingle found him about ten P.M., but apparently he didn't see anybody on the beach." He looked at Alberg inquiringly.

"That's right. That's what he said."

"Neither did anybody else. I've been up and down, talked to somebody in every house along there. Nobody saw anything, heard anything, knows anything." He paused. "They asked me what it was all about, of course."

"And what did you tell them?"

"Just routine. That's what I told them. Some of them wanted more. Two ladies, live in a little place not far from Golden Arms. They wanted more. So I told them."

"Told them what?"

"That I was investigating the death of a dog. They were very impressed."

"Terrific," said Alberg.

"They've got a couple of canaries," said Sanducci.

"Great," said Alberg. "I hope to hell nothing ever happens to their damn canaries."

"Anyway," said Sanducci, "then I went to the scene of the crime."

Sokolowski scowled at him.

"Get on with it," said Alberg wearily.

"Sorry." Sanducci looked at his notes. "It happened above the high-tide mark, in some brush at the bottom of that little cliff. There's broken branches, a lot of blood, signs of scuffling; but no footprints, there's too much sand, and no weapon. But I saved the best part for last."

Alberg looked at him. "What best part?"

"The dog wore a collar. The lab boys found a good print—left thumb. It's not Hingle's, I checked. Could be his wife's, I guess. But somebody took hold of the dog by the collar, at the back. And it wasn't Hingle."

"I don't see how it's going to help us," said Alberg, shaking his head. "Even if we eventually get a match-up. It won't prove anything except that somebody grabbed the dog's collar. There's no tie-in to the woman's death at all." He looked at Sokolowski. "What do you think, Sid? You think it means anything?"

"I think we better talk to Hingle," said the sergeant slowly. "Find out how many people were that friendly with his dog. That's all I think right now."

"Yeah," said Alberg, nodding. "And we might as well get Mr. Galbraith's prints in the meantime. Tell him we've got new evidence." He glanced again at the portrait on his wall. "No need to tell him what it is. If he and Corkindale are lying, maybe taking his prints will put a big enough scare into him to panic him."

"Yeah. Right onto the next ferry," said Sanducci.

"Maybe," said Alberg.

He stood and took down the portrait. Something about it had lately been setting his teeth on edge.

He stared at it for a long moment.

No. It wasn't the portrait.

It was the sketch. Something about Alfred Hingle's sketch.

CHAPTER 28

Tommy Cummings' picture had brought it back and now Norma couldn't get it out of her mind: the sound of Alfred keening.

She hadn't allowed herself to think about it at the time; she was far too distraught about Clyde's death.

He'd made the same sound the night he was arrested. And when Clyde was murdered she heard it again, coming from behind the closed door of Alfred's shed, and for a moment she'd thought it was Clyde, not quite dead, howling out his pain.

But it was Alfred's howling, and Alfred's pain.

He had come directly to Norma, that night more than twenty-five years ago, and he'd told her what he'd done. He was drunk and crying when he told her; drunk when he did it, too, but probably not crying.

It shouldn't even have been counted as a weapon. A Swiss army knife is all it was, and he'd never opened it up, never threatened the girl with it, he'd said, and Norma had believed him. It fell out of his pocket, and she saw it, the girl did, and thought he was going to use it, but it was never his intention to use it, he'd even forgotten he'd had it with him, Alfred told her, and Norma had believed him, and she still did.

The girl hadn't believed him, though. And neither had the police.

He had never said a word to make her think so, not a single solitary word, but Norma had wondered how much of the whole terrible business might have been her fault, for denying Alfred her body before they got married. Of course she knew better now. She knew that people had to accept responsibility for what they did, and that there was nothing, nothing, to excuse a man for assaulting someone. Even if the someone was a girl he met in a bar, and got drunk with, and who asked him flat out for a ride home.

And he did take her home, too. Afterwards. But she was very upset. And he knew what was going to happen. So he went to Norma's little basement apartment in that run-down house in East Vancouver and he told her all about it and when he'd finished, he was kneeling on the floor in front of her and he put his face in her lap and he made that peculiar keening sound, almost music, it was, but the saddest music a person was ever likely to hear.

Of course she waited for him. Of course she married him. She loved him, didn't she? And if you loved somebody it was through thick and thin, for better or for worse.

She couldn't seem to get herself organized to do anything useful today. Ever since Tommy Cummings left she'd just been sitting at the little desk in the kitchen, thinking about nothing at all, really. Except Alfred, out in his shed.

Maybe, she thought, she should try to get on at the hospital full time again.

Norma hadn't worked full time since the previous spring, when she'd marked her fifty-fifth birthday by volunteering to participate in a work-sharing plan the hospital had set up in an attempt to cut down on expenses. She now shared her job with a recent nursing school graduate whose relief at having gotten even half-time work was considerable.

Norma still wasn't sure why she had decided to cut down on her working days. She thought she was as efficient and energetic as ever. Maybe she just wanted to stay that way.

Or maybe she was afraid that if she hadn't offered to work less the hospital administration would have made the decision for her. Norma had a lot of pride.

When for the second time that morning someone knocked on the door it still didn't occur to her seriously that it might be Roger, even though it was his day to come calling. He'd missed last Wednesday, and what with all the turmoil in his life—the gossip was all over town—Norma hadn't been surprised. She wouldn't be surprised if she never saw him again.

And of course that would be a good thing: Alfred could well do without the irritation of his wife's friendship with a man he stubbornly, irrationally insisted was a murderer.

But it was Roger at the door, all right.

"Ah, Norma," he said. "I've missed you." She thought he looked wrung out, drained, even though he was smiling.

"Alfred's here," said Norma. Then she blushed, furious with herself, because she'd made it sound like they had some kind of clandestine relationship.

Roger's smile faded. He glanced behind Norma into the hall.

"He's in the shed. His truck's parked in behind there, behind the shed. That's why you didn't see it."

"What's he doing home on a workday?"

"His dog died."

Roger looked at her uncomprehendingly. "His dog died?"

"Somebody killed him." She remembered the sight of them, Alfred struggling across the yard through the moonlight with Clyde in his arms, calling out to her in his pain and fury.

"Somebody killed his dog?" said Roger, incredulous.

"That's what I said." Maybe Alfred would recover, though, Norma thought. After Tommy Cummings left he'd looked at the picture for a long time and then he'd actually said, "Remember last summer when Clyde took off into the woods after that rabbit?" And Norma had given a relieved, tremulous laugh and said, "And he came back looking so bewildered, with dirt all over his muzzle and thistles stuck to him."

"Christ," muttered Roger.

Norma decided to ignore the profanity. "Alfred thinks," she said, "that whoever did it was the one who killed your—your friend, too."

He glanced at her quickly. "I was afraid you'd heard about that. I was going to tell you about her," he said.

"What was she doing up here, anyway?"

"I don't know," said Roger. He ran his fingers through his black curls. "I honestly don't know."

She looked at him thoughtfully. She was entitled, after

all, to her friendships. "Well, don't just stand there. Come on in."

She poured some coffee and they sat down at the kitchen table.

"You didn't know she was here, then?" said Norma.

He shook his head.

"How did you find out?"

"That portrait." He got up and looked out the window toward the shed.

"I guess the police have questioned you."

He turned around. "Oh, yeah. Mainly a guy named Alberg."

"I know Mr. Alberg. Alfred and I, we know him. Have you got an alibi?"

He looked at her with a grin and sat down, straddling the chair. "Do you read a lot of mysteries or something?"

Norma turned her coffee mug around and around on the tabletop. "Of course I know about alibis. Alfred and I, we know about them." She looked up at him. "You can't have been in Sechelt for two months or three months or whatever it is and not heard about Alfred."

Roger didn't comment.

"He got sent to jail," said Norma. "It was a long time ago. But I guess it'll never be over." She was breathing quickly and tried to calm herself. She was aware of Roger watching her.

"So you waited for him, while he was in jail."

"Of course I waited for him," she said.

Roger shook his head. He folded his arms on the back of the chair. "You're quite a woman, Norma McKenzie," he said.

"I'm Norma Hingle," she said quietly. "And I'm just ordinary."

Roger got up to get the coffeepot from the stove. He refilled Norma's mug, then his. "That's how come you know this Alberg, then," he said, sitting down again.

Norma nodded.

"So we've both been grilled by the same cop. Me and Alfred." He looked amazed and then burst into laughter.

Norma was at first offended, irritated by his irreverance. But he kept on laughing, and soon she found herself joining him.

Eventually he stopped and looked at her almost absently. “Well I didn’t do it,” he said. “And I know you don’t think Alfred did it. So I wonder who did?”

“I don’t know,” said Norma wearily. “And I’m afraid they’re never going to find out.”

“They’d better find out,” said Roger grimly. “And damned soon, too. I’ve gotta get out of here. I’ve gotta get home.” He rested his arms on the back of the chair. “Gotta get me some work. Get me some money. I’m fast running out of funds, Norma McKenzie.”

Suddenly the kitchen door opened and Alfred was standing there. For a minute the three of them didn’t move. Then, “Jesus Christ!” roared Alfred. He advanced upon Roger, enraged.

“Alfred,” said Norma, moving quickly between them. “That’s enough, now.”

Roger edged around behind Norma, heading for the hallway to the front door.

“Alfred, get hold of yourself,” said Norma. She was trying to sound stern, but could tell that her voice had risen, and had a quiver in it.

Without looking at her, Alfred took Norma by the shoulders and moved her aside. “I know all about you,” he said in a black voice to Roger. “I’ve heard all about you. That woman, that actress—she came all the way up here looking for you. Well she found you, didn’t she? Didn’t she? She found you all right, the poor bitch.”

“No,” said Roger. “She didn’t find me. I wish she had.”

“And my dog,” said Alfred, slowly, each word falling like a chunk of stone. “My dog.”

Roger began to shuffle slowly, cautiously toward the door. Alfred watched him for a second longer; Norma saw that her husband’s big hands were clenched into fists, and the veins in his neck stood out, and his body was canted forward. She kept very still, hardly daring to breathe.

Then Roger got to the door and opened it, and a late-afternoon shaft of sunlight hurled itself down the hall, and as though this were some sort of signal, Alfred let out a bellow and pounded after Roger; Norma could have sworn that the whole house shook.

"Alfred!" she shouted, and ran after them.

"Alfred!" she cried from the porch.

Roger was running now, full tilt, heading for the yellow Hornet that belonged to the librarian. And then Alfred, only yards behind him, hurtled into the air and with a yell brought Roger down onto the dirt.

CHAPTER 29

The first thing Alberg saw when he pulled over on the access road in front of Alfred Hingle's house was Cassandra's car, parked behind Norma's Mini on the loop of rutted driveway.

He was pretty sure that Cassandra wasn't acquainted with the Hingles. And besides, he never saw the Hornet now without thinking of Roger Galbraith. But before he could even start to feel anger with Cassandra for persisting in lending her car to that damned actor—a suspected murderer, for God's sake—long before he could begin to wonder what business the actor might have with Alfred Hingle, the front door of the house flew open and Roger Galbraith burst onto the porch and broke into a run for the Hornet.

Then Alfred Hingle bolted through the door and with a roar threw himself into the air; he landed on top of Galbraith and they toppled to the ground.

Alberg, now running, heard curses and grunts from the two men rolling around in the dirt. Norma was standing on the porch shaking her hands wildly and uttering piercing cries.

"Okay, break it up," said Alberg as he got nearer. "Break it up, I said," he shouted.

Alfred, clearly in control, was astride Roger Galbraith, who was clumsily trying to grab at Alfred's arms.

"Police!" roared Alberg in exasperation, coming to a stop beside them. He reached down and grabbed at Alfred's shoulder. Hingle shook him off and hit Galbraith again, in the side of the head.

"Alfred, goddamn it," Alberg bellowed, "get off him!"

Hingle looked up at him. "He's a no-good killer," he said, panting.

"Get up. Come on, get up." Alberg took him by the arm. "And you, stay where you are," he said to the actor. "Don't move." He pulled Alfred to his feet and got him over to Norma, who had come down from the porch.

"Oh Alfred," said Norma, who was crying, "I'm mortified." Alfred put an arm around her and stared down at Roger, who was still on the ground, braced on his elbow in a half-sitting position.

"Okay," said Alberg. He stretched out his hand to Roger. "Get up."

Roger ignored the hand and scrambled to his feet. He had a reddening welt on his temple and his nose was bleeding. "You stupid fucker," he said, glaring at Alfred, breathing heavily. "You want to walk in my shoes, then walk in them! I'll give you them, you stupid fucker—you don't need to kill me for them." He brushed with shaking hands at his loose blue shirt. It didn't have a collar. Alberg wondered if the guy ever wore a tie. "Fuck it," said Roger to Alfred. "You're crazy, you're a fucking lunatic."

"I don't want your damn shoes," said Alfred furiously. "What the hell are you talking about? What the hell's he talking about?" he said to Alberg, who didn't bother to reply. "And it's you who's a killer," said Alfred to Roger. "Not me, you murdering swine!"

"I never killed anything in my life!" Roger yelled. He wiped blood from his face with the back of a hand. "What about you, you son-of-a-bitch! You're the one found her body, for Christ's sake. You're the one with the record. Not me!"

Alberg pulled a handkerchief from his pocket and gave it to him.

"What the hell's going on here?" said Alberg.

"It's a misunderstanding, Mr. Alberg," said Norma. She left Alfred's side and took Alberg by the sleeve. "Really, that's all it is. Nothing at all. A misunderstanding."

"Jesus," said Roger, his voice muffled by Alberg's handkerchief, which was pressed against his nose. "Some misunderstanding. The guy just attacked me, for no reason. That's what happened. Jesus."

"I never want to see you," said Alfred, slowly, dangerously, "in my house again."

"I was visiting your wife," said Roger, with a certain amount of dignity. "Your wife and I are friends." He turned to Alberg, his dark eyes looking pleadingly over the top of the handkerchief, now splotched with blood. "I come to visit her, now and then. We have coffee together. I have a lot of friends in this town."

Alberg looked at him grimly. The sooner this jerk left the Sunshine Coast, he thought, the better off everyone would be.

"Okay," said Alberg. "Get out of here."

The three of them watched silently while Roger got into the Hornet. He started the motor with a roar and lurched the car in reverse along the ruts to the access road.

"That man," said Alfred, "murdered my dog."

"You go around saying things like that," said Alberg mildly, "and you're gonna get yourself in trouble."

"It's ridiculous," said Norma, tears springing to her eyes. She stomped up the steps to the porch and into the house, slamming the door behind her.

"She's embarrassed," said Alfred, watching the Hornet as it headed rapidly down the access road.

"Can't say I blame her," said Alberg.

"It's probably a good thing you happened along. I was set to flatten him."

"He looked pretty flattened when I got here," said Alberg.

"I've got a bad temper," said Alfred heavily. "I know it."

"I didn't just happen along," said Alberg. "I came on purpose. I have some news for you. And I want to ask you a favor."

The Hornet had disappeared. Alfred turned to look at the staff sergeant. "What kind of a favor?"

"That sketch in your shed. The one of the dead woman. I'd like to borrow it."

Hingle thought about it. "Why?"

Alberg shrugged. "Don't know, exactly. I just want to have it around for a while."

Hingle turned away and started walking toward the shed. "Have you searched where that actor's staying?" he said over his shoulder.

"Yeah," said Alberg, trudging after him.

"Did you find anything?"

"What do you think?"

"You wouldn't tell me anyway," said Alfred. He grunted. "He's probably gotten rid of it by now. The weapon. Probably threw it in the ocean, after he murdered my dog."

Alberg stopped. They were about fifty yards from the shed. "Alfred."

Alfred turned around.

"You've got to stop that. Making accusations. I told you, it's going to get you into trouble. Serious trouble. The guy could lay a charge."

"I'd like to see him try," said Alfred.

"Or I could," said Alberg pleasantly.

Alfred considered this. Then he turned and continued toward the shed. "What I say in the privacy of my own home," Alberg heard him mutter, "is my own business."

When they got into the shed he removed the sketch from the wall and handed it to Alberg. "I'll let you have it. As long as you bring it back when you're finished with it."

Alberg looked down at it. Pencil lines on now grubby paper, that's all it was. Why the hell had he thought he wanted it? What the hell was he going to do with it?

"Thanks, Alfred," he said tiredly. "Now, I've got something to tell you about Clyde. It won't help you one bit. But at least you'll know we're working on it."

CHAPTER 30

Thursday night was clear but cold. Most of the cars lined up at Langdale, waiting for the last ferry to Vancouver, had their motors running. Inside them people drank coffee from the vending machines located in a building near the dock, tried to read newspapers in the light from the lampposts stationed around the terminal area, talked, listened to their radios.

Off to one side were vehicles whose occupants were there to pick up relatives and friends who were expected as foot passengers returning home from Vancouver, or points beyond.

There was a man sitting alone in his car who, as he waited, never took his eyes from the black sea, and it was he who first saw the lights of the ferry approaching, between Gambier Island to the north and the much smaller Keats Island to the south.

"Ferry" didn't seem a large enough word to describe the ship, which was 457 feet long and weighed 6,500 tons. It had three car decks, a promenade deck with a cafeteria and a snack bar and numerous lounges, and a top outside deck. It was capable of carrying 1,400 passengers and 362 automobiles.

But it wasn't heavily laden, this dark midweek evening in November.

The foot passengers disembarked first, and the man spotted the waitress, Sunny, easily; her bright hair shone as she passed beneath the lights. She was dragging two large suitcases and laughing with a dark-haired girl who walked with her, equally burdened.

The man eased his car toward them as they entered a roofed corridor extending along the side of the parking area. Then they rushed past him and began to wave and beckon excitedly. He looked over his shoulder and saw the driver of a small truck reach across the front seat to open the passenger door, and in the glow of the inside light when the door opened the man saw that it was Sunny's father.

He turned around quickly and watched in the rearview mirror as the girls threw their luggage into the uncanopied back of the truck and clambered in next to the driver.

The man waited until the truck had passed him, then pulled out to follow it. Both vehicles got caught in the stream of traffic now flowing off the ferry. It seemed a long time before they reached the exit from the terminal and turned onto the highway.

He followed them through Gibsons, and Sechelt; he followed them all the way to Halfmoon Bay. He watched while they stopped to let off Sunny's friend.

When they got to the cafe, he pulled off the road and cut the motor and the headlights. He watched as Sunny's father got the luggage from the back of the truck, and took it into their house, Sunny beside him, still chattering and laughing excitedly. The door closed behind them.

The man waited.

The house was behind and to one side of the cafe, which was dark except for an outside light that illuminated the CLOSED sign on the front door.

After a while the father appeared on the front step of the house. He was holding the door open, talking to Sunny, who was inside, out of sight.

The man knew that the two of them lived alone. Sunny had no brothers or sisters, and her mother had died ten years earlier, when Sunny was eight. Everybody on the coast knew this, and everybody on the coast talked about everybody else.

He waited for the father to leave, to trudge across the gravel separating the house and his place of business and open the cafe.

But when he left, Sunny's father took his protesting daughter with him. He had her by the arm and was propelling her firmly across the gravel to the back entrance to the cafe. Sunny was clearly not happy about it.

But nevertheless, she went.

In his car the man put his hands on the top of the steering

wheel and rested his forehead on his hands. He remained in that position for several minutes. Then he lifted his head, started the car, made a U-turn, and drove off down the highway toward Sechelt.

CHAPTER 31

It was late Friday morning. Alberg hadn't been in to work yet, but Isabella knew where to find him, if he was needed. He was sitting at a table in the back of Earl's Cafe.

He was on his third mug of Earl's coffee when he saw Sanducci stroll along the street and through the door. As soon as he saw Alberg, Sanducci hesitated, then came over and stood by the staff sergeant's chair. He took off his hat and revealed his hair, thick and black and wavy.

"Hi, Staff," he said.

Alberg eyed him gloomily. He hated it when he envied Sanducci. For he did envy him, sometimes. He envied Sanducci's dark good looks, and his easy success with women who were too young for Alberg but who interested him all the same.

Sanducci was also, by virtue of his youth, impatient with compromise, ignorant of anguish, unacquainted with disillusionment. And of course he was unworried by his failures, because his future would certainly have none of those in it. Alberg remembered how confidently he had once believed in the limitlessness of his own success, in a future that would by definition be an extravagant improvement over the present. When he was dissatisfied with himself it was this confidence, this happy ignorance in Sanducci, that he most coveted. He recognized his occasional envy for what it was—a hapless rejection of his own maturity. And it angered and embarrassed him.

At least, thought Alberg, I'm taller than he is.

"Sit down," he said grudgingly.

Sanducci sat.

"Coffee?" said Earl, the Chinese proprietor, appearing with the pot and another mug.

"Yeah, thanks," said the corporal.

"And I'll have a refill, since you're here," said Alberg. "Did you get Galbraith's prints?" he said when Earl had left.

"He's supposed to come in this morning. He bitched about it, naturally. Wanted to know why, what's this new evidence. I fudged it. He's coming."

"What about the picture?" said Alberg. "Any more sightings? Jesus, it sounds like we're whale-watching."

Sanducci shook his head. "Nothing. We've found some more people who talked to her, but nobody's got anything new. It looks like she vanished into the air in Madeira Park."

"And then turned up dead in Sechelt." Alberg poured sugar and cream into his coffee and stirred. He sighed. "Talk about something else," he said. "Bring me up to date."

"I'm going up the coast tomorrow, to check out that so-called vandalism," said Sanducci after tasting his coffee, which Alberg noticed with disgust he drank black. This reminded him of Cassandra, and his spirits sank even lower.

"Good," he said absently.

"We've got rid of the crazy lady in the trailer," said Sanducci.

"Yeah?" said Alberg, with more interest.

Sanducci nodded. "Her parents have agreed to take her back. And she's agreed to go. At least for a while."

Everyone agreed that the young woman in the trailer was mentally disturbed: her parents, her doctor, the officials who provided her with welfare money because she refused to live at home and her parents couldn't afford to support her anywhere else.

She was prone to violent rages. So far these had not been directed against other people. But the frequent eruption of shrieks and screams from the trailer she rented, accompanied by the sound of breaking glass and china, was highly disruptive to the lives of the elderly couple who lived in the small house next door to her.

"She frightens my wife," the husband had told Alberg apologetically. He had hesitated, then added, "Today she tore out of her place and headed over here—we'd heard her yelling so we were looking out the window—and my wife started running around hiding the bread knives. But she stopped at the edge of our property and then she ripped out all the flowers that were growing along there. Primroses and some winter pansies. Just ripped them out. Then she started to cry. Well, it was a wailing sound, more or less. And then she dug a big hole, with her hands, in the dirt, and buried all the plants in them, howling all the time. So I thought it was time I called the police. A person can stand just so much of that. Never knowing what she's going to do: it gets on your nerves, after a while."

Once the Super-Valu had called the detachment because she'd written them a $5,000 check for her groceries and gotten angry when they'd tried to point out her error.

Sometimes for no apparent reason she'd run out onto the highway, waving her hands and screeching at the traffic.

"I thought she was supposed to be on drugs," said Alberg irritably to Sanducci. "To keep her evened out, or some damn thing."

"Yeah. But I guess she only takes them when she feels like it. She's going to hurt herself eventually, that's what they're worried about."

Alberg found this profoundly depressing.

"So she goes back to her parents," said Sanducci. "And if that doesn't work out, into the hospital again."

"Shit." Alberg had always thought of her as an inoffensive creature. She had long, thin, light-brown hair, an elongated face, small eyes. She looked like she'd snap in two if you brushed against her. But he'd been told it took two men to subdue her when she was enraged.

Nobody could understand what it was that set her off. Between eruptions she was still obviously not quite normal, but at least she was quiet. You'd pass her on the street and she'd be smiling to herself, peering around with a look on her face that suggested that you and she weren't seeing the same world, and for a minute you wished she could see what she did.

She was much preferable, in this respect, thought Alberg, to the crazy people who kept their madness hidden until it blew them apart and resulted in catastrophe. Death.

Alberg wondered if a person like that could have made a brief appearance on the Sunshine Coast; just long enough to slit Sally Dublin's throat.

Or perhaps he was still here, discreetly clothed in apparent normalcy, his madness temporarily alleviated by murder.

Earl's Cafe was getting crowded, now, with people who had come in for lunch from the shops and businesses up and down the street. Alberg was digging in his pocket for change to leave on the table when he saw Tommy Cummings come through the door. The art teacher looked around, spotted Alberg, and, like Sanducci before him, hesitated, then moved toward the staff sergeant.

"Sit down, Tommy," said Alberg, pushing a chair out from the table. He introduced the teacher to Sanducci, who then got up to leave. Alberg wanted to go too, but he stayed where he was. "You here for lunch?" he asked Tommy, who nodded.

"Sometimes I like to get away," he said. His hands were smoothing the tabletop in front of him as if there were a cloth there and he was trying to iron out its wrinkles with his fingertips.

Alberg vividly remembered the school staff room.

"Have a hamburger," he said. "Earl makes great hamburgers."

Tommy dutifully ordered a hamburger, then said to Alberg, "How are you getting along with—"

Alberg quickly held up a hand. "Don't ask," he said. "Do not ask."

"Sorry."

Alberg thought about the pencil sketch of the dead woman,

now tacked up on his office wall next to the portrait. He wanted to ask Cummings how the one ever grew into the other, but he couldn't do so without letting him know that Alfred Hingle had filched it from the teacher's garbage.

Tommy's hamburger was set before him on a platter along with coleslaw and French fries.

"Jesus," said Alberg, staring at it. "Bring me one of those, too, Earl, will you?" He looked morosely at Tommy. "I promised myself I'd just have a salad."

"Have a salad for dinner," said Tommy. He picked up half of his hamburger, put it down again, picked up a fork, and took a mouthful of coleslaw.

"Yeah," said Alberg, watching him eat. "Yeah, that's a good plan."

It was a small place, Earl's Cafe. Earl had once explained to Alberg that he liked being a one-man operation, except for the cook. He didn't have a family to support, for some reason, so he didn't need much money. This was the busiest time of the day, at Earl's. At the table next to the window Alberg recognized a young saleswoman from the bookstore across the street, huddled over soup with a mechanic who worked at the gas station on the corner. On stools at the counter were an elderly man reading the morning paper, two women with plastic supermarket bags at their feet, and a teller from the Royal Bank. Alberg was checking out the people at the other four or five tables when Cassandra walked in, with the actor.

"Shit," said Alberg.

As they looked around the cafe and almost immediately caught his eye, Alberg felt like some kind of potentate. All morning long, it seemed, he'd been sitting there. All morning long, people he knew had come in, spotted him, their faces had fallen, and they'd found it necessary to shuffle reluctantly over to greet him. He didn't want their damn greetings. He watched balefully as Cassandra walked toward him, the frizzy-haired actor following with obvious reluctance.

"Karl," said Cassandra coolly.

"Cassandra," said Alberg, equally cool.

The actor didn't say anything at all.

"May we join you?" said Cassandra, as Alberg's hamburger arrived. "There aren't any empty tables."

Alberg glanced at Galbraith. There was still a welt on the side of his face where one of Alfred Hingle's blows had landed, and his nose was swollen. "I don't mind," he said to Roger, "if you don't," and the actor shrugged and the two of them sat down.

"Roger," said Cassandra, putting her hand on his shoulder, "this is Tommy Cummings." She smiled at the art teacher. "Tommy, Roger Galbraith."

Alberg watched with interest as the two men acknowledged her introduction. They had reached automatically across the table to shake hands before they seemed to remember what they had in common. Both hesitated, then completed the handshake. Tommy put his hands in his lap and concentrated on his French fries. Roger stared at him intently.

Cassandra was chattering about the menu. She stumbled over her words sometimes; Alberg figured she had begun to realize this might not have been the brightest of ideas.

Alberg leaned back happily and lit a cigarette.

"You're the guy who did the portrait," said Roger.

Tommy nodded.

"I knew her, you know."

Tommy looked hopelessly around the cafe. He hadn't eaten a thing, Alberg realized, except for one forkful of salad. "I heard that," said the teacher.

"She was a friend of mine," said Roger.

Tommy looked desperately at Alberg.

"You did that thing after she was dead," said Roger. He sat on the edge of the chair, tensed as if to spring straight into the air. His hands were flat on his thighs, elbows slightly out.

"So what?" said Alberg.

Roger turned to look at him. "He stole a second of her fucking life, drawing that fucking picture. His filthy hands all over her life, after she was dead, for Christ's sake."

"Roger," said Cassandra, red-faced.

Tommy fumbled in the back pocket of his trousers for his wallet.

"Hmmm," said Alberg. "You're not making much sense, Galbraith."

"Roger," said Cassandra again. "Please." She turned to Tommy. "I'm looking forward to your show," she said warmly.

Tommy looked at the bill and pulled money from his wallet. "Thank you," he said with a strained smile.

"Everyone will be there," said Cassandra confidently. She looked at Alberg. "Even the staff sergeant, here, I'll bet."

Roger shuddered. "Not me. I damn near had a fucking heart attack, the first time I saw one of his paintings."

Tommy looked at him quickly and smiled. He seemed genuinely amused.

Alberg regarded the art teacher thoughtfully. "Are they for sale?" he said. "The stuff you'll have on display?"

"If anybody wants to buy them," said Tommy. He gave an involuntary shudder.

"Pretty nervous, are you?" said Alberg.

"Yes. Pretty nervous."

"Yeah," said Alberg to Cassandra. He stubbed out his cigarette. "I'll be there." He turned to Roger. "Okay," he said abruptly. "You've got a date at the detachment, remember? Come on. I'll escort you over to the ink."

He laughed out loud at the alarm that swept across Galbraith's face.

What the hell could they do, anyway, if the prints matched? Charge him? With what?

But Alberg could smell the fear on the guy.

He threw money on the table. He'd damn well enjoy this jerk's terror as long as it lasted.

He got up. "Come on, Roger. Let's go."

"This is harassment," he heard Cassandra announce coldly, as they left. "This is definitely harassment."

CHAPTER 32

That night the man drove up the highway to Halfmoon Bay and again parked on the side of the road, opposite the cafe. He could see through its large windows that Sunny was inside, wiping the tables. There were no customers.

He went a little farther up the highway and found a place to turn around. Then he parked where he could see the back of the cafe and the front door of the house. There were no lights on in the house. He waited.

He waited for more than five hours, until the place closed at midnight.

Trucks drove in, now and then. And cars filled with raucous teenagers. Sometimes couples stopped at the cafe. Sometimes men traveling alone.

It was never very busy. Often Sunny had no customers at all. But these periods lasted only a few minutes.

He couldn't tell whether her father was in the cafe. He hadn't seen him enter or leave the building, or the house either. Maybe he'd gone out, the man thought with a surge of hope. His truck didn't seem to be anywhere around.

So if Sunny was alone in the cafe, which was never empty long enough for the man to be certain of being able to accomplish what he had to accomplish, maybe she'd be alone once she got inside the house, too.

If only her father would stay away long enough.

Without turning on his headlights he moved the car into the parking lot, closer to the house, but far enough away from the cafe so that nobody inside could see him. He slouched low in his seat whenever anyone went in or out, so they would think his car was unoccupied.

He waited and watched.

At midnight Sunny's father still hadn't appeared. The man

saw Sunny shoo the last customer outside, laughing. He was obviously reluctant to leave. But finally he climbed into his logging truck, blasted his horn at her as she stood waving in the doorway, and drove onto the highway heading south, spewing gravel as he roared out of the parking lot.

The man saw Sunny turn over the OPEN sign so that it read CLOSED. He watched as the lights were switched off.

Then the light over the back door of the cafe came on. It was very bright, and in its glow the man saw the back fender of Sunny's father's truck sticking out from its parking place between the far side of the house and the woods.

And he saw Sunny leave from the back door of the cafe with her father right behind her.

He laughed out loud in his anger, and banged his fists on the steering wheel, and although he was sure they hadn't been able to hear him they turned, together, and looked toward his car, which was facing them. He ducked down behind the steering wheel. He waited in the dark, hardly daring to breathe, but no one approached the car.

After a while, cautiously, he sat up. The parking lot was dark and empty. Lights had been turned on in the house.

He started the car and got out of there.

On his way home he realized that she was altogether too well protected, and he didn't have time to wait until her father might relax his vigilance.

He would have to do them both. Somehow. He would have to break into the house and wait for them there, hiding; and then wait until they were asleep. He would have to do it as soon as possible.

Tomorrow.

CHAPTER 33

Sanducci went up the highway Saturday evening to check on the vandalism complaint from the lumber company and see for himself the spikes that had been driven into its Douglas firs.

On his way back down to Sechelt he decided to stop for coffee at Halfmoon Bay. Sunny might be back by now, he thought; and sure enough, she was.

Her blonde hair was streaked white-gold and her skin had a sheen of tropical sunlight upon it. When Sanducci walked into the cafe and saw her behind the counter, reaching for a banana cream pie on a mirrored shelf, his heart shifted in his chest and he felt suddenly flushed and awkward and about seventeen years old.

Which, he reminded himself grimly, was only a year younger than Sunny.

She looked over when he came through the door, causing the bell to ring. It was extremely important that he interpret correctly the expression on her face when she recognized him. He stared back at her so intently that he failed to respond to her friendly "hi."

He sat down and put his hat on the counter. Had there been something special in her friendliness? It was impossible to tell. She seemed glad to see him, he thought, watching her slice a piece of pie and transfer it deftly to a plate. But she was the kind of person who seemed glad to see anybody. There was no use kidding himself about that.

She went around the counter to take the pie to a woman sitting at a table with a child about ten years old. The kid was slouched in his chair looking sullenly at the tabletop. Occasionally he kicked the leg of the table or leaned back so far that his chair was balanced on two legs. His mother didn't need the banana cream pie, in Sanducci's opinion, but she was eating it anyhow.

Sunny went back behind the counter. "So what'll you have?" she said with a smile. Surely she didn't turn that particular smile on just anyone.

"Just coffee, please," said Sanducci, and she brought him some. "How was Hawaii?"

"It was great. Just great." She sighed and flicked a dishcloth at the counter. "I could have stayed forever." She was smiling again. This time Sanducci didn't think it was such a terrific smile. God knew who she'd met down there. He was surprised that her father the cook, even now clanging things around in the kitchen, had let her go.

He tried to look at her critically. Her nose was a touch too big. Her eyes were a paler blue than he usually liked. And his preference was certainly for women a little taller than her five foot three or four. Her hair, however, was perfect. Lots of shades of blonde, from sun-bleached gold to something like the color of taffy. Today she wore it down around her shoulders. It was very wavy and caught the light and flickered like yellow fire.

He drank his coffee and smiled back at her and marveled at her body, soft slopes here and firm curves there, and tried not to think about the fact that she was eighteen years old and, if he really studied the situation, not all that bright.

The kid at the table teetered too far and his chair crashed to the floor and him with it. His mother began haranguing him. The child was trying to get to his feet, trying not to cry. "I told you," said his mother furiously. "I told you that would happen."

Sunny went over to help the kid up. This required that she lean over, which gave Sanducci a good look at the backs of her knees and thighs. He smothered a groan and gulped down the rest of his coffee.

"It's all right," said Sunny, brushing briskly at the boy's trousers. "Nothing damaged, right? Not even the chair." She laughed and set the chair upright.

Soon afterward the mother finished her pie, paid the bill,

and left with her child. Sunny gave the boy a wink when from the door he looked back at her with an almost furtive grin, and then she laughed again.

They were alone in the cafe now, except for Papa behind the service hatch; his white cook's cap bobbed in and out of the fringes of Sanducci's vision.

Sunny tidied up behind the counter, humming to herself. Sanducci decided to ask her out. But before he got his mouth open he realized that he hadn't worked out where to take her. She wasn't old enough to go to a Vancouver club, and besides, it would be just his luck to miss the last ferry and end up stranding the two of them over there; he shuddered to think what her father's reaction would be. They could go out to dinner, but that meant a lot of conversation and he wasn't at all sure Sunny was up to that. Or they could go to a movie. He had already seen the movie that was playing in Gibsons and there wasn't another theater for miles, but he'd sit through anything for a second time if it meant he could sit next to warm fragrant Sunny for a couple of hours.

He decided to do it.

"Would you like to go to a movie?" he said. It came out sounding rather brisk and formal.

"I can't," she said calmly, wiping a glass sugar container. "I'm working late."

"What about tomorrow?"

"It's Sunday. Sundays we have supper at my aunt's."

"What about Monday?"

"Monday I go to the dentist." She replaced the sugar and wielded her cloth on a salt shaker.

"At night?" said Sanducci bitterly.

She lifted her head and laughed. "Of course not. In the afternoon. But I've gotta have a tooth out. After that all I'm gonna want to do is go to bed."

"Do you think," said Sanducci, "that you're likely to have recovered by next Saturday?"

"Sunny!" It was her father, whose face was now framed in the service hatch. "I need some help back here." He glowered at Sanducci, who nodded as if in dignified acknowledgment of a greeting.

She filled up his cup before she left and gave him another smile. Her smiles were beginning to irritate him.

He sat there moodily for five minutes or so, knowing he ought to be on his way but unwilling or unable to just slap fifty cents down on the counter and leave. Then she came back and he decided instantly to keep at it until she had agreed to go out with him.

"Did you hear about the murder?" she said. There was a stool behind the counter. She wriggled up onto it and crossed her legs at the ankles and put her hands demurely in her lap.

Sanducci looked at her in disbelief. He felt disoriented. Didn't she know he was a cop, for God's sake?

"The one down in Sechelt," Sunny explained kindly. "The woman." She leaned toward him and her pink-and-white front-buttoned dress gaped at the neck; he saw that where her tan ended her flesh was honey-colored, chaste and incorruptible. "They say somebody slit her throat," Sunny whispered. Then she sat up straight again. "That's why my dad's so uptight," she confided. "He picks us up at the ferry, do I get time to have me a nice hot bath? Forget it. He hauls me straight in here, puts me to work. Doesn't want me to be alone, he says. Jeez, we just live across the parking lot." She leaned forward again, lowering her voice. Sanducci's gaze burrowed into the half-visible cleft between her breasts. "I gotta admit, though. Yesterday, it was weird. There was this car out in the parking lot, after we closed. We looked over there, at the car, wondering who it was, you know? The driver was in it, he ducks down so we can't see him. Can you imagine? Then we go into the house, and we hear him roaring away." She sat up straight, thrusting her breast against the front of her waitress's uniform, and looked at Sanducci expectantly. "So, did you hear about it? The murder? It happened down in Sechelt."

"Yeah," said Sanducci thickly. "I'm a cop, remember? It's my detachment that's handling it."

Her eyes got bigger and he realized that until this moment

he had had, as a specific male person, less than her complete attention.

"Was it you came up here with a picture, then?" said Sunny.

Sanducci shook his head.

"Somebody did. Some Mountie. To see if anybody remembered seeing her."

"Yeah. It wasn't me." He felt heavy with stupidity, trying to think how he could bring the conversation back where he wanted it.

"Nobody did, though, Dad says. What did she look like, anyway?"

"How about next Saturday?"

Sunny frowned in bewilderment.

The door crashed open and three teenagers came in, all male. Sunny's father appeared immediately in the service hatch.

"Sunny Sunny Sunny!" crowed the biggest and grimiest of the three boys. He spotted Sanducci and put on a sneer.

"Jesus Christ," said Sanducci. He got fifty cents out of his pocket and dropped it on the counter.

"What *about* Saturday?" called Sunny as Sanducci pushed between two of the denim-vested boys; one sported a sparse mustache and was something of a comedian; as Sanducci passed he staggered backwards with a yelp and clutched at his chest as though he'd been shot.

"Forget it," muttered Sanducci.

"What?" said Sunny.

"Forget it!" hollered Sanducci, and flung open the door. He would have slammed it shut, except that it was on a spring and controlled its own manner of closing.

He drove more than a mile, smoldering.

Then he began to calm down.

And a few miles north of Sechelt his mind started to work again.

He pulled off the road, thought furiously for a few minutes, turned the patrol car around, and, trying to suppress his excitement, headed back to the cafe at Halfmoon Bay.

CHAPTER 34

The place was shaped like a clamshell. At the hinge was a small raised stage upon which had been placed several long tables holding coffee urns and plates of cakes and cookies. Several women were bustling around up there, setting out stacks of Styrofoam cups and bowls of sugar and pitchers of milk and making sure there were plenty of paper plates and napkins. Adjacent to the semicircular walls, freestanding panels had been set up on which were displayed Tommy Cummings' paintings.

By the time Alberg arrived a respectable crowd had gathered, and they'd been there long enough to have begun to relax. People were wandering slowly among the panels, looking at the paintings, or sitting talking on the chairs and sofas that had been arranged in the center of the hall.

Right by the door a table had been set up for the artist, who sat there pale and twitchy, probably from the strain of sitting on display alongside his work. He was trying to manufacture calm by humming quietly to himself.

"Sold anything yet?" Alberg said to him.

"Not yet," said Tommy with a tight smile. He was perched upon a straight-backed wooden chair in a manner that suggested imminent departure.

"Don't you have any brochures or anything?" said Alberg.

Tommy gripped the edge of the table, upon which someone had optimistically arranged a receipt book and a ballpoint pen, and shook his head, and resumed his humming.

The door was opening frequently to admit more of the curious or the artistically inclined, and Alberg saw that Tommy was shivering in the draft despite the Harris tweed jacket he wore over a shirt, a sweater vest, and a tie. Occasionally his hand fluttered to his face and rubbed distractedly at the scar almost hidden beneath the hair that fell over his forehead.

Alberg, who thought the light ought to have been better, wandered restlessly away from Cummings. He was unexpectedly suffused with sadness, and silently in his head ran a tune from his childhood. His father had sung it to him. It astonished him that he could even now remember the words: "Down goes the bright sun bearing his light, blazing the sky with his last fiery beams; down goes the bright sun bearing his light, leaving the world to darkness and dreams." Over and over, they repeated themselves, until he shook his head and determinedly turned to the paintings.

He let his newly acquired information about art churn around in his mind, hoping for insight. He could distinguish among the watercolors, oils, and pastels, but he thought he could probably have done that before he'd done his reading.

He looked for the source of light in a small painting of a huge old cedar tree, wearily a-lean, which was being inexorably strangled by an ancient, thick-stemmed, densely blossoming wisteria.

He tried to figure out which colors had been combined to create the satiny glow of petals in the oil painting of some deep red tulips; they were scattered in a vacant lot among weeds, empty crumpled cans of Diet Pepsi, and glittering fragments of broken glass.

Alberg had expected to see a few things that were familiar from his visits to Tommy's apartment, but all the work was new to him. He knew Tommy wasn't likely to have created twenty new paintings in a couple of weeks; he must have had most of them stored away someplace. Alberg wondered idly how that was accomplished. Did Tommy just stack them in a heap in his spare bedroom? Or were they perhaps hung on the walls there, floor to ceiling, row upon row?

He didn't stop long in front of any of them, because there was always somebody huddled at his elbow or breathing in his ear or chattering to a friend.

And besides, he was disappointed in the paintings. He didn't like them any more than he had the ones he'd seen in

Tommy's home. None had the vividness, the immediacy, the heart-stopping animation of the portrait of Sally Dublin. They were workmanlike, identifiable, even pleasant to look upon. But none of them was inspired. Alberg felt a curious uneasy embarrassment about this, as though he were somehow to blame. He had just begun to wonder how soon he could politely leave when he glimpsed upon one of the panels a painting about twenty inches square that exuded a profound stillness. He made his way through the crowd toward it, realizing that motion, though illusory, managed to exist in most of Tommy's work.

Not in this one, though. He stood before it in dismay and wondered what on earth it was doing there. It was a lifeless portrait of an elderly woman sitting in a high-backed wooden chair. She was wearing a dark brown dress with paler brown lace at the throat and on the cuffs of the sleeves. Her hands were folded in her lap. There was no background, no obvious source of light. The painting had been executed with meticulous attention to detail, yet Alberg stared at it dispassionately. He felt nothing, looking at it.

"Do you think that's his old mom?" said a mellifluous voice in his ear, and Alberg whirled around to see Roger Galbraith grinning at him. He was holding Cassandra's hand. "Not much love lost between them, if it is," said the actor, turning back to the painting. "Jesus."

Galbraith was decked out in narrow black pants, black boots, a full-sleeved white shirt, and a long white thing around his neck that tied in front in a floppy bow. Alberg looked at him in disbelief.

Cassandra withdrew her hand from Roger's and pushed, unnecessarily, at her hair. She noticed that Alberg had taken some pains with his appearance tonight. Instead of corduroy pants and a poplin jacket he was wearing dark brown trousers, a sports jacket, a white shirt, and a tie. His blond hair gleamed in the lights, which were aimed, not always accurately, at the paintings.

"It's not one of his best, is it?" she said, nodding at the portrait.

"He says portraits aren't his strong point," said Alberg. "I guess he's right." He looked at Roger. "I guess he just got lucky with Sally."

Galbraith's face flushed. He stared at the picture of the old woman and said nothing.

"By the way, I've got some news for you," said Alberg to the actor. He glanced around, then gestured toward the far side of the hall. "Would you excuse us for a minute, Cassandra?"

Cassandra got some coffee and sat on an unoccupied sofa.

She put her feet together and thought about how fine she looked in the red silk dress she'd bought the last time she was in Vancouver. It went well with her dark hair.

Across the room she watched them, Alberg lounging against the wall, talking, his hands in his pockets; Roger standing stiffly in front of him.

And she'd managed her makeup successfully, too, thought Cassandra. Her hazel eyes had looked large and even enticing, when she looked into her mirror.

But none of this did any good. She thought about his leaving—because he would eventually be permitted to leave; he was no murderer, she was certain of that—and panic fluttered like a scavenger around her heart.

Roger was leaning toward Alberg now, as if to hear him better. Then he said something, and Karl shrugged and nodded.

Sunday dinners with her mother, long days looking through the rain-streaked windows of the library, empty evenings with the television set: Cassandra felt these things would seize her, when Roger left.

She knew she was being imprecise; she knew she had been relatively content, before he came. But she was afraid to recall in detail what her life had been like then. She knew only that she had had a focus, in him; that he had illuminated her days and warmed her nights, and that the prospect of days and nights without him threatened her well-being.

Yet a small part of her was relieved that he was going. She tried to nurture it, but apparently it was on some schedule of its own. It shrank when she encouraged it, bloomed fleetingly at moments when she had forgotten it was there.

She reached to get her small black handbag from the floor where it sat next to her fashionable black shoes—the red dress had slim black piping around the neck, and the cuffs of its wide sleeves—and burrowed inside it for something, anything.

She told herself that she just had to get through the next few days. She just had to hang on until he left. She'd arrange to take a few days off, then. She'd go away, somewhere. Maybe to Victoria. She'd have tea at the Empress and drinks at a pub and walk the streets and at night she'd lie in her hotel room bed and weep. And then she'd come home and do something assertive and positive to change her life.

Roger appeared next to her, a grin on his face, and squatted down so that he could look into her face. "Corkindale came through," he said quietly. "And whatever fucking new evidence they think they've got, it's not my fucking prints that're all over it."

"Oh Roger," she said. "Thank God." And she meant it, too.

He shot to his feet and whooped with joy, startling several clusters of art appreciators.

It's going to be dreadful for him, Cassandra thought clearly, when he gets home and his friend Sally isn't there.

He had brought tumult and suspicion and dreadful worry into her life. But he had brought laughter, too. And sex. Oh, sex.

Roger hurried off to find his sister, who was somewhere in the crowd. Cassandra stood up and saw Alberg watching her from across the room. She couldn't tell what thoughts were in his mind. She seldom could, unless he spoke them aloud. Then, suddenly, he winked at her. She waved, tentatively, and he smiled, an open, friendly, joyous smile.

CHAPTER 35

If he was right, thought Sanducci, racing along the highway, then she could be in danger; and he thought about the car she'd told him about, the one waiting in the parking lot of the cafe. Her father would protect her, he thought. In the kitchen he would have weapons.

But out in the parking lot, or on the streets, there he would not have a weapon. And what could a father's flailing fists do against a knife?

She was safe right now, he thought, driving fast along the two-lane highway. The cafe didn't close until midnight, and it was only nine-fifteen. There was no need for this excessive speed.

And besides, there was probably nothing to his idea at all, it was just a damn fool time-wasting idea, just an excuse to get him back there, that's all it probably was.

He pulled up in front of the cafe, the patrol car spewing gravel, and was relieved to see that the parking lot was empty.

Inside the cafe Sunny was alone, sitting on her stool behind the counter, reading a paperback. She put it down as soon as he came in. Sanducci saw that the cover showed a nightgown-clad woman with long dark curly hair and a dark-haired man whose face was not visible, buried as it was in the woman's breasts.

He put the portrait on the counter, face down, and looked at Sunny.

"You want coffee?" she said.

He shook his head.

"Something to eat? The apple pie's good."

He shook his head again.

She frowned at him. "What's the matter with you?"

"Sunny. When did they come around with the picture of that woman? The one who was murdered in Sechelt. You didn't see it, did you?"

She got up and went over to the serving hatch. "Dad? When did that Mountie come with the picture?"

Her father came through the door from the kitchen. "It wasn't him," he said, looking at Sanducci.

"No, sir, it wasn't," said Sanducci. "It was somebody else from my detachment. When he showed you the picture, Sunny had left on her holiday by then, hadn't she?"

"Yeah," said Sunny's father. "So what?"

Sanducci turned over the portrait. "Sunny. Have you ever seen this woman?"

Sunny looked. Then she looked up at Sanducci, her face lit with excitement. "Yeah. Yes, I have. She was in here the night before I went away. I told her all about my holiday. She'd been to Hawaii. She said I'd love it. She was right, too."

"I've never seen her," said Sunny's father, peering down at the picture. "I told that other fellow. I never saw her."

"Oh you weren't even here yet, Dad," said Sunny impatiently.

"Sunny," said Sanducci. "Was she alone?"

"Oh no," said Sunny promptly. "There was a guy with her."

"Can you describe him?"

"Oh sure," said Sunny. "Sure I can."

CHAPTER 36

Alberg in the crowd admiring the paintings was aware of muted conversations, the discreet gurglings of private amusements, the rustlings of women's dresses and the fragrance of their intermingled perfumes. He knew—and Tommy Cummings must also know—that what had brought most of these people here, dressed in their best, was a frankly morbid curiosity. Had they expected to see the original portrait of the murdered woman on the wall, among the roses and the Douglas firs and the seascapes and the driftwood?

He glanced over at Tommy's table and saw the art teacher in conversation with Alfred and Norma Hingle, who had apparently just arrived. When they had left to join the crowd, Alberg ambled over to Tommy's table. "How are you doing?" he said.

Tommy looked up, his face flushed. "I've sold three of them."

"Christ," said Alberg. "Congratulations. You might make a packet tonight, Tommy."

The artist's bright-eyed gaze flickered beyond Alberg and then quickly down at the tabletop, where his hands still clutched the receipt book, and in the same moment Alberg became aware of Cassandra at his side, and Roger Galbraith next to her.

"That picture of the old woman," said Roger. "Who is she, anyway?"

Tommy looked up. "She's my mother," he said.

"What did I say?" Roger crowed to Alberg and Cassandra. "It's his old mom! Didn't I say so?" He rested his hands on the table, to lean closer. "Tell me, Tommy," he said confidentially, "did you love your old mom?"

Tommy let go of the receipt book and placed it carefully, exactly, in front of him.

Roger laughed and lifted his hands. "Hey, man. It's a joke, you know?"

"You are rude and obtrusive, Mr. Galbraith," said Tommy. He spoke slowly, deliberately, with an iciness that surprised Alberg.

"You," said a bitter voice, and Alberg turned to see Alfred Hingle staring at Roger. "Everywhere I go," said Hingle, "there you are."

"Alfred," said Alberg quietly. "Come on over here. I want to talk to you." He tried to lead the man away, but Hingle stood firm.

"Damn your murdering soul," said Alfred. Roger backed up until he was pressed against the table.

"Watch your mouth, fella," said the actor. "Why don't you arrest this guy?" he said to Alberg.

"He didn't do it, Alfred," said the staff sergeant. "He let us take his prints. They didn't match."

Hingle's face sagged. He stared at Alberg.

"Didn't do what?" said Tommy. "What prints?"

"The fellow who killed my dog," said Alfred. "He left his fingerprints on Clyde's collar."

"You mean you fingerprinted a dog's collar?" said Tommy Cummings, incredulous.

Alberg lifted his shoulders, spread his hands, and smiled.

"But why?" said Tommy. He gave a little laugh which obviously irritated Alfred Hingle.

"Because it's their duty to find out who murdered him, that's why," said Alfred. "It's their goddamned duty."

Alberg put a hand on his shoulder. "Come on, now, Alfred," he said. "Calm down." He walked him a few feet away from the others. "I know you don't like the guy. I don't like him either. But he didn't kill the woman and he didn't kill Clyde, either. So stop giving him a bad time, okay?"

Alfred didn't reply.

"Come on. Let's look at the pictures," said Alberg, glancing over his shoulder. The actor was staring at Hingle's back. "I haven't seen the ones at the far end, yet." Firmly he led Alfred along the panels until they reached the last one. "The guy's pretty good, isn't he?" They were looking at a painting of a raccoon. Alberg looked closer. "Jesus," he said, bewildered.

"He did one of Clyde," said Hingle, nodding at the painting. "He looks alive in it. Just like that raccoon."

"Jesus," said Alberg, staring.

"Just arrived with it under his arm," said Hingle. "On Wednesday, it was."

Alberg slowly turned to look at him.

"I don't much like the rest of this stuff," said Hingle. "But I like this. This one's good."

Alberg stepped cautiously around the panel to look at the painting that hung on the other side. "Jesus Christ," he said under his breath.

Hingled joined him. "Very pretty," he said approvingly. "Must be his niece or something. He's not married, is he?"

The painting was of a young woman in her late teens or early twenties. It was head and shoulders, about eight inches by ten. Her shoulders were turned slightly away, but her green eyes gazed straight at Alberg. She had short, wavy brown hair. She wasn't smiling. One side of her face was sunlit, and her eyes glowed with life.

Something icy flooded Alberg's spine. He leaned against the wall and kept his voice casual when he said to Hingle, "You didn't happen to find any sketches in his garbage this time, did you? Sketches of Clyde?"

Alfred shook his head. "I've been in mourning. Haven't been to work since Monday."

Alberg nodded absently. He saw Cassandra working her way through the crowd toward them.

"Have you got any aspirin, Karl?" she said when she reached them.

Alberg pushed himself away from the wall. "What's the problem?" he said.

"Tommy's got a headache. He wants to leave. I said I'd try to get him some aspirin."

"It must be a terrible pressure on a man," said Alfred thoughtfully, "to have a creative urge."

"Yeah," said Alberg. "I've got some aspirin. Tell him I'll be right there. Why don't you go get him some water?"

Cassandra hurried off, and Alberg turned to Hingle. "Alfred, when do you make your collections in town? I mean, the stores, that part of town?"

"On Mondays," said Alfred. "Why?"

Alberg shook his head. He started moving through the crowd to the front of the hall. He noticed Galbraith flirting with the bank manager's wife. He wondered if Cassandra had noticed. Or the bank manager.

Monday, he thought. Jesus Christ. Jesus H. Christ.

He was close enough now to see the artist sitting at his table. Tommy Cummings was watching him approach, rigid in his chair.

Alberg walked slowly toward him. Tommy stood up.

Alberg reached the table. "Oh Tommy," he said softly. "Oh, but you are in such deep shit."

Tommy flicked a switch somewhere in the center of him. The inaudible clangings and clatterings that Alberg had sensed throughout the evening, and accounted for as a kind of stage fright, were abruptly silenced. He breathed, but he did not blink. He watched, but he did not speak. And his stillness felt to Alberg like quicksilver.

"And you seemed like such a nice man, too," said Alberg.

Tommy smiled. "I am a nice man."

Alberg moved around the table. He put a hand on Tommy's shoulder and felt him shudder. "You need a break. We'll go get ourselves a cup of coffee."

They met Cassandra, carrying a cup of water. Alberg took it from her with a smile. "Go hold the fort for Tommy, will you?" he said, and kept moving, his hand on Cummings' shoulder.

"It's almost ten," said Tommy as they crossed the hall toward the stage and the coffee urns. Heads turned as they passed, smiles were smiled, congratulations were murmured. Tommy ignored it all. "The show's over at ten," he said. "I'm leaving then."

"Sure," said Alberg. "Fine." He put down the water, got a cup of coffee and handed it to Tommy. "Come on," he said, and steered him to a corner near the stage, away from the paintings, away from the cluster of people in the center of the hall.

Tommy stationed himself with his back to the wall and sipped at his coffee.

"Is your mother alive, Tommy?"

"Of course. She lives in Surrey. In a condominium there. I see her regularly. Several times a year." He glanced up at

Alberg. His face had a glaze upon it. Only his eyes seemed alive, and they darted and danced and sputtered like candle flames in a breeze.

"You did a piss-poor painting of her, Tommy," said Alberg. "How come?"

Tommy smiled at him. "I don't like her," he said gently. He took another drink of his coffee. "Awful," he said with a grimace, and looked around for somewhere to put the cup. But they were standing near the bare wall, and there wasn't a table around, so he elected to hang on to it.

"Some of this stuff is pretty good, though," said Alberg.

"Thank you," said Tommy. He was smiling again.

"Like the raccoon," said Alberg. "And the girl with the curly hair."

Tommy placed his right hand over his mouth. It reminded Alberg of his daughters as children, the hand as agent of conscience over a recalcitrant tongue.

"Do you call it a portrait," said Alberg, "when it's only a picture of a raccoon? Or a dog?"

Tommy whipped his hand away. "Of course I do."

"You use the same techniques as when you're painting a person?"

"Of course," said Tommy.

"And if it's going to be good," said Alberg, "really good, I mean, the necessary element is the same?"

"Oh yes," said Tommy. "You're right, of course. I have to like the person. Or the dog. That's true," he said seriously. "That's why the portrait of the girl worked. And the one of my mother didn't." He shook his head regretfully.

"I don't think so," said Alberg.

"You don't think so."

"No. I don't think you have to like them."

"You don't?"

"No."

"What *do* you think, then, Mr. Alberg?"

Alberg saw Sanducci come into the hall. He spotted Alberg and Tommy and came quickly toward them. For one terrible second Alberg imagined that another body had been found, another woman's throat slit, and that he was wrong about Cummings. But then he looked back at Tommy.

Who was waiting with empty eyes.

"I think," said Alberg softly, "that you have to kill them."

It was as though Tommy hadn't heard him. He looked at his watch. "It's ten o'clock," he said to Alberg.

Sanducci was almost upon them. Alberg fixed him with a stony gaze and he stopped. The crowd was watching the corporal with wary bemusement; a uniformed police officer was apparently not welcome among a congregation of art lovers.

"You must have a lot more paintings at home," Alberg said to Tommy.

"I have more, yes." He seemed unaware of Sanducci.

"Let me look at them," said Alberg.

"I'm afraid I can't," said Tommy politely. "I have to go now."

"We'll go together."

"No. You don't understand. I'm not going home. I have to go somewhere else first." He took a step away from Alberg.

The staff sergeant quickly put an arm around Tommy's shoulder and turned him so that his back was to Sanducci and the crowd; Alberg felt their curiosity now focused like a rifle or a microphone directly upon him and the artist.

"Tommy," said the staff sergeant. "Alfred Hingle sometimes pokes through the garbage he collects. Did you know that?"

Tommy glanced distractedly over his shoulder. "Look at all those people."

"He found some drawings in your garbage," said Alberg. "Sketches of Sally Dublin."

"That's all right," said Tommy. "I don't mind." He rubbed at his forehead. "I have to go now. Really."

Alberg took him by the shoulders. "Tommy. Look at me."

Tommy looked at him. "Oh God," he said. "Oh God."

"He picks up your trash on Mondays. She was killed Sunday night. You didn't sketch her in the hospital until Tuesday."

"Yes," said Tommy. "Yes. I see." His arms were limp at his sides. He lowered his head. "I think I'm going to fall down."

Alberg looked over at Sanducci. "Corporal," he said. "Come here."

Sanducci hurried over to them. "Staff," he said. "This guy. Cummings." He looked at Tommy, then back at Alberg. "We've got an identification." He was glowing.

"That's good, Sanducci," said Alberg. "That's very good work. Take his other arm, will you? Come on, Tommy," he said. "Let's go. Easy, now. Let's go." And they led him through the uneasy, muttering crowd toward the door.

CHAPTER 37

STATEMENT OF THOMAS WILLIAM CUMMINGS: PART 1

"Okay, Tommy, you understand everything we've said to you, do you?"

"Yes."

"You understand that you're under arrest, that you have the right to counsel, and that you don't have to speak to us."

"I understand."

"And you want to make a statement, is that right?"

"That's right. Yes. I do."

"It's a voluntary statement. No threats, including the threat of the use of force, have been made to persuade you to make this statement. Right?"

"That's right."

"Okay. This officer will take down what you say as you say it. And the tape recorder is running, too. When we get your statement transcribed, we'll ask you to read it over and sign it. I may interrupt you from time to time, to ask a question—"

"No."

"No? No what?"

"No, don't interrupt me. Ask me questions afterwards, if you like. But when I start telling you about it, I don't want you to interrupt me."

"Okay. We won't interrupt you."

"Thank you."

"Take your time. Start whenever you're ready."

"I'm ready now.

"I've got a place near Pender Harbor where I go for weekends. To work. It's very pretty around there. Lots of lakes and inlets and islands and peninsulas and bays. Sometimes I rent a boat and go by water to Garden Bay or Madeira Park. Or maybe up Gunboat Bay, and I'll stop in a cove and take out my sketch pad. The rain doesn't bother me. I take along an umbrella and I prop it up so it covers the sketch pad.

"I was on my way home from Pender Harbor.

"At first I thought somebody had had car trouble.

"I'd just gotten past Madeira Park when I saw her by the side of the road. I knew there wasn't a gas station until Secret Cove; that's six or seven miles, and it was raining, and getting dark.

"That was the first thing I thought of, once I knew she was hitchhiking. That she'd have a hard time getting a ride. There wasn't much traffic. It was not a nice night, and it would be a long, long walk to Secret Cove.

"Maybe I should go back, first. Should I go back?"

"Whatever you like. Tell it whatever way you like."

"I think I should go back."

"Okay."

"I keep looking in my art classes for kids like I was but I don't find them. Most of them don't like drawing. Or looking at paintings. They just want to slosh colors around on paper.

"Drawing is hard to learn.

"I wanted to do portraits. You have to draw very well, to be able to do portraits.

"One night—it was almost twenty years ago—I went to

Blaine with some other people. We went to some pubs. Do people still do that? Cross the border to drink in American bars?"

"I think so."

"It's such a stupid thing to do. It doesn't make any sense.

"I was at art school then.

"But I have to go further back. Please."

"It's all right, Tommy. We've got lots of time."

"Thank you.

"I wanted to be a portraitist. I always liked that word, 'portraitist.' At art school in Vancouver we did a lot of life drawings, but that's not the same thing as a portrait.

"Friends would pose for me, though. It didn't go well. At first I thought it was because I didn't draw well enough. But I got better and better at drawing. And I still couldn't do portraits.

"I tried to do animals. I thought if I could get animals right, maybe that would teach me how to do people. But it didn't work. Animals and people, both; they looked like—there was no technical explanation for it. I don't know. They didn't live.

"Then one day I found a seagull on the beach. It was dead, and there were those tiny little crabs all over it, and it had been wet and sand had stuck to it and now the sand had dried. It was very ugly. But its head wasn't ugly. I did a sketch of it and at home I did a painting. First I painted it the way it was, lying dead on the beach, covered with sand and little rushing crabs. And then I decided just to do the head. I decided to try to make it look like it was still alive. And when I'd finished it did look alive. I was very surprised. I showed it to my instructor, and some other people. They liked it very much.

"Some time later I was driving along First Avenue to the freeway. I don't remember why. It was at night. And something darted out in front of my car, and my car hit it. I pulled over right away and got out. There was an animal on the street, back where my car had hit it, and it hadn't died yet. It was writhing all over the road, smearing its blood on the pavement. Cars were going by on the other side of the boulevard but there didn't happen to be any traffic on my side, just then. I wished somebody would come along to help me. I didn't know what to do. In a minute or so it stopped moving and I went close to it and saw that it was a raccoon. I didn't think raccoons would live in the middle of a populated area like that. But apparently they do.

"There was an old blanket in the trunk of my car. I got it out and put it over the raccoon and picked it up and moved it onto the boulevard. Just then a car drove along and stopped. I told the driver what had happened. She said she'd call the S.P.C.A. so they would come and get the body. And then she drove away.

"I was crouched on the grass under a tree next to the raccoon. I pulled the blanket back a little way—I didn't want to see where its body had been injured, but I wanted to look at its face. Its eyes were open. I looked at it for several minutes. There was enough light, from the streetlamp.

"My sketch pad was in my car. I made several sketches of it, and at home I did a painting, just of its head. I pretended like I had with the seagull that it was still alive.

"It was astonishing, how good it was. Well, you saw it. At the show tonight."

"Yes. It was good."

"People didn't want to sit for me anymore, because I never showed them anything I did. They had become impatient, and thought I must have become a portraitist who only did animals. And of course that was true.

"And then we went to Blaine that night, to drink beer. I stopped enjoying myself early in the evening and left the place and went back across the border. I was driving along the highway to Vancouver—there are all sorts of yellowish lights planted along it—and I saw a young woman, hitchhiking. I had never picked up a hitchhiker before but it was a white foggy night and she was trudging along looking small and forlorn so I stopped.

"She got in and I drove on up the highway. She said she wanted to go—I can't remember where, someplace in the Valley, I think; anyway, not Vancouver. I said I could give her a ride to Vancouver and she could hitch another ride from there. She looked very tired and tried to persuade me to take her all the way but I said no, I couldn't. I thought it was very brash of her to ask me. I was just about to say that I'd give her money for bus fare—when she . . . she offered me herself. She offered me her body. If I would take her where she wanted to go.

"I was very disgusted. I don't remember if I said anything but I was very surprised and very disgusted. I didn't want a person like that in my car. I started to slow down and pull off to the side of the road and she became very angry. She became abusive, in fact.

"When the car was stopped I reached across her to open the door and then I tried to push her out. She resisted. She was actually trying, forcibly, to stay in my car. I became angry myself then. I punched at her and finally I knocked her out of the car.

"She struck her head, somehow. Maybe on the edge of the door, or maybe on the pavement. I got out of the car and rushed around to where she was lying on the shoulder of the road. And I saw that she was dead. I tried to take her pulse, but there wasn't any. She was lying on her back and I could see in the yellow light that she was bleeding from the side of her head. I was astonished. The whole thing was so clumsy, so silly. I found it so hard to believe that she was dead.

"Cars drove past but nobody stopped. Maybe they weren't looking at me, because of worrying about the fog. It wasn't very thick fog. But maybe they thought it was going to get thicker any minute.

"I drove away quickly. But I stopped after a couple of miles to do some sketches. From memory.

"At home I was excited and apprehensive. Both. Because I didn't know if it would work with people.

"But I was very pleased with the portrait.

"Of course I didn't let anyone else see it. It was an accident, so I didn't have anything to feel uncomfortable about.

"But I knew that other people probably wouldn't agree."

CHAPTER 38

It was about one-thirty on Sunday afternoon when Norma, who was outside vigorously sweeping the front porch, saw the librarian's car appear on the access road.

It turned off onto the half-circle carved over time in front of the Hingles' house and slowly lurched over the ruts until it came to a stop behind Norma's Mini, which was parked behind Alfred's pickup. This front yard is beginning to look like a parking lot, thought Norma irritably as first Roger and then the librarian got out of the Hornet.

She waited on the porch, leaning lightly on her broom.

"I'm catching the two-thirty ferry, Norma McKenzie," said Roger. "I'm going home to L.A." He glanced behind him at the librarian, who was still coming up the steps. "Have you ever properly met my friend Cassandra? Cassandra Mitchell, this is Norma McKenzie Hingle."

The librarian stretched out her hand. "I feel as though I've met you," she said with a smile, "but I guess I haven't, not really."

Norma shook her hand. "I can't ask you in for tea," she said, "because Alfred is in something of a state."

"I can imagine," said Cassandra. "What did he do with the portrait?"

"Hung it in his shed, I bet," said Roger, glancing over in that direction. "He seems to spend most of his time there."

"He burned it," said Norma.

"Burned it!" said Roger.

"That's what I'd have done, too," said Cassandra.

"I wish I could ask you in for tea," said Norma after a minute.

"We haven't got time, anyway, Mrs. Hingle," said Cassandra.

Norma looked at her curiously. "You haven't been delivering him all over town, I hope, while he said his goodbyes."

Cassandra reddened, but laughed. "No, no. You're the only one he wants to say goodbye to, he says." She looked at Roger. "I'll wait in the car."

"She seems a fairly nice woman," said Norma, watching Cassandra open the car door and get into the Hornet. She turned back to Roger. "Well, you've got a nasty tongue in your mouth, I've discovered, and a nasty streak in your character, too, I wouldn't be surprised." She set the broom aside and put her arms around him and gave him a firm hug. "You'd better be off," she said, pulling away.

"Ah, Norma," he said, and his eyes got all wet. He took her hands and kissed the backs of them and said a few soppy things and then he climbed into the librarian's car and it pitched uncertainly in reverse gear back along the ruts to the access road and soon was gone.

Norma picked up the broom and began sweeping, hard. She heard the front door open but ignored Alfred until he took the broom out of her hand and turned her around and embraced her. They stood there for quite a while, not saying anything, until Norma had blinked all the tears out of her eyes and they had dried on her cheeks.

"Staff Sergeant Alberg tells me," said Alfred finally, "that he's taken my name off the list. So as long as he stays here, I guess we won't be bothered anymore."

Norma tried to feel glad, hearing this news.

But for the first time she wondered if maybe they'd be better off moving someplace else. Maybe it wasn't too late. Maybe Alfred could change his name and they could start all over again. Have a grand new life, somewhere else, with lots of future and no past at all.

She was very tired. She could not remember ever having been so tired.

CHAPTER 39

STATEMENT OF THOMAS WILLIAM CUMMINGS: PART 2

"After I finished art school I went to university. My mother had been urging me to go and finally I did. I got an education degree and started teaching at a school in Chilliwack. I moved out there, because I didn't want to commute sixty miles every day, but I went back to Vancouver most weekends. I had a good friend there. He was at art school with me. By now he was working in an advertising agency. Commercial art, that's what he had always wanted to do. He was very good.

"On my way in to Vancouver one Friday night I picked up a hitchhiker and I stabbed her with a screwdriver. I didn't plan to do it. But I knew that another accident probably wouldn't happen.

"It was terrible. It was violent, and there was a great deal of blood, and I was extremely upset. But I didn't want to hit her on the head in case I smashed it.

"I shone my flashlight on her face and did some sketches, and then I put her in a boggy place off a side road.

"But I didn't just dump her there. I want to be sure you understand that. I knew from the sketches that the painting was going to be good and I was very grateful. I can't say that I was sad that she was dead, because I didn't even know her. But I felt badly. So I sang her a lullaby. It was all I could think of to do.

"I went to a gas station in Vancouver and cleaned up the inside of the car with a lot of paper towels. Nobody paid any attention. And then the next day I bought seat covers and put them on. But soon afterwards I sold the car to a wrecker. It was an old car anyway.

"Of course I had to keep that portrait hidden, too. She was a girl from Abbotsford, which is only twenty miles from

Chilliwack, and her photograph was all over the local paper when it came out.

"I kept it hidden until tonight.

"I don't know why I decided to show it to people tonight."

CHAPTER 40

They didn't say much during the half hour drive to the ferry. Cassandra tried to think about the weather, which was cloudy, and the road, which was twisty, but the weather wasn't important and she knew the road as well as she knew her way around her own house.

She tried not to think about whether she would ever see him again after today, but that was impossible. She was, she thought disgustedly, a ridiculously optimistic person. There were wells of hope within her that had no business being there.

But surely this was her salvation, too, Cassandra told herself. She probably wouldn't be capable of getting through this day if it weren't for her inability to accept the finality of it.

He reached over once or twice to squeeze her thigh, and when he did she turned to smile at him, trying to make it a bright smile and a warm one, a smile with no tears in it.

At the terminal he said, "Let's not drag it out, Cassandra," and she agreed. They wouldn't wait together in her car for the ferry to arrive; he would join the other foot passengers in the small shed filled with vending machines and overflowing ashtrays and she would leave right away.

She got out of the car to open the trunk, so he could get his bags. There were only two of them. She marveled at this. How had he gotten so many clothes into only two bags? She swore she'd never seen him in the same things twice, in the whole three months she'd known him.

He took her by the shoulders and smiled into her face and

she felt warm and broken. He looked rested, polished, pressed, crisp, shiny and ready for adventure. Cassandra hated to think about how she might look to him.

They hadn't slept together since he'd first been questioned by the police. She tried to remember their last time in bed together, but because she hadn't known that it was going to be the last time, this was not possible. Maybe, she thought, as he pulled her into his arms, she would be able to remember it later.

"Take care, Cassandra," he said, hugging her tightly.

And that was all.

And then he was gone.

CHAPTER 41

STATEMENT OF THOMAS WILLIAM CUMMINGS: PART 3

"Eventually I applied for a teaching position here. I wanted to come here mostly because of the quality of the light. And the sea. I used to come here with my friend, when I was in Chilliwack and he was at the advertising agency. When we had the accident, when he was killed and I was hurt, we were on our way to Horseshoe Bay, to the ferry, to come over here for the weekend.

"When I recovered, I tried to do his portrait. From photographs and sketches I'd made before the accident. But it didn't work. I couldn't make him live.

"I came here to Sechelt, and four years or so went by before it happened again. This time it was that woman from Roberts Creek, Wendy something. I knew her slightly—I didn't know her at all, actually; she was just a waitress in a restaurant where I sometimes ate. She was hitchhiking to Gibsons.

"This time I used a knife and I was calmer and I didn't forget what I'd learned in art school about anatomy so it was less messy, less dreadful in that way.

"I don't think I had ever intended to do it again. And yet I must have known that I might do it, because I had a knife in the car. I sang to her, too. I sang to her while I sketched her, and I sang to her afterwards, too.

"But it was a mistake, because she lived right here on the Sunshine Coast. I guess the others hadn't seemed real to me.

"No that isn't quite accurate. I have to be accurate. As soon as they died, they stopped being real. The portraits were something distinct from them. The portraits were what was real.

"At least that's what I thought then.

"But this woman—her realness continued, because of the furor, because the furor even enveloped me. Nobody saw her in my car and nobody was ever suspicious of me, but the police questioned everyone she knew and this included me. I was terrified.

"Five years ago I went to the Island for the Easter vacation. I gave a ride to a young woman who lived in Courtenay. She was going to Nanaimo to catch the ferry to the mainland. I was going on to Victoria.

"The portrait was very good. Very good. Each one in fact was better than the one before."

CHAPTER 42

"There was a picture of every one of those girls," said Sanducci on Sunday afternoon. "Stashed away in his spare room closet. And the knife's in the glove compartment of his car. I bet the lab finds hair samples, too. And there's some stuff from her bag. He kept every piece of I.D., every traveler's check—it's all there." He stretched out his legs. "Jesus," he said, with what Alberg considered unnecessary self-satisfaction. "It's all sewed up, Staff. We've got him."

"You did good, Sanducci," said Alberg.

Sanducci smiled.

"Now get out of here. Write up your report. Close the door on your way out."

When he'd left, Alberg reached into the bottom drawer of his desk and pulled out the portrait. It looked the same, but of course it wasn't, because now Alberg knew that Cummings hadn't created it from sketches made in that hospital room. He'd done it before he ever got to the hospital room; he'd done it Monday, when he got home from school, using sketches he'd made by flashlight the night before, sketches of Sally Dublin propped up against a tree, her face cleaned of blood with rain-soaked tissues.

He said he'd thought of doing another one, using the new drawings. But he was pleased with the original. He liked the idea, he said, that it would be seen, widely distributed, possibly admired. So that's the one he'd given Alberg.

The sketch retrieved by Alfred Hingle had been one of those done in the cafe at Halfmoon Bay. Sunny said that Cummings had been drawing constantly while he and Sally Dublin were having coffee, and that Sally hadn't seemed uncomfortable about this at all; in fact she had laughed and struck poses for him.

It was a slow night, Sunny had said. There was a truck driver, and then he left, and a short while later Cummings and Sally arrived. And an hour or so after they left Sanducci was there for a while, and another truck driver arrived as he was leaving, and that was all the customers she had that night, she said.

Alberg began to tear the portrait in half. But he stopped, and put it in a large manila envelope, and put the envelope in the bottom drawer of his desk.

He didn't want to keep it. But he couldn't destroy it, either. Not just yet. And maybe not ever.

CHAPTER 43

STATEMENT OF THOMAS WILLIAM CUMMINGS: PART 4

"I was determined that it would never again happen on the Sunshine Coast. I realized, of course, that it was a kind of compulsion. But it wasn't something that happened every day, or every month. Several years passed between incidents. For several years at a time I could be extremely content painting all kinds of things other than portraits.

"I could usually tell when I was likely to be—when my concentration was liable to fix itself on the need to do a portrait. I'd find myself doodling on scraps of paper, which is not unusual for me, of course. But when I looked at what I'd done I'd see that it was drawings of the details in a face: noses, or lips, or jawlines, or ears; never eyes, though. And then I knew that I was going to be in danger again soon.

"I know you'll want details about that evening. I'll try to remember things as plainly as I can.

"But I must say again, first, that when I saw her by the side of the road the reason I automatically slowed down was that I thought she must have car trouble. Because she didn't just have her thumb stuck out, she was waving vigorously with her whole arm. So when I pulled over I didn't know she was a hitchhiker. That's an important point, I think.

"I reached across to roll down the window on the passenger side. She stuck her head in. I turned on the inside light and saw her smiling at me. Beaming, really.

"It would have been difficult to refuse her a ride, because I had already pulled over.

"And then when she said she was a stranger, from California, who didn't know a soul on the coast except one person who didn't even know she was coming—obviously events were conspiring, and I wished that it wasn't my habit to always keep a knife in my glove compartment, but I knew it didn't matter, I'd just have used something else.

"I wish I hadn't killed Alfred Hingle's dog. Oh I wish I hadn't done that. Because it didn't help. It wasn't necessary. Not really. Because I already knew. I just didn't want to admit it."

"Are you all right, Tommy? Tommy?"

"Yes. I'm all right.

"She asked me where I was going and I said Sechelt. She said that was where she was going, too, and she asked me if I'd give her a ride.

"She saw my sketch pad and easel and things in the back seat. She told me that she'd done some modeling for life drawing classes when she was starting out as an actress.

"She laughed a lot. I liked her.

"We stopped for coffee at Halfmoon Bay. Now you can see, from that, that I really didn't expect anything to happen. I wouldn't have let myself be seen with her if I'd expected anything to happen. And when it did, then I knew that I'd have to kill that waitress, too; oh the whole thing just got bigger and bigger and more and more awful, having to sketch her in the hospital—I couldn't think of a way to say no to you, Mr. Alberg—and then knowing I'd have to kill that waitress, too, because she was the only one who'd seen me with her. Oh. Oh.

"Just give me a minute. I'll be all right."

"Take your time."

"Yes. I will. There.

"I sketched her at the restaurant. They were terrible sketches. Terrible. I got so frustrated, so angry.

"When I pulled off the road at the clearing I told her it was because I'd heard something funny and wanted to check out the engine and that was true, right up until I'd turned off the motor. But as soon as I did that I reached for the glove compartment to get the knife. It was only then. Only then.

"But it's like that every time. I just forget, when it's over, that at some point I must have decided to do it.

"She was quicker than me. She had enjoyed my company, I think, but when I said I was going to pull over she stopped talking and straightened up and sat at an angle. She was older than most hitchhikers. I guess she knew more about people. And then she was an actress, too. Maybe I didn't sound convincing.

"While I was reaching for the glove compartment she was getting out of the car. She hadn't put her seat belt on. I had told her it was the law, in B.C., but she just laughed and said they chafed her. So she didn't have to fumble around undoing it, she opened the door and jumped out, quick as anything.

"This had never happened before.

"And I followed her.

"It was dark and rainy and she didn't know where she was going. Maybe she expected to find a house in those trees, or a cave to hide in. But there was nothing like that. I could hear her thrashing around in the trees and yelling for help. I was very calm. Exhilarated. That had never happened before, either.

"And when I finally caught her . . . 'It's this part I like.' I remember thinking that. 'This is the part that I like.'

"I went ahead anyway. I did it. And I got my umbrella and my sketch pad and my pencil from the car and I shone my flashlight on her face and I sketched her, and this time of course I liked the drawings, they were good.

"I liked her. Really. I gave her one of the stones that I'd picked up on the beach that afternoon.

"And I sang to her.

"I was going to hide her body somewhere. I hadn't figured out where. I hadn't had time. And then I thought I heard somebody coming, an animal, or a large person, coming through the woods. So I had to just leave her there, and run for my car.

"You see . . . 'It's this part I like.' That's what was so terrible. To find myself thinking that.

"The portraits, they had become ritual. Ritual. Secondary.

"I didn't want to believe that. So I killed the dog. It was

an experiment, I told myself. But even while I was doing it, I knew that it wasn't necessary.

"And then I really didn't know anymore what I'd been doing all this time."

CHAPTER 44

Where the highway dipped close to the ocean at Davis Bay Alberg saw Cassandra's yellow Hornet parked at the side of the road. He slowed, hesitated, almost drove on; but then he saw her out on the beach, walking slowly, her hands in the pockets of her jacket and her eyes on the sand. So he parked, too, and got out and walked toward her, not quickly, but faster than she was walking, so that eventually she heard his footsteps and looked over her shoulder. She stopped and turned to face him.

She looked melancholy, he thought, but not incurable.

"I just took Roger to the ferry," she said.

He nodded. "Do you mind if I walk along with you?"

"No. Of course not."

Their feet crunched along the sand, and the scent of the sea was strong. It was a gentle sea today, talking to itself in a preoccupied whisper as it swept onto the sand, and away, and back again.

When they got to the end of the sand, where the rocks took over and trees grew closer to the water, Alberg sat down on a log and looked out at the water.

He wanted Cassandra to sit beside him, so that he could feel the warmth of her. There was a coldness deep inside him that he thought might be eased by the touch of her body against his. But for some reason he wasn't able to ask anything of her, not even that she sit down next to him.

For a long time, it seemed, he sat on the log and she stood nearby, too far away. Then she stretched out her hand

and touched his cheek, running her fingers slowly from the corner of his eye to the edge of his jaw. "Let's go back," she said, and he nodded and stood up.

They turned around, heading west, where the sky was a bright, pearly panorma of light-curdled cloud.

Off on the water Alberg thought he saw a puff of smoke. "Jesus," he said, coming to a halt, looking for a boat in trouble.

It came again, and again.

"Oh, God!" said Cassandra. "It's the whales! The orcas!"

There was a pod of them, their massive tails thrusting head and flippers clear of the water, blowing clouds of mist into the bright winter air.

"I heard they were coming," said Cassandra. "Somebody up the coast called a friend down here. She was in the library yesterday, talking about it." She turned to Alberg. "I've never seen them before." Her face was shining.

They were frolicking in the water, six or more of them, only about fifty feet from shore. Alberg looked behind him to see people hurrying across the highway; they must have seen the whales from their windows. Soon there was a group of about fifteen people on the beach, looking out to sea.

Some of the orcas were enormous, with fins which when they leapt from the water must have measured twelve feet. The pod was moving slowly along the coastline—blowing, leaping, disappearing beneath the sea, only to leap high once more, as if their exuberance were too great to keep them underwater.

"The woman in the library," said Cassandra, "she said they only appear off this coast about once every five years."

They watched until the pod was out of sight.

Then they went to Earl's for a hamburger.

TIME FOR BED

A lullaby known throughout Europe and North America. With different words, it appears in John Gay's *The Beggar's Opera*.

Time for bed, now, it is night.
Come, no tears or sorrow!
You will wake with morning's light
And play all day tomorrow.

The silver moon will guard your sleep.
The golden sun will wake you.
Sleep, my dear one, please don't cry,
Sleep, while I sing a lullaby.